BOGEY'S
FINAL GIFT

JOHN MEEKS

WASHINGTON, DC, 2011

ISBN: 1456312405
ISBN-13: 9781456312404

DEDICATION

In memory of Harrison E. Johnson who taught me that the horse is more important than the race.

ACKNOWLEDGEMENTS

For all that is good in this book I owe many people.

John McKee and Cyndy O'Bannon have taught me about horses and about Charles Town. Dr. Francis Daniel has supplied veterinarian insights. Andrea Adler helped me get untracked early with editorial and content hints.

I owe a special debt to my two wonderful horse partners and friends, Dr. Howard Hoffman and Dr. Allen Cahill, who have shared the highs and lows of thoroughbred breeding and racing with me for a quarter century and taught me much in the process.

I also am grateful to the honest horses who gave their best for me, bringing color and excitement into my life and inspiring this feeble effort to honor them. Northern Wolf might have been the best but Waller was the most engaging. I have to apologize to his memory since, in the book, I credit him with less than half of what he actually earned in order to keep Bogey as poor as I needed him to be. Waller had that success in spite of a serious bout of EPM (Equine Protozoal Myeloencephalitis) during his second year of life. Tough guy.

Finally, as always, my wife Anita offered the perfect mixture of support and pointed suggestions that always help me do the best job I can.

For all that is bad in the book I can only blame myself, but I do that with no regrets. The process of creation was a joy.

PROLOGUE

BALTIMORE, FALL 1990

Humphrey Dawson sat at a bar table in Baltimore's Harbor Court Hotel, sipping on his third martini and smiling vacuously at Claudia Huddleston, the beautiful woman across the table. How could he get a conversation going?

Edmond Huddleston, her uncle and his biggest client, had put him in this spot. "Come on Humphrey," Huddleston had told him this morning, "If you go home, you'll just toss and turn worrying over some nonexistent problem with Sentinel's Cry. Besides, I need your help entertaining my niece. She's hard to get out of the house, but I talked her into coming to see our colt run tomorrow. She'll have more fun if she gets to know you. She's cute and a sweet girl but so shy it's hard to get a sentence out of her. Maybe you can get her to talk."

Claudia was as socially inept as Huddleston promised. Humphrey was bashful himself, especially when meeting new people, but compared to her he was a chatty extrovert. Her reticence was particularly confusing in view of her looks. Claudia wasn't cute. She was spectacularly, exotically gorgeous. He had never seen anyone like her. She was slender, about his height at five four, and as she walked into the bar, her simple black silk dress outlined an enticing figure. Her face was even more striking. Her skin color was unlike any he had ever seen. It was tawny and luminous and glowed as though backlit. The radiance of her face set off large eyes that flitted between green and blue with each change in expression. Her honey blonde hair flowed around her face, moving in silken concert with her smallest gesture. It was difficult to resist the urge to stare at her, especially since there was little conversation to distract him. He drained the last of his third drink and signaled the attentive waiter for another.

"I'm sorry I'm not great company tonight," he said. "I'm worried about the race tomorrow."

"It's okay. I don't talk much either," she managed. "Why are you worried?"

"I thought I felt a little heat in the horse's foot this morning. It's probably just nerves. The vet says he's okay, and I trotted him on asphalt behind the barn and couldn't see any lameness."

"But you're still worried," she said. "I worry a lot. It's hard to stop once you start."

She was right about it being difficult to get the colt off his mind, but he decided to try. "So where's your uncle? Have you heard from him?" he said lightly.

Claudia seemed distressed by the question. "I'm so sorry. You can't always count on my uncle. I guess he's just so busy. You don't have to stay if I'm holding you up."

Humphrey looked at her incredulously. "Are you kidding? Every man in the room wishes he could change places with me. You are beautiful," he blurted.

She reacted with acute embarrassment. Gaze lowered, she murmured, "I don't know what to say."

Humphrey blushed. "I'm sorry. I didn't mean to upset you."

He was still smarting over his failed effort to connect with Becky Friedman, and this blunder reminded him again that he simply didn't know how to talk to women. He really cared about the exercise rider. She was a kindred spirit, someone who both loved and understood horses, but it wasn't just that shared interest. He admired her spirit and toughness. Her outspoken manner helped him speak up, and her sparkling dark eyes and ebony tresses stirred almost irresistible urges to draw her into his arms. But when he haltingly asked her out, she seemed annoyed by his awkward overture and turned him down flat with an abrupt, "No. I can't do that."

He came back to the present and heard Claudia say softly, "I'm not upset. I just have trouble with compliments." Her eyes shone moist and blue and deep. "Maybe I should have another drink, relax and just enjoy it," she said with a brave little smile.

Humphrey decided to join her. After his fifth martini, he joined her when she apologized for being a little tipsy and asked him to escort her to her room, when she invited him in and when she leaned into him and kissed him. Then he joined her in bed.

* * *

Humphrey awakened at first light and dragged himself out of bed. Claudia was sleeping peacefully. By the time he dressed and drove home, he was sober. His head throbbed painfully. Dizziness and nausea left him barely able to stagger to the bathroom for aspirins and a shower.

If possible, he was even more sickened by guilt and regret. Not only did his drunken state lead him to take advantage of an intoxicated younger woman, it left him with the bizarre but still intense conviction that he had been unfaithful. In his mind, the wronged woman was Becky Friedman. Logic reminded him that Becky had refused to go out with him and that he owed her nothing, but reason didn't dull the pain.

He dressed hurriedly and headed for the track, donning sunglasses to hide his bloodshot eyes even though the day was dark and cloudy. At least he should get back to his job and be sure Sentinel's Cry was healthy enough to run.

The colt was waiting at his stall door looking bright and on his toes. The horse always seemed to know when it was race day. Humphrey led him out onto the tarmac just as he had yesterday afternoon. He walked him up and down a few times and then began to trot with him.

"Jeez! Don't wear the horse out before the race. Put him up and let him relax."

Humphrey looked up to see Edmond Huddleston grinning at him. As always, he was accompanied by Otey Musgrove, the huge man who had played beside him when they were with the Baltimore Colts football team and now served as his driver and general flunkey. Humphrey looked at the two men who had assumed such importance in his life. They were a study in contrast. Huddleston was big man but trim and always immaculately dressed in designer suits. He told the trainer that he worked out daily and had gained only five pounds since retiring from professional football. Otey, on the other hand, always looked scruffy and ill-kempt. He had been corpulent even in his playing days and now was grossly obese. Dawson wasn't fond of the horse owner or his sidekick, but he had to admit Huddleston's money and his willingness to spend it for good horseflesh was a major factor in the success he now enjoyed.

"He seems to be going okay," Humphrey said.

Huddleston walked closer, admiring the colt. "Of course he is. Look at him! Perfection." He looked more closely at Humphrey. "You on the other hand don't look too great. My little niece keep you up too late?" Humphrey blushed. "At least you're here. She checked out and disappeared this morning." He went on. "I'm sorry I got shanghaied in a business meeting, but she's a little cutey, isn't she? I thought you'd get by without me." He clapped Humphrey on the shoulder. "Never mind, let's win a horse race and head for the big time."

Humphrey couldn't argue. The horse didn't show any discomfort. There was no lameness.

Sentinel's Cry would start in the Futurity.

However, the colt did not finish.

He came into the stretch with a five length lead, running easily. Suddenly he seemed to stumble and break stride. The horse was clearly lame, and the jockey had no choice but to pull him up. By the time the colt came to a halt, he was holding his right leg in the air, refusing to put weight on it. The skies opened and a lancing rain slashed the track surface.

No one in the owner's box noticed the downpour. Huddleston was apoplectic. "God damn it," he screamed. "That little son of a bitch was setting a track record! Shit." He slammed his binoculars down. "This really screws up my plans."

Humphrey was in shock, his whole body numbed by the horror he felt. How could this be happening? The colt had jogged across rock hard asphalt without flinching. His hoof had not bothered him. Now Sentinel's Cry could not stand on it. He looked over at the vet, hoping for an answer. The man avoided his gaze. Suddenly Humphrey understood.

The creep blocked the nerve in the colt's ankle. Sentinel's Cry jogged sound because he couldn't feel the pain in his hoof.

Humphrey's decision was instantaneous. He spun on the owner, who was still cursing under his breath. "I can't train for you any longer, Mr. Huddleston. You'll have to find someone else. Have them come and get your horses."

He started to leave the box to see after Sentinel's Cry, who was already being loaded into a horse ambulance. Huddleston grabbed his arm.

"Who the hell do you think you're talking to? You little prick, you can't fire me. Who do you think you are?"

Humphrey gathered his courage. "I think you told the vet to clear the horse to race. I think you had the vet give him a Novocain injection to block his nerve so that I couldn't see that he was off. I think you told the track superintendent to make the track hard and fast to get the track record. I think you caused this horse to break down."

Huddleston's face grew even redder. His eyes bulged and his grip on Humphrey tightened painfully. He was shouting at the trainer, bits of spittle flying into Humphrey's face.

"You're making accusations? You're firing me?" His eyes narrowed and his voice became very cold and calm. "You know what you are? You're nothing. You're no one. I'm going to let everyone know that."

He released Humphrey and gave him a shove that almost made him fall. "Get the hell out of here!"

* * *

Just before the start of the Futurity, Becky Friedman made up her mind that she would not be controlled by her family's objections. She was going to go out with Humphrey Dawson. She felt bad about that decision. Hadn't she already caused her mother enough embarrassment? But for heavens sake, she wasn't marrying the man. Maybe this was the best way to follow mother's wishes without regrets. If she could spend time with Dawson socially, away from the track, in the real world, the strong attraction she felt for him would probably prove to be the foolish crush her mother labeled it. She would realize that there were problems in a relationship with a gentile that she hadn't anticipated. And maybe his short stature would bother her when they were in public as a couple. As her brother had mockingly warned her, "If you date him, you can never wear high heels." She didn't even like high heels, but the jibe hit a nerve.

On the other hand, if her heart could be trusted, well, she needed to know that and then work it out with her mother later. Dawson had caught her off guard when he abruptly asked her out. Coming out of the blue like that, she had come out with the culturally programmed rejection she now regretted.

She headed toward his seat in the grandstand, hoping to add her congratulations if Sentinel's Cry won as she expected. The colt was really special. She paused on the way as the race started and then watched in horror as the colt pulled up lame. This changed everything. Now she had to comfort Humphrey, see if she could help in some way with the injured horse. Humphrey would be devastated.

She was a few feet from Huddleston's box when she heard the owner shout, "You know who you are? You're nothing. You're no one. I'm going to let everyone know that. Get the hell out of here!"

Becky was stunned. Humphrey looked angry enough to kill. He stormed by her in a blind rage. He didn't even notice she was there.

* * *

Two days later, an article appeared in the *Daily Racing Form*. The headline read, "Huddleston Fires Trainer, Cites Incompetent Management". The piece went on to describe the breakdown of Sentinel's Cry and the personal sense of pain and loss the owner had felt. Huddleston was quoted, "I loved that animal. I trusted him to that kid, and this is the sorrowful reward I get for trying to give the boy a chance. The vet says that Sentinel's Cry fractured his coffin bone right at the joint. He will never race again."

A week later, the *Baltimore Sun* carried a story on the front page of the Sports section revealing that Edmond Huddleston was considering a lawsuit against Humphrey Dawson for negligence and possible fraudulent behavior related to several thoroughbred horse purchases. Mr. Huddleston's attorney was investigating possible kickbacks and other questionable behaviors.

The next day, Humphrey was called into the track CEO's office. A copy of the paper was on the table. Caleb Briarson, proper in tailored brown pinstripe, was frowning. He tapped the newspaper with a stiff forefinger. "We cannot have you on the grounds until these alarming allegations are resolved."

Humphrey didn't even bother to speak. He knew he was suspended. Telling his side of the story to this Huddleston sycophant was pointless.

Humphrey drove to his apartment and stayed drunk for three days. His phone rang off and on, but he didn't answer it. On the fourth day, Fats Sheppard pounded on his door until he had to answer it.

Fats stood in the doorway and looked him over. He shook his head.

"Jeez, I go out of the country for a few days and you end up looking and smelling like this. Leave the drinking to me."

Fats stayed several days demanding that Humphrey get back on his feet; brushing aside any need to get back to his business in California.

"Millie can handle things there," he said. He constantly pushed his friend to come up with a new life plan. Any idea that did not involve racing was immediately rejected.

"It's your gift, your destiny," Fats told him.

Humphrey had one mare that he had purchased when her racing days ended. She had been a hard knocking race horse, but in the breeding shed she was difficult to get in foal. Her one foal was an unraced three year old gelding named Waller.

Fats learned online that Sentinel's Cry was catalogued as a stallion prospect in the winter horse sale at Timonium.

"You can buy him cheap," Fats told Humphrey. "He doesn't have much earnings or black type on his page, and only you know his real promise. You could breed him to that good mare of yours."

Humphrey put a down payment on a small tract of land in West Virginia. That took most of his remaining cash, but he couldn't get the handsome colt off his mind. At the last moment, he sent Fats to the sale, where he bought the once promising horse for peanuts.

CHAPTER 1

MAY, 1994, CHARLES TOWN, WEST VIRGINIA

Bogey Dawson had never felt fear on horseback, but he felt it now. The two-year-old filly, Final Gift, was a handful, but she had settled, and he leaned into her, urging her down the track toward the laughing, jeering crowd by the trainer's stand.

On the track across from them, he could see Becky Friedman, her delicate frame being tossed like a rag doll as she struggled to stay astride the huge gelding named Waller. He silently cursed himself for hiring her to exercise him.

As Bogey rode closer, he steeled himself against tragedy. But Becky was smiling. Bogey glared at the knot of people yelling at her and fought his urge to scream at them.

As quickly and unexpectedly as he had begun to buck, Waller stopped misbehaving. The huge gelding headed down the ramp to the stable barns as though nothing had happened.

Becky reined him in. She spun him around and walked him back onto the track toward the band of men and women crowding the rail, who were suddenly quiet. She sat erect and proud in the saddle, the horse totally under her control. She stopped in front of the crowd.

"We will be performing again tomorrow morning at approximately the same time. Tell your friends," she said with a smile and then walked Waller down the hill to the barn.

Bogey's heart was still pounding as he followed her. The tightness in his chest eased and he drew deep breathes, trying to calm himself. In the crisp, sunny spring morning the scene before him was the corner of Charles Town race track he viewed every day – the same tired grey barn, beginning to lean, the narrow outhouse behind it and the rows of equally worn and faded barns beyond. The brilliant sun, just over the horizon, pushed barn shadows toward the stands and the offices within, as though the buildings were reaching feebly for help. Most track workers found this 1994 back-stretch scene depressing, its squalid neglect more evidence that the track owners had given up. Bogey, on the other hand, usually found the bleak tableau comforting; a quiet refuge after the hectic years in Maryland. The thoroughbreds in those decrepit barns were blue collar, often nicked up but hard knocking, honest and, most important, free of media hype and demanding owners.

At this moment, however, calm and comfort eluded him. Both his relief that Becky was safe and the alarm he had felt when she seemed in danger were disturbing. Since she came to Charles Town race track two years ago he had carefully avoided her, reasoning that if she rejected him when he was at the top of his game, she would surely have no use for him now. And what if she somehow learned of his shameful treatment of Claudia Huddleston? While suffering from a desperate hunger for her that would not go away, he was too embarrassed to look her in the eye.

Things changed when he brought Final Gift to the track. The filly was green and headstrong. Bogey didn't mind that. In fact her mental toughness was just further proof to him she would be special.

Soon after arriving at the track the filly latched onto Waller. Bogey wasn't sure why horses connected like that. Waller was her half brother but unrelated horses or even chickens, goats, cats or other creatures were often chosen as buddies. Who knew why?

Two days of trying to force the promising two year old to go to the track without Waller ended with Bogey and the filly both soaked in sweat. She battled him while Waller's shrieks of protest over the threatened separation tortured Bogey's frayed nerves and fanned the filly's frenzy.

He knew all the exercise boys at Charles Town and none of them would be able to stay on Waller. He thought Becky Friedman could. At age thirty eight, broke and with only three horses in his shabby stable he had to hire help. And he was so stuck on his employee he couldn't look her in the eye without blushing. Ridiculous.

Since Becky knew Bogey didn't have any stable help, she volunteered to cool out and bathe Waller while he took care of Final Gift. When they finished with the horses and put them in their stalls, they walked out onto the soggy drive in front of the barn. Recent spring rains had turned the once-graveled surface to puddles and mud.

Becky took off her riding helmet and smiled at Bogey, her black eyes sparkling with mischief.

"Your little maverick put it to you today," she said. Bogey glanced at her. Her black pony tail swung and sparkled in the sunlight as she tilted her head playfully. She had a dazzling smile.

"Final Gift is not a maverick."

"She acts pretty crazy."

Bogey looked her in the eye.

"She's just green. Training asks stuff of horses that go against centuries of instinct."

"Her instinct is to try to kill you."

As usual she was teasing him, nimble and light footed and he was biting, plodding and pedantic. He tried flattery. "You did a great job with Waller. I've never seen him that bad," he said.

Waller saw no purpose in morning workouts. He never caused trouble in the barn or at race time, but each morning the old devil behaved until it was time to go back to the barn. At the top of the ramp he extracted revenge for being put through the pointless effort by going into his bronco act, doing his best to buck off his rider. With anyone except Bogey, and now the girl, he usually succeeded.

She waved aside the praise. "He was just going through the motions. He knows he can't get me off." She pointed a finger at him. "By the way, not that you're a bad rider, but I have a tip for you. You sit a little stiff, like a guy clutching the bar on a roller coaster. Relax, don't try to stay on top of the horse, just let your body move to keep the horse under you."

She's giving me riding lessons?

He tried to hide his outrage but her sly grin told him she had read the reaction on his face. He controlled himself and said, "You were always able to handle the tough ones in Maryland. But I got a little scared this morning. Waller's over the top."

"That's what I wanted to discuss." She wasn't joking now. "He's a special case. Could you pay me seven a ride instead of five? Everyone around here is cutting back and I'm having trouble making ends meet. John McKee gave me a lot of business but he took a bunch of his horses up to Penn National. I've been waitressing some over at the Turf but they only need me now and then. This whole town is fading away."

Bogey was in a bind. He didn't want to say no but he couldn't even afford the five dollars a day he had agreed to pay. Waller was his only meal ticket aside from the training fees he got from his one and only owner. The pantry was pretty bare.

He hedged. "I'm on the run today. Can we talk tomorrow?"

She was screwing up her face, probably preparing a wisecrack, when a big black Mercedes pulled up beside them. Bogey recognized it as a brand new 1994 E500, a car he had dreamed of but could never afford.

Morning sun glinted off the windshield making it impossible to see inside. After a pause the driver emerged. First a soccer ball head partly covered with wisps of lank hair poked out. Powerful thick shoulders, almost too wide for the door opening followed. A bulging abdomen and then massive legs ending in clown sized sneakers completed the arrival.

Otey Musgrove. The man mountain with the mudslide belly. Bogey stared at him in disbelief. The huge man with the tiny eyes spat a brown stream into a puddle at his feet. His round face wore an evil smirk.

"Hi, Shrimp," he said. He turned and opened the back door for Edmond Huddleston. Bogey's fists and his stomach knotted.

Even four years after he last saw him, Huddleston still looked fit enough to take off his tailored grey suit, change into uniform and play professional football again.

"Hello Humphrey," Huddleston said. He looked down with obvious distaste at the mud oozing up the sides of his expensive shoes and then up at the shabby, grey siding of the barn with the hand painted sign: Bogey Dawson Stable.

"Nice place."

His craggy face, tapering from a wide flat forehead to a hatchet chin, was twisted in an ironic smile that did nothing to warm cold green eyes.

"Hello Huddleston," Bogey said. He pointed to the sign. "Call me Bogey. I don't answer to Humphrey any more."

"Well a lot has changed, hasn't it? I used to be Mr. Huddleston. You used to be a very polite Humphrey - when you said anything at all. Now you're a dead movie hero or a bad golf score?" The morning sun in his eyes caused an angry squint.

"I wonder what changed me."

Becky Friedman's face reflected polite inquiry. "Could it have anything to do with the time this rich crook screwed you at Laurel Raceway?" she asked Bogey.

"Looks like we got a couple of smart alecs, boss," Otey growled. "At least one of them looks good." He moved toward Becky and poked her chest with a huge finger. "What you got under that flack jacket, honey?"

"Come close enough to see and I'll scratch your eyes out," she told him conversationally.

Otey backed off in mock terror. "Whoa. Got a tiger here." He kept backing away, leaving the three of them.

Huddleston spoke calmly. "Look, er-Bogey, we don't need all this. Your father warned me that you might still have some kind of grudge, but he thought we should talk."

Bogey remained silent, his face a stony mask.

"Don't be difficult. I'm here to do you a favor," Huddleston said gently.

"I don't need any favors."

"No? I guess my source was wrong." Huddleston held up fingers and ticked off points. "He said you're broke, about to get in trouble with the mortgage on your little farm. He said you only have one horse racing. On top of everything, this track is about to go bankrupt and shut down." He thrust the three fingers at Bogey who ignored them.

"If your source was my father you should know that he always worries about his baby boy. He offers help when none is needed."

"I have other sources. I have friends everywhere. I have friends right here." Huddleston waved around in an expansive gesture.

"How much did they cost you?"

The other man flinched in mock pain. "Damn, you *have* turned snippy. No matter. Here's the important thing. My friend tells me that Sentinel's Cry has bred you a promising filly. I'm here to offer you the chance to avoid what happened to her father. He broke down. If that happens with her you go broke. There goes the farm, there goes your career."

Becky chimed in again. "Wow, Bogey. Things are okay now. You know you can trust this guy."

Huddleston frowned at her but looked back pleasantly at Bogey. "Hear me out," he said. "I am here to offer you a more than fair price for the filly. I will also give you a good profit on what you paid for Sentinel's Cry, even though you took advantage of my grief and virtually stole him. To show there are no hard feelings, I'll give you a job. Not as my trainer, of course, but as an assistant who can advise me on horse selection."

"Flying around the country to horse sales in your private jet. Just like old times."

Huddleston ignored the sarcasm. "Just like old times," he agreed. "Just with new women." He waved casually toward Becky. "She can be one of them if you want but don't expect to see my niece. She's pretty traumatized by what you did."

Becky Friedman was tapping Bogey on the arm. He shrugged her off and glared at Huddleston. "There is a favor you can do for me."

"Name it."

"Tell my father this. If his idea of helping is to send you then don't help."

Becky's nudging became more insistent. "The fat guy went in your barn," she hissed.

Bogey spun and sprinted toward the barn. He was only steps away when Otey shot out the door cursing loudly. "That damn horse is nuts. She tried to kill me."

"What were you doing in there?"

"Just trying to get a look at that horse the boss wants. She turned her butt on me and tried to kick my head off."

The big man's face was crimson, the flush rising beyond his hairline and peeking through the thin hair on his spherical dome. "I don't care what the boss says; I don't want to be anywhere near that rogue!"

"Don't worry. You won't be around her," Bogey said. "Put your boss back in the car and get the hell out of here."

Huddleston strolled up wearing a friendly smile. "Everybody calm down. Otey please don't tell me what you will and won't do. Just get in the car. We're leaving." He gazed calmly at Bogey. "And Humphrey, don't let your past trip you up. Just think about what I said. You'll realize you need this deal. We can negotiate the money amount."

He started walking away and then turned back. "Besides, Humphrey, you, of all people, should know that I get what I want. And I want that filly."

"That sounds like a threat."

"Not a threat, Humphrey, just a reminder."

"You're not dealing with Humphrey. I'm Bogey now. Just a reminder."

The owner stopped at the car door and shook his head sadly. Bogey knew that look. It came when someone wouldn't do things Huddleston's way. It told the poor guy "You have only yourself to blame for what I'm going to do to you".

As the car drove away Becky faced Bogey, her eyes wide. "Wow, Count Dracula and his oaf. They're kinda scary up close. What did he mean with that last comment? And about his niece?"

Bogey shrugged. He knew all too well what Huddleston meant on both counts, but if he talked about it his voice might betray nervousness and guilt. After a pause Becky went on. "Well, Dawson, you stood up to them. To tell you the truth I thought Humphrey wimped out back in Maryland. This guy Bogey may be a different dude."

She punched him on the shoulder and it felt good.

How dumb is that? Turning a punch into a caress. Remember, fool, she's a little too young and a lot too pretty for the likes of you. She turned you down, remember?

"Look, I have to get out of here. I have a ton of work that's waiting, for goodness sakes," he stammered. His eyes were back on the ground.

She raised an eyebrow. "That Bogey guy; he looks you in the eye when he's talking horses or kicking bad guys' asses. You should cut him loose for small talk too."

Yeah, small talk. That's what it was to her. He ignored her comment and hurried to his old Mustang, hoping she didn't think he was fleeing. He *was* fleeing; he just hoped she didn't realize it.

The Bogey guy needed some time alone. Time to lick his wounds and mend his defenses.

CHAPTER 2

Becky shook her head as she watched Bogey trot to his car.

Why do I scare the poor man? Probably shouldn't have asked for the raise. He seemed to like my spunky act back in Maryland. Now it seemed to push him away. Will he ever ask me out again?

She shrugged. No matter, she had to get on with things. One more horse to work at Harry Collins' barn then hustle over to her rented room, clean up and put on her waitress outfit for an afternoon shift at the restaurant. She needed the hours, and Sarah would kill her if she got there late. It wasn't that Sarah was unkind; it was just that she had gone out on a limb and risked her job of forty years to recommend the inexperienced girl from the big city.

Becky's last mount was a kind old mare. This one wouldn't be bucking and tearing around the track like Waller. In fact, the only caution needed was to be sure to go slowly until the old gal was thoroughly warmed up. It took time to humor all the minor aches and pains accumulated in her years of competition.

Becky eased the mare around the track while stealing glances at the Blue Ridge foothills and letting her mind wander.

The last hour had been exciting and unsettling. She was honored that Dawson had chosen her to ride Waller. The old gelding's cantankerous habits were well known around the track, so the trainer's trust in her was gratifying. It was also the reason the crowd on hand this morning was hoping to see her fail. She wasn't really popular at Charles Town, a situation she had worked diligently to engineer. Half the rowdy crowd was made up of male exercise boys who hated to admit that a female was a better rider than any of them. The other half was split between males whose advances she had spurned and envious females who wanted the attention Becky was scorning.

Her thoughts lingered on Bogey Dawson. He was the best horseman she had ever known. When they were both in Maryland, she had watched him rise to the top of the trainer rankings on his ability to select good horses and an uncanny ability to understand their needs and foibles once they were in his care. She admired him and she liked him. Even when he was the toast of Maryland racing, he was shy and modest. He never tried to seduce her, a refreshing change from many of the men she encountered at the race track and elsewhere.

That gallantry was endearing but a little wimpy. This morning she had seen another, very different side of the man. When Huddleston and his goon came around, Dawson became steel. She now regretted accusing him of giving up too easily in Maryland. After all, the media and his own father and brother had sided with Huddleston.

Then the talk about other women. It made the man interesting. Apparently he wasn't always shy. She felt surprisingly jealous of those faceless other gals, including Huddleston's niece.

Becky admitted to herself that she was fascinated and intrigued by the paradoxes that were Bogey Dawson. He even looked interesting. His short sandy hair looked like he chopped it himself. His blue eyes were too big for his lean face.

It's too bad he's a short gentile.

Don't kid yourself, Becky Friedman. He is a truly good man, an admired friend, and appealing in some way she couldn't fully define. She felt admiration for him and aching sympathy for the raw deal he got in Maryland. And, if he asked, she would jump at the chance to go out with him.

CHAPTER 3

It was dark when Bogey finished at the farm and bedtime when he returned from feeding the three horses at the track. He was exhausted, and four a.m. would come early, but he called his father anyway. The old attorney answered on the second ring. Richard Dawson was famous for his instant availability day or night.

"Hello, Father."

"Humphrey, nice to hear from you. How are things?"

"Not so good. Huddleston showed up here today."

"Yes. He told me he was going to talk to you about a horse he wants to buy. Did he make you a good offer?"

"I don't know. I don't want to hear any offer from him."

There was a long pause. Bogey knew his father was carefully crafting a statement. He also knew the messages that followed pauses like this one were never complimentary. "Humphrey, I hate to offer advice to a forty-year-old man."

"Thirty-eight. I'm thirty-eight. Dickey is forty."

"Edmond Huddleston took you to the edge of fame and prosperity before you insulted him. The desperate straits you find yourself in at this time are the result of your self-righteous bullheadedness."

"What happened to Sentinel's Cry was Huddleston's fault. I couldn't keep training for a man like that."

"You couldn't keep training for him for the simple reason that he fired you."

"Yeah, right after I fired him."

"The predominance of evidence suggested that the horse was injured because of you, not because of anything Mr. Huddleston did."

"Bull. He rigged all that."

"Son, I am trying to protect you."

"Are you going to send me back to karate class? Are you going to get me another tutor? You referred Huddleston to me in the first place. I was getting by without him. He deliberately risked the health of a fine race horse, and when things blew up, he blamed it on me. Whose side are you on?"

The old man sighed. "I'm on your side, Humphrey. I'm your father. I'm trying to protect you from yourself."

For the hundredth time, Bogey said, "There's nothing wrong with myself."

"I don't say this to hurt you, but look at the facts. Your intelligence tests are outstanding, but you barely managed a C average in high school. I thought a tutor would help. You were the target of bullying and physical attacks in school. Dickey was tired of protecting you. I thought karate lessons might help you. How was I to know you would lose your temper and misuse those skills?"

"You didn't see what those kids were doing to Fats that day – and Dickey was one of them."

"That's not what Dickey tells me. According to him, you went berserk when the boys were only joking around. Never mind. The real point is that you have never given yourself a chance. You dropped out of college after three months and went to do menial labor at the race track. The only time you've made a living wage is when you trained for Edmond Huddleston. You're on the edge of bankruptcy now. Mr. Huddleston is tossing you a life line, and you call me to whine and complain about it."

"Father, forget it. Whenever I try to talk to you, I end up on trial. Okay, I plead guilty. You don't need to cross examine me."

"Humphrey, you won't let anyone help you."

Bogey gave up and let him have the last word. "You're probably right. Goodnight Father."

Calling his father had been a mistake. Four a.m. was even closer, but now he was wide awake, his gut tight, his thoughts whirling. The solid defences he offered his father didn't work inside his mind. There he faced endless questions.

Sleep had to wait.

CHAPTER 4

"God, you look awful. I know you work hard, but don't you sleep sometimes?" Becky asked during the morning gallop.

"Not last night," he answered truthfully.

"Thinking about Huddleston's offer?" Gesturing toward Final Gift, she asked. "How much do you think he would give you for Miss Lightning in a Jar?"

It was easier talking on horseback. He didn't have to look at her. "A lot. Huddleston would cheat you out of a nickel, but he'll pay a million for a horse without blinking. I never saw him get outbid on one he really wanted."

"So why don't you put an outrageous price on her?"

"Because he'd pay it."

"Then at least you could pay me my money," she said with a grin.

"I've got you tomorrow, honest. Marshall sent his check, and I'll deposit it this morning and get some cash."

"Thank goodness for your one and only owner. How is that scarecrow horse of his doing?"

"I think there's a race horse in there even if he is bony. He's bulking up some."

"What about this young wild woman you're riding? How can you be so sure she's the real deal? How can you turn down big money for her when she hasn't even breezed, much less run in a race?"

"I know horses." He was surprised to hear the quiet confidence in his words. "She's going to be a wonder. You watch."

"Maybe. If she runs to her looks. Wayne Lucas said a good filly should have 'face of an angel and ass of a washerwoman'. She fits - if you can teach her some manners." She loped ahead on Waller.

A siren blasted, shattering the morning calm. A recorded voice boomed over the track public address. "Loose horse! Warning. Loose horse."

Bogey heard a commotion behind him and looked back to see a riderless horse bearing down on him. The animal was totally spooked, running blind, eyes wide but unseeing and white with alarm. An outrider was swinging into pursuit but was no where near the panicked creature.

He shouted to Becky. "Run. Run." At the same time, he shook the reins and kicked Final Gift, signalling her to move out of harm's way.

Bogey was totally unprepared for what happened next. In front of him, he saw Becky tap Waller and leap ahead. The filly under him seemed to drop her body toward the surface of the track and lean forward. With a deceptive smoothness, she accelerated toward the old gelding and then instantly was past him. The only sensation of speed was the air rushing over Bogey's skin like a gale, but in a flash they were around the turn and past the finish line. He glanced back and saw Becky and Waller running hard at the head of the stretch, ten lengths behind him. He reined in the filly with some difficulty. A quick survey assured him that the loose horse had been corralled by the outrider.

Becky rode up. "What the hell did I just see?" she asked.

"I hope you didn't see a good horse destroy herself."

"Come on, man. Not many stakes horses have that turn of foot. I think she *is* a wonder horse."

"I just hope she didn't buck shins or worse."

Back in the barn, Bogey checked the filly, checked her again after hot walking her, and once more after her bath. Becky had to work a horse for a different trainer but came back when she finished.

"Is she okay?" she asked.

"For now. Lots of times trouble doesn't show till the next day."

"I won't argue with you Old Man Gloom, but this filly looks tough." She paused. "I admit that what happened today wasn't as funny as the day Waller got loose. That was the last time I heard the siren until this morning."

The memory made Bogey grin.

A few months ago, he had decided to risk Waller in a claiming race. He thought there was no chance that anyone would buy Waller. All of the other trainers knew the horse's reputation. They wouldn't take the old maverick.

Bogey's reasoning was wrong. Harry Collins claimed Waller and led him away to his barn. Word spread around the track that Harry's main exercise boy had bragged he could stay on any horse and urged the trainer to take the big gelding.

Bogey kicked himself for losing his old friend and only dependable meal ticket, but he didn't give up hope. He watched for Waller every morning. On the fourth day after the claim, the old gelding reappeared, showing perfect manners under the smiling, triumphant exercise lad. The kid gave a special wave to Bogey and a snappy salute to his own trainer standing a little further down the rail.

Around the track Waller trotted, warming up and then galloping with neck bent, straining at the bit like a good horse. Bogey was heartened by what he saw. When Waller behaved this well in the morning you could bet he was plotting something really special.

When horse and rider finished their first circuit of the track and came even with the ramp to the barn, Waller suddenly sprang, not upward but sideways. Caught completely off guard, the rider lost one stirrup but hung on. Waller then shot skyward, his back arched. The rider flew backward and landed hard. Waller circled toward him menacingly and, as the boy tried to scurry away, landed a kick solidly on his backside that sent the rider sprawling. The kid let out a yell and crawled under the rail to safety, too frightened to notice everyone laughing at him.

The siren and canned warning blared, but Waller was satisfied with his work. He trotted down the hill and returned, not to Harry's barn, but to Bogey's.

Harry, wearing a rueful grin, strolled over to Bogey. "Want to buy a nice gelding, dirt cheap? I think that horse is saying he'd rather live in your house." He looked over at his exercise boy who was gingerly rubbing his behind. "It turns out no one wants to argue with him."

Bogey smiled at the recollection of that episode, only one of Waller's legendary performances.

"If I were a better person, I'd feel sorry for that smartass kid," Becky said. "I'm not and I don't. It worked out for me. The loudmouth couldn't take the ribbing so he quit, and Harry started using me on his horses."

"Waller is trying to support both of us."

"Yeah. I'm glad you brought in Wild Wonder Woman. It gave me the chance to get to know the old rascal."

"Quit calling my filly names," Bogey said, an edge in his tone.

"I'm not going to call her Final Gift. Morbid. Where did you get a sad name like that anyhow?"

"Her dam, my one and only mare, colicked and died just after weaning her."

"More morbid. Too morbid." She thought a moment and said, "She needs a barn name, something happy." She paused a moment. "I have it! Rosie."

"Rosie? Where did that come from?"

"From you. That song you serenade her with. 'Don't know what to call you, but you're mighty like a rose.' She's Rosie."

He rolled his eyes. She gave him a level stare filled with mock gravity. "You know, this guy Bogey, when he jumps into small talk, let him try on a sense of humor."

That was a big order. All his life he hated being laughed at. Now this pushy gal wanted him to laugh at himself.

Over the next few days, it became apparent that Final Gift had not injured herself bolting away from the runaway. Her limbs and joints remained cool to the touch, and she showed no evidence of tenderness or pain. However, she *was* a thoroughbred so, of course, that worry was replaced by another. She began to show subtle signs of malaise. To Bogey's eye, she seemed to droop and her coat lost luster.

When he mentioned his concerns to Becky, she disagreed. "Rosie is settling in, acting less like a nut. You should be glad."

He wanted to believe her. But then the strapping filly started eating poorly, leaving the bottom of her feed tub untouched. It was clear that something was going wrong.

In the Maryland glory days, Humphrey Dawson would have asked the veterinarian for a complete evaluation, blood work included. Bogey didn't have the money. These days he did everything himself, from mucking stalls to hot walking to blacksmithing and now medical evaluation. He checked the filly's vital signs and listened to chest and belly. He conducted a meticulous search for swelling, discharge or heat anywhere on the filly's body. As far as he could tell, everything was fine.

Except that the filly continued to fade. Now she left half her oats, and the dullness of her coat was apparent even to Becky. She studied the filly as Bogey led her from the stall.

"You were right. Our girl Rosie is going bad. When are you going to send her to a vet?"

"I couldn't pay him. Besides, she has no symptoms, no fever, nothing."

"So what are you going to do? She's not just in a bad mood you know," she said a little sharply.

He spun to look at her, his eyes brightening. "Actually I think she might be – in a bad mood I mean. Barn sour."

"Come on, get serious."

"I am serious. Her dam was by Broad Brush, and I had to keep her entertained. Broad Brush himself was the same way. His trainer used to van him out to the airport to watch the planes take off and land." He turned to the filly. "Rosie girl, tomorrow we're going on a field trip."

Two weeks later, when Rosie returned from her vacation at the farm, Becky could hardly believe the change. Even under a dark, lowering sky, the filly's coat glowed and her eyes were bright.

Becky shook her head. "Barn sour. Well I live and learn."

The implied praise warmed Bogey, but he covered his delight by voicing another worry.

"We'll see how she holds up when I let her start doing something. I've got to cut her loose before she pulls my shoulders out of their sockets."

There was another reason Bogey was reluctant to let Rosie breeze. The possibility of injury was real, but he was also concerned positive reports on her works would bring Huddleston back.

Bogey had spent some time wondering about the identity of Huddleston's informant at Charles Town. The person had to be someone who was privy to track information and rumor, maybe someone discerning enough to recognize a young horse with the potential to be special – a runner that "could be any kind", as the cliché had it. There weren't a lot of matches. One possibility was the old fellow who sat in the press box high above the track and recorded the time on morning workouts. If he was the guilty party, then flares and rockets would go up when Rosie flew through her first formal work.

Bogey also realized that one of his fellow trainers could be the spy. They were up at the rail each morning, and most of them would be able to spot a good horse. They would also be even more impressed when she breezed.

He ruled out the other backstretch people. Grooms, hotwalkers and exercise riders wouldn't have the needed expertise.

Except for one exercise rider. One who knew his high opinion of his filly. One who saw her up close everyday.

Rebecca Friedman.

The suspicion caused him great pain. Unfortunately, it made a lot of sense. She knew Huddleston. She was short on cash.

Hadn't she tried to talk him into selling Final Gift to Huddleston?

As hard as he tried to put the idea out of mind, it still hung around. She had seemed to resent what Huddleston had done to him. When Huddleston came to the barn, she had been cuttingly hostile to the man. But that could be an act. It wouldn't be the first time that someone he thought was an ally turned out to be a traitor. Paradoxically, the suspicion made it easier to talk with her. Instead of trying to hide his secret infatuation, he now watched her closely for clues to treachery.

* * *

By Friday he was out of excuses. The weather had turned springtime gorgeous, the track surface couldn't be better, and Rosie was kicking the barn down, bursting with pent up energy that revved her almost beyond his control. On the track, he could barely hold her back. Even after her long daily gallops she tugged at the reins, begging to do more.

God, she was beautiful. After her brief food strike, she had filled out and now had the substance to match her unusual height and length. In the warm spring air, she had shed her winter overcoat and donned a slick ebony shine that highlighted her perfect confirmation. The tall, gawky adolescent was now a beautiful lady.

"I'd say she looks gorgeous. I've never seen a finer looking two-year-old," he told Becky as they bathed Waller and her on Thursday.

She nodded thoughtfully. "She's a picture all right. You have to breeze her."

"Yeah, she's going to hurt me or herself."

As if to illustrate his point, Rosie went up on her hind legs and pawed the air. She came back down fighting Bogey's control. He spoke calmly, moving with her as Becky backed off cautiously. The filly settled and let him swipe off the excess water from her coat. He sang softly to her, and with only a little bucking and kicking, she let Bogey take her to her stall.

Becky and Waller followed them in. "Looks like tomorrow's the day," she said. "Will you work Waller with her?"

Bogey answered immediately. "We'll warm them up together, and I'll break her off at the three-eights pole. Her competitive nature will take it from there."

"What makes you so sure," Becky asked.

"I see it in her eyes," Bogey replied.

"The wizard has spoken," Becky said, bowing with her hands together in a pose of worship.

* * *

The next morning started as always with Becky on Waller and Bogey riding Rosie. On the second turn around the track, Bogey nodded to Becky and loosened Rosie's reins. He leaned forward slightly in the saddle.

For several strides he didn't notice any difference. Rosie still seemed to be galloping. But somehow she was pulling away from Waller. Bogey could feel that she was flatter to the track, and her stride had lengthened. Suddenly she was gaining on the breezing thoroughbred that had pounded past them seconds before. That horse's rider had been pumping hard on his neck and clucking loudly, asking for everything the chestnut horse could bring.

Bogey was doing nothing of the kind. He was sitting relaxed, silent and still. Rosie was not pounding the track. Her hoof beats were quiet, almost muffled. In spite of her relaxed mode, she overtook the horse in front of her in a few long strides and flew by him as she crossed the finish line in front of the stands.

Bogey began to rein her in. Rosie resisted him for several frightening strides. "Please, please," he pleaded under his breath. She responded to his direction and slowed to a gallop. Bogey let out a loud sigh, realizing that he had been holding his breath.

Becky and Waller were waiting for him. They slowed to a walk as they came past the stands. From the press box high above the finish line, the clocker yelled down. "Who the hell was that, Bogey? I got him in 35. That gets the bullet by a second and change. Fastest work by far."

Bogey laughed loudly and yelled back. "It's a she, not a he. Her name is Final Gift, and I would be excited about the time except that she only went two furlongs."

After a moment of silence, the clocker spoke. He sounded very puzzled. "I thought I saw you break her off three furlongs out."

Bogey laughed again. "Don't I wish," he said.

"Well, okay," the clocker yelled. "There is a lot of action down there. I guess I mixed you up with another horse." After a moment, he added, "Makes sense. She didn't seem to be going very fast."

Becky looked over at Bogey and raised her eyebrows. "This Bogey character is coming along. Pretty skillful lying."

"Sarge is dirt poor. I still see him at the betting windows every night. If I admitted Rosie was that fast, Sarge wouldn't be able to resist selling the tip. I've wondered if he might be the "friend" Huddleston mentioned. If so, this info would be worth big bucks."

"God, you are full of it! Enemies all around you. It's bullshit anyway. You can't hide the horse. I don't know of any secret races with big purses. Sooner or later he'll know what you have. So what? Just keep telling him no deal."

"You don't know Huddleston."

"Come on. What's he going to do?"

"I don't know. That's what worries me."

CHAPTER 5

BALTIMORE

Edmond Huddleston fixed his attorneys with a flat gaze, watching their reactions carefully. It was difficult to keep them in simultaneous focus since the senior partner was behind his crescent mahogany desk, while he and the man's son were in chairs on the other side. Huddleston didn't mind. The old man was the key.

As always, the senior Dawson was the picture of elegant rectitude; slender, immaculate in his pinstripe grey suit, old eyes still sharp and confident behind rimless spectacles – the very image of a trustworthy barrister. The attorney's office, with its subtle elegance and soft aromas of wood and old leather, always made Huddleston comfortable and confident. Even if the old man talked as if he were reading from the law review, he had his uses. His kid was another matter. If he was a chip off the old block, something had leached the fiber from him. Dickey Dawson tried to copy his father, but his suits never looked as sharp on his athletic frame that had thickened around the middle. His eye glasses, identical to his father's, were often smudged. Huddleston wrote him off long ago.

"So, have you heard anything from Humphrey," Huddleston asked the senior Dawson.

"Yes. He called."

"Has he thought about my offer?"

"I would say no. He hasn't thought. He has reacted, but that is not the same thing."

"So he's still trying to blame me? He's still angry?"

"Yes. My son is too often ruled by emotion rather than reason. I told him that you were offering him a way out of his predicament."

Huddleston spread his hands in a bewildered gesture. "A way out? Hell I'm showing him the yellow brick road. How could he want anything more than I've offered him? Money, a future, a secure job."

"As I said. My son is not always rational."

Richard Dawson, Jr., spoke for the first time. "Not always?" he asked sarcastically.

"Dickey, he is your brother," the old man said.

"Sorry," Bogey's older brother muttered without contrition.

Huddleston cut into the family interaction. "What I need is some way to make him see the light. You two know him. Surely you can come up with a plan."

"Perhaps the best thing is to wait. After all, if the horse comes up with an injury you wouldn't want it. Even if Humphrey has some success, you can just raise your price, knowing that the animal is more valuable to you. What do you have to lose?"

"Time. That's what I have to lose. I have plans for that race horse. Besides, Richard, you know that I don't like to wait. I am not a patient man."

"Edmond, I would be remiss as your attorney if I didn't remind you that on more than one occasion, that impatience has led to complications for you."

Huddleston grinned at him. "That's when you guys make your money."

Dickey spoke up, talking to Huddleston but glancing frequently toward his father. Huddleston suppressed a grin. Dickey's shifting attention was reminiscent of a spectator at a tennis match – except this spectator's main interest was at one end of the court – his father's end. "I hate to be the one to say this, but my brother is not only emotional, he is very stubborn. It will take strong measures to move him."

Dickey's father frowned but said nothing.

"So what kind of pressure do you suggest?"

"Humphrey has always lived in a pretend world. He is ignoring the hopelessness of his situation clinging to the fantasy that one good horse can make everything right."

"It is my understanding that one very good horse can mend many fences," his father said.

"If the horse is *very* good. If the horse doesn't break down. Lots of ifs," Dickey said.

"I ask again: what kind of pressure?" Huddleston asked impatiently.

"My brother needs to be reminded of reality. It has to be forcefully pushed on him. It has to be shoved in his face."

"You were often happy to do that for your little brother when you were children," his father said drily.

"Come on. Mother played along with his games. You didn't want to upset her. The kid was spoiled rotten. Someone had to try to set him straight," Dickey protested.

"You and your friends weren't always kind about it."

Huddleston stood up, waving his hands above his head in surrender. "Let me out of this family feud!" He inclined his head toward the elder Dawson. "No offense, Richard, but I have to say that my experience with Humphrey leads me to agree with Dickey. Your baby boy is a wooly-headed dreamer."

Richard Dawson, Sr. looked at him suspiciously. "So what do you plan to do?"

"I'm not sure," Huddleston told him. "But it won't be just waiting around."

* * *

What Huddleston decided to do was to call Dickey Dawson the following day.

"Dickey, my friend. I have a question. When you were playing quarterback for our old alma mater, what did you do when the other team kept blitzing you?"

"Change calls. You know the drill. Why do you ask?"

"Because you know your brother. How do we blitz him so he changes his call?"

"We need to make his money problems real to him."

"Suggestions?"

"Let me see what I can come up with," the attorney said.

Huddleston could hear the satisfaction in the man's voice. Give Dickey Boy a chance to smack down little brother and supplant Poppa Bear in one move. He had been sure that Richard Jr. would jump at the chance.

Edmond Huddleston put down the phone, enjoying the moment. He would have made a great coach, he thought. Moving personnel into the right positions and then motivating them to perform; he definitely had the skills.

CHAPTER 6
CHARLES TOWN

As the weeks slid by, Bogey became more sure that Final Gift was a gift indeed. The filly he now called Rosie – the barn name Becky had coined - learned quickly. The starting gate, a menacing metallic monster for many young horses, merely piqued her curiosity. He let her circle the machine, smell it, decide to walk into it and then trot away from it. She seemed satisfied that this new enclosure held no more danger than her stall. Soon she had demonstrated her mastery to the gate crew and was granted a gate card, clearing her to race.

Her abilities were now common knowledge around Charles Town. For one thing, she continued to grow and muscle up. A massive Amazon encased in shining black patent leather is difficult to ignore. Bogey tried to avoid a timed morning drill. He planned to use fast gallops – the two minute lick, as it was known – to round her into racing condition. Unfortunately, her gait was so deceptively smooth that she loped past other horses who were working all out.

Even Becky's skeptical wisecracks stopped. As June gave way to July, she began to press Bogey about his plans. Bogey had just finished Rosie's bath and was staring at her worshipfully. She stopped hosing Waller.

"So, Bogey man, are you going to race this girl or just keep standing around admiring her? Maybe you should have her stuffed. Stand her in your living room. Look at her all day and all night."

"I guess she is about ready, but it's complicated."

"What's so complicated? You get a condition book, pick a race, enter the horse. Not rocket science."

"Which condition book? I don't want to run her here."

"Why not? She'll inhale any of the babies here."

Bogey hesitated, embarrassed. "I need to cash a bet on her," he finally said.

"I get it. Everybody here knows about her, eh? No odds."

"I don't have a lot to bet."

"Don't I know it? Hard time scratching up my paltry five bucks half the time."

She lifted her scraper and drew it across Waller's broad back, pulling a cascade of water onto the pavement. The gelding stood quiet, enjoying the attention and the warmth of the summer sun. Becky stopped in her task and fixed Bogey with an understanding gaze.

"I see the complication. You don't want to run in Maryland. I get that." She went back to scraping water off Waller, but Bogey could see she was thinking. "I'm sure you've considered Saratoga," she finally said.

"I don't know. I've never even been there."

"You never raced up there?"

He shook his head. "Wouldn't even know how to get there."

She rolled her eyes. "There are maps. I went there twice when I was working horses in Maryland. It's beautiful. I loved being there."

"How did your horses do?"

"Both owners were dreaming. Their stock didn't belong in that league."

"I think Rosie can handle it."

"So do it," she said.

"I don't know. I'd have to take Waller to keep her company, or she wouldn't be happy. Besides, if I take Tommy up there he would be way over his head. I mean he's a good jock here. He's done a good job on Waller, but he might get the filly beat. She's not going to be easy to manage."

"Now you admit it. She's crazy."

"No. Not crazy, just smart."

"Just joking. You're right about the rider. She deserves an experienced, talented New York jock."

Bogey shook his head. "Yeah, but no one like that would take the mount on a first time starter from Charles Town.".

"Bogey Man, this is your lucky day – maybe. I'll let you know."

He looked at her in total confusion. She turned and led Waller away, grinning back at him like a mischievous little girl.

CHAPTER 7

Becky was more worried about this phone call than she had expected to be. She had put it off until after her shift at the Turf and was still dragging her feet. She looked around at her rented room. It was small, just a guest bedroom in the house off Washington Avenue where the widow Winslow lived alone. The flowered wallpaper and the dumpy old furniture would have offended Rebecca Friedman's mother beyond measure, but Becky liked it. She also liked Mrs. Winslow, and the price was right.

The room in many ways symbolized her present attitude toward Charles Town – the town in general and the racetrack in particular. Both had been difficult to get used to when she left Pimlico racetrack and her parents' home, but they both suited her now.

Fitting in at the track had been tougher than she expected. It was always a little rough on any backstretch for an attractive female. What was forbidden as sexual harassment in more polite settings was common place at most tracks. But Charles Town! This place took the cake. And it wasn't just the guys. The females were always shooting off their mouths about their sexual conquests and their speculations about the intimate liaisons between their peers. To hear the talk, the joint was awash in swirling hormones.

Becky had her defenses. She could out trash any fool who tried his crude comments on her. She was also master of the chilly brush off for those who were more gallant in their approach. These skills had led to two nicknames: The Galloping Mouth and The Icebox. Becky was glad her message was getting out clearly.

Now she had another line of defense. The rumor mill had her connected with Bogey Dawson. She did nothing to dispute the notion that they were an item. Unfortunately, it wasn't true.

She did enjoy his company. The man was so shy! He could hardly look her in the eye. After all the bold guys who crossed her path, his blushing confusion was refreshing, even somewhat appealing. God! If her brother ever saw them together, he would chew the little guy up and spit out the mangled remains. Not to mention what her mother would do to him.

But she did look forward to the time she spent with him each morning. And why had she been so pleased when he started calling his big horse Rosie – the name she suggested?

Maybe it's not him. Maybe it's just that crazy Rosie who is also crazy good. And, of course, my grumpy old sweetheart Waller. It's so sweet, the way he takes care of his demented little sister.

Bull, admit it, she looked up to Bogey. He didn't even have to whisper to the horses. He and the animals were in each other's heads automatically – or after a song or two. But respecting a guy didn't translate directly into romance. But it was a start. As the song said, maybe the start of something big.

She told herself that she was making this phone call for her own reasons, not for Bogey Dawson. Still, she realized that if things didn't work out, she would dread telling him. She was putting off the possibility of letting him down. The phone was in the hall outside her room. She forced herself off the bed and marched herself to the telephone. The window at the end of the hall was pitch black.

Maybe she was calling her friend too late at night.

Come on! Quit stalling.

"Hello," the voice on the other end said. Becky listened intently for any sign she might have awakened her, but Judith Patton sounded wide awake. In fact, Judy's squeaky voice sounded cheerful, alert and excited. Just as she always sounded.

"Hi, Judy. It's me," Becky said.

"You're kidding! Becky! What finally moved you? Questions about the O.J. case or Lisa Marie marrying Michael? Obviously you must need something. You never call," she said sarcastically.

"Me? Why me? You don't have a phone?"

Judy laughed. "You're a Jew. Guilt is supposed to work, but it never does. I'm delighted you called. I think about you every day. How are you doing? Still hiding out at Charles Town?"

"Still here. Hanging on by a thread. I don't have to ask what you're up to. It's in the *Racing Form*. You're riding the hide off of them. Finished second in the Belmont standings! General Patton, they're calling you. Not bad for one of Bouncer's Bimbos."

"That little guy got me on the right track. Not only that, but he brought me my best friend ever. I really wish we could see each other more. I miss you."

"Funny you should mention that. I *do* need something. I'm calling to see if we could arrange that very thing. A nice little visit."

"Well, I'm heading up to Saratoga in a couple of days," Judy said uncertainly.

"Exactly what I was counting on."

CHAPTER 8

TO SARATOGA SPRINGS, NEW YORK

Rosie was on the muscle. It took every ounce of Bogey's strength and all his skill to maintain control of her. By the time he got her safely back to the barn, his arms and shoulders ached and tingled. This filly definitely needed a race.

Becky Friedman dismounted from Waller and looked at him with a mixture of pity and amusement. "Pretty good workout, eh?"

He nodded glumly, resisting the urge to massage his aching muscles.

"So have you chosen a race? She's begging for one."

"I got a Saratoga condition book."

"And?" she prompted impatiently.

"They have a seven furlong maiden for fillies next week. That should fit her."

"Just need a jockey, right?" She grinned at him, dragging this out.

He hung his head. "Yeah."

"I have an old friend who rides up there that you might use."

"Is he just trying to catch on?"

"No. It's a she and she's experienced."

"Who?" he asked.

"Judith Patton is her name."

"Dang! You know Judy Patton? The General?"

"She calls me her best friend. 'Course lots of folks do."

"Do you think she'd ride Rosie? Will her agent let her do that?"

Becky snorted. "Her agent will let his meal ticket do whatever she wants to do. And Judy told me she would be delighted to ride Rosie at Saratoga."

Bogey leapt toward her and hugged her tightly. "Oh my God! Thank you! Thank you!" he shouted. His excitement led to the impulsive embrace, but once in his arms, her closeness was a bigger thrill. Momentarily it seemed she relaxed and pressed into him. She pulled away so quickly he later doubted what he had felt.

"Down boy. Easy with the groping," she said. "A simple thanks and a handshake would have done nicely."

"I'm sorry," he said meekly.

"Look, I have to go all the way to upstate New York with you. At least I guess I do. Waller needs to take the trip too, doesn't he?"

He tried to gather his senses. "Yes. Yes. It would be better if he went with us. Be good if he ponied her. She would be upset without him," he stammered.

"Okay. I don't want to have to be watching your hands the whole time. Understand?"

He told himself there was banter under her grave tone, but he couldn't take any chances. "I hear you," he said humbly.

* * *

By five p.m. on Wednesday of the next week, they pulled into Saratoga Springs. Becky had agreed that she would not be paid for her time unless the filly finished on the board – first, second or third. However, if she did, Bogey would pay her twice the amount she could have earned galloping horses at Charles Town. They settled Rosie and Waller in their stalls, left the old horse trailer at the receiving barn, and drove the Mustang to the rambling structure where Judy Patton had reserved two rooms for them. The house was outside of town on Lake George. It was run as a bed and breakfast and was filled by track people during the summer meet. They separated to freshen up, agreeing to meet again in half an hour.

Becky was a little late. She entered smiling. "I've been on the phone talking to Judy. She's invited us to meet her further up the lake at Mario's.

Dinner's on her." She checked her watch. "We have a half hour. Want to go for a walk?"

Bogey tried not to sound too eager. "Yeah, I wouldn't mind looking around a bit."

They went outside and discovered a path down to an empty pier. They walked out to the end and gazed around the lake's perimeter. There were houses all around the smooth expanse of water. Some of them were simple and rustic, while a few were larger and fancier. Most of them had piers, and boats were heading toward them as the day came to its close.

Bogey could not resist looking at Becky. In the fading daylight her face was lit as though by candle light. Her glowing beauty made his heart ache. He had to look away.

For awhile they watched the lowering sun paint the lake in shades of orange. A cool breeze stirred and rippled the water as it came to them. He glanced at Becky, who seemed to be deep in thought, a soft smile playing at the corners of her mouth.

"Look at all those kids in the boats. Aren't they having a fine time," she said dreamily.

He fought to find his voice. He nodded, "Yeah. Yeah. It's great." He managed to say.

She looked at him quizzically. "Are you all right?" she asked.

"Oh, sure. I'm just worried about the race tomorrow," he improvised. "Can Rosie really do this?"

Becky laughed and patted him on the back. His heart skipped a beat at her touch. "Of course she can. Rosie can do anything."

"She'll have to run against a bunch of million dollar fillies, trained to peak for this racing meet by the best trainers in the game."

"So what? She's worth a million or more, and she has been trained by the greatest horseman I know."

She was kidding him again. "Come on. Be serious. You know how she hates new things. She's not accustomed to this track, and she doesn't know the jockey."

"She knows us. She knows Waller, and he will be her lead pony. Judy knows horses. She and Rosie'll make friends right away."

"I hope you're right."

"We better head for the restaurant," she said. "You'll feel better after you meet Judy. Just relax and enjoy the scenery."

He couldn't trust himself to look at the most beautiful scenery. The vision walking beside him.

* * *

Bogey liked Mario's right away. During the halcyon days with Huddleston, he had been to many expensive, usually pretentious, restaurants. There was nothing pretentious about this Italian café on the lake, but the aromas wafting from the restaurant into the parking lot were mouth watering. The interior was homey and pleasant with a comfortable welcoming atmosphere.

There were several divided seating areas and the hostess took them back to the table where Judy was already seated. She jumped to her feet when she saw Becky and ran to meet her. The two women hugged warmly, and then Becky introduced Bogey to the jockey.

Patton was a petit, attractive blonde. She put her arm around Becky's shoulder, having to reach up a little since Becky was an inch taller. "I love this gal," she said. "In junior high she kept the big gals from beating me up."

"Yeah, right. Even then you could have bench pressed two of them."

"That's me, the old muscle bound tomboy."

"Tomboy nothing, even the high school boys were circling around you."

"They got a kick out of my voice. Like someone who had inhaled helium."

Bogey sat back and watched the two friends kid around. The little jockey did have a very high pitched voice, almost a squeak. Her joke about it reminded him of Jim Sheppard's tongue-in-cheek ambition to be a ballet dancer when they were in high school. "No reason why I couldn't. Right?" he'd say, spinning his globular bulk around the room. Bogey wished his friend was here to heckle and be heckled.

Bogey pulled himself back to the present and the threesome around the table. Once the waiter had everyone's order, Bogey steeled himself and spoke. "Miss Patton, I am glad you will ride my horse tomorrow."

"My name is Judy, and I believe I will be thanking you before this time tomorrow. Becky tells me she is the second coming."

"I'll stick by that. She is special," Becky said.

Judy turned back to Bogey. "What do you have to say? You're the one who's around her every day. Is she as good as Becky thinks she is?" she asked him.

Bogey looked Judy in the eye and said, "I've been around a lot of horses. She's by far the best I've ever seen. You have to respect her. She can't be forced into anything until she decides that it's safe. Give her her head, and she is well behaved and totally honest. Just don't try to make her do anything she isn't ready to do."

Judy gave him an appraising look. "I see why Becky is impressed with you. Thanks for the information. I'll keep it in mind."

She looked around the table. "Is there anything else I need to know?" Becky spoke up. "Just one thing. I'll be riding her lead pony. He's actually a hard-headed old race horse but he and – well, we call her Rosie – are inseparable. He's a pain in the ass when she's not around, but a sweet older brother to her."

"I'll let you handle that. If there is nothing else, I see the food coming. It's great here, and fortunately I'm not one of those jocks who have to starve themselves to make weight."

Bogey watched in amazement as Judy devoured her salad and made her way through the veal course with the help of a huge slice of garlic bread. He was stuffed, but the tiny jockey insisted everyone had to have a slice of strawberry pie. Becky was grinning widely.

"I see you're a little off your feed," she told Judy. "I'll have the vet check you out tomorrow."

* * *

Bogey woke early the next morning to find everyone, including Becky, in the big kitchen enjoying coffee and doughnuts. Outside the window, a heavy fog hung over the lake. Becky read the concern in his face.

"It's nothing," she said. "You have it most mornings up here. Burns off before noon."

Actually, most of it was gone by the time they finished caring for the horses. It was cooler here than at Charles Town, but the sun was bright above scattered light clouds.

By ten a.m., Bogey was restless. He saw Becky watching him.

"Let's walk over on the route Rosie will travel," she said. "Your familiarity will help her acclimate. Besides, you've got to see this place since you've never been here."

"One owner tried to get me to bring a couple of his horses up here, but I talked him out of it. They weren't good enough for one thing."

She waited for him to go on. When he didn't, she prompted," And the other reason?"

"I didn't want to leave the other horses for that long."

"That's what I thought," she said.

They wandered around the grounds. Families were already arriving, laying claim to their favorite spots under the towering old trees. Most of them came equipped with folding chairs, coolers and other supplies needed for comfort. Some families had young children, who laughed and played on the shady grass. Television sets were suspended in the trees throughout the area. On the screens, two men were talking about the day's races. They stopped a moment to see what they would say about Rosie's chances in the second race, but they were already dissecting the third race. "Wonder what they said about Rosie," he asked.

"Not much, I'm sure," Becky said. She drank in the whole scene. "Now this is what horse races should be," she said.

"Yeah. I always heard about this place, but the real thing is something to see."

They circled around, passing a building where colorful silks could be seen in the windows, past an outdoor strip of betting windows and then to the paddock. The enclosure had a walking ring and spacious outdoor saddling areas in addition to the usual row of wooden stalls.

"Nice," said Bogey.

"A few years ago it was even nicer. Before the crowds got so large, they saddled the horses out in the open." She pointed back where they had seen the families. "Back there under the trees."

They presented their identification badges to an usher and entered the grandstand. It was a wooden structure that spoke of stately tradition. Becky pointed down the row of seats to enclosed boxes below. "Gentlemen lucky enough to sit there will be required to wear jackets. Their lady folk will be equally grand. This is the grandstand. Over to our right is the clubhouse. Everyone there will be properly attired, or they will be politely sent away. No shorts anywhere, thank you."

Bogey laughed. "So all those boxes and the clubhouse are reserved seats?"

"Dear boy. All the seats are reserved. Only the picnic area and the standing room between the stands and the rail are general admission."

"Wow. You have to pay for seats here in the grandstand?"

"Of course. If you can get your hands on a ticket, that is. Early every morning they sell any returned tickets at a booth by the street. On a weekday you can usually pick one up, but good luck on a Saturday."

"What makes it so popular?"

"Good marketing and good racing. The best horses from all over the country come here. There's a stakes race just about every day, two or more on weekends. The best maiden two-year-olds usually appear first right here."

"Like the bunch Rosie will have to run against."

"Like the bunch that Rosie will dust."

"Nothing like confidence," Bogey said.

Later, at the barn, Bogey waited for the command to bring the horses to the paddock. He had put on a coat and tie and made an effort to slick down his unruly hair. Becky gave him an amused glance. "The big shot is back in the big time," she teased. For some reason the jab helped him relax.

Finally the call came. With Bogey leading Rosie and Becky leading Waller they started the long walk to the paddock. The grounds were now crowded with people who smiled and pointed as they walked along the path to the saddling area. Becky mounted Waller and rode out on the track to wait. Rosie accepted her pal's departure calmly, just glancing his way to be sure where he was headed.

As race time approached, Judy Patton appeared wearing Bogey's racing silks. He was embarrassed that his brown and gold vertical stripes showed their age after many trips through the wash. Judy didn't seem concerned. After a brief handshake, she only had eyes for Rosie.

"She certainly looks the part."

Bogey nodded. "Works to her looks. I hope she runs to them too."

"Any more instructions for me after looking at the past performances?"

"I didn't look at them. Just ride her like she wants to go," he said. He knew his voice sounded tight.

The "riders up" command came. Bogey led Rosie forward and boosted Judy into the saddle. She leaned forward and winked at him. "I'll try not to fall off," she said in her piping voice.

Bogey walked them out to the track and handed the reins to Becky. As they trotted away, he looked at the tote board in the infield. Rosie's odds were fifty to one.

That was a worthwhile bet, and he hurried to get it down at the outdoor windows. That done, he walked to the rail, finding a spot where he would be able to see the length of the stretch and the finish line.

When the gate opened, Rosie ambled out dead last. His heart was in his throat.

Maybe the odds were correct.

Maybe she didn't have a chance against these fancy fillies. Maybe he should have told Judy to rush her out of the gate. She was already five lengths behind the field as they headed down the backstretch. Maybe he should have worked her out of the gate more, taught her to break faster.

Judy was doing what he said, and it sure as hell wasn't working. The jock was sitting quiet and still on Rosie's back, apparently not noticing that her mount seemed off balance. Rosie was showing none of her long, ground devouring stride. Her gait was choppy and awkward. Oh my God, thought Bogey. Did she hurt herself in the gate?

Becky had walked up and was standing beside Bogey. That made things even worse. It was embarrassing. He had talked up Rosie extravagantly. Mister Big Shot. That was him all right.

After the first quarter mile Rosie had dropped further back. As she went into the turn Bogey could see that she was looking around, ears pricked and twisting from side to side. She looked at the horses in front of her and then turned her head to look at the crowd. That assembly was now cheering lustily for the favorite who was inching away on the lead.

In this moment of despair, Bogey saw a change in Rosie. She seemed satisfied with her appraisal. Her ears flattened, and her gaze fixed on the horses ahead of her. He thought he understood that look. It said this place is all right. I can operate here. Time to get down to business.

He watched her begin to gather herself. The choppiness disappeared as she flattened out and began to glide over the ground. Judy's only response was to lean closer on her neck. Still she and the horse were only half way around the turn.

Bogey chanced a glance at the horses ahead of her. No use. She had found herself, but it was too late. Way too late. She was still last by more than fifteen lengths and the favorite was running easily on the front, straightening down the long stretch and headed for the finish line.

But she *was* beginning to run, and he had to mumble encouragement under his breath, hoping against hope. As she approached the quarter pole, Rosie caught up with the pack. As usual, her pace seemed relaxed and unhurried, but she was passing the other fillies one by one. He began to shout his encouragement, and Becky chimed in. As Rosie straightened into the stretch, only three horses were in front of her.

That situation did not continue. As the leading filly came to the sixteenth pole, Rosie moved to the outside and swept by everyone, untouched by the jockey's whip. She won the race by widening daylight.

Except for Bogey and Becky, the crowd was strangely silent. The masterful NYRA race caller spoke for them on the public address system. "Well, Final Gift in her first start gave us all a gift. The gift of a new star in the racing firmament. The final time of her race was just off Came Home's time record for the Hopeful Stakes at the same distance. Even the colts had better watch out for this girl."

Bogey was jumping around like a mad man. "She did it! She did it!" He shouted and grabbed Becky in a bear hug. She was laughing crazily as they danced around together.

"Did you hear what he said? The boys better watch out for our girl!" she yelled in his ear.

Behind him Bogey heard a familiar voice.

"Humphrey, hey Humphrey! We're rich again."

Puzzled, Bogey turned to see Fats Sheppard rushing toward him. His old friend had changed a lot over the years, even in the three years since he had stepped in at Dawson's low point in Baltimore. Today Fats, who usually wore tee shirts and jeans, was sharply dressed in a tan sport coat and tie. Some things never changed; as always, his broad face was split in a brilliant smile, his auburn hair was tousled and his eyes glowed with excitement.

He gave Bogey a hug and launched into a breathless monologue. "Where have you been anyway? I don't have your phone number. Never mind, we can get to that. Tell me about this filly of yours. Dynamite! Lucky I was here for the week on business and good thing I saw you. I managed to get a pretty good bet down on her. You should have told me you were bringing this one up here, or have you forgotten all your old friends?"

Bogey had to break in. "Fats, listen for a minute." He pointed to Becky. "This is Becky Friedman. We work together. This is my old friend Fats Sheppard," he told her.

Jim turned an appreciative eye on the exercise girl. "Nice working conditions."

She smiled at him. "I don't really work with him. I work for him. Why does he call you Fats? You look pretty cut to me."

Jim laughed. "Before I discovered healthy food and running, I deserved the nickname. Believe you me."

Bogey felt a twinge of jealousy. These two were hitting it off too well. He was relieved to see Judy Patton and Rosie circling back. Even with the distraction, Bogey had kept an eye on the filly as she pulled up smoothly and headed back with her head held high.

"Fats, I have to take care of the horse. I'll catch you up later."

"Come by our box. We're right at the finish line."

"Fats, as soon as we get the filly cooled out and tested, we'll probably load up and head back home," he told him firmly, intending the message for Becky as well.

"Okay, okay. Take my card. Call me on the eight hundred number. I'm still out in California, at least I will be on Monday."

Bogey nodded and shook Jim's hand. He hurried over to lead Rosie into the winner's circle. Judy was smiling down at him.

"You've got one here. She just flicks the track behind her. I mean she barely touches the dirt," she said.

As Bogey led Rosie to the winner's circle, the jockey added, "Think of me the next time you race her, okay?"

* * *

When Bogey came out of the test barn with the filly, Becky was waiting for him. "How about you, Rosie!" she said enthusiastically "You are the greatest. The greatest! Waller was very proud of you." Smiling, her wide full lips framed perfect teeth, and Bogey went limp with longing for her.

She cocked her head to one side and studied Bogey. "You're mighty glum for a guy who's got the best two-year-old filly in the land."

He plodded toward their trailer, head down. "I've had time to think about what's coming down the road after this."

"Like when Sentinel's Cry made such a splash?"

He nodded. As they neared the barn where Waller awaited them, he said, "Crazy things happen around a great thoroughbred. Bad things can happen."

"They're about to start," Becky said and pointed to the black Mercedes parked beside the barn. Otey Musgrove leaned against it.

Rosie flattened her ears and squealed, dancing backward.

Otey opened the back door for Huddleston.

"Well, congratulations," Huddleston said. "We have a very nice filly here. I'm thinking I need to raise my price."

"*We* don't have anything," Bogey said.

"Come on, Shrimp," Otey laughed. "You're just one sensible move away from being a rich man."

"Just go away," Bogey said evenly.

Huddleston's voice was the essence of calm reason. "You can't afford that attitude of yours, Humphrey. This filly ran green. I could put her with a top-notch trainer. You're way out of your league with a horse like this one."

"You'll never get her," Bogey said coldly.

"Look, we can do this nicely, and you walk away with a fat check, or we can let you drown in debt. Either way, I get that filly and her daddy."

Huddleston turned on his heel and walked to the car. Otey opened the door for him and then feigned a sudden move toward Rosie. The filly went up on her rear legs and lurched toward the car. Otey jumped in hurriedly. When he had the door safely shut, he rolled down the window and leered at them. "I'll see you two and that crazy horse later, Shrimp."

CHAPTER 9

They didn't talk during the first hour of the drive back to Charles Town. Bogey stared ahead in glum silence except for terse remarks into his cell phone when someone called. After the third call, Becky spoke up.

"Pull over and let me drive. Between your mood and the phone, we're going to end up in the ditch."

He was glad they made the switch because the phone continued to emit his "Call to the Post" ring tone as soon as he hung up on the previous call.

"Damn," he muttered as the phone rang once again.

"You could turn it off," Becky pointed out.

"I got this thing thinking I would have owners wanting to keep in touch. After Rosie's show, I'm hoping to get a new client or two. I can't afford to miss that call."

"How many of those calls were owners?"

"Zero," he said glumly.

"Who is calling?"

"A few old friends, owners and fellow trainers from Maryland."

"That's nice."

"Would have been nicer if they called when I was getting skinned."

She shrugged. "Everybody loves a winner."

"Yeah. And nobody wants you when you're down and out."

"Hum a few bars," she joked. and he actually grinned again.

"All the other calls were about buying Rosie."

"This soon? Wow!"

"All of them were bloodstock agents. Those guys are just fishing," Bogey said. "The serious ones will come later after the big money does research."

"Will they want her? She doesn't have that much pedigree."

"She's by a son of Seattle Slew. Waller's her brother, and he's stakes placed with over a hundred thousand in winnings. After her show today, that will probably be enough to tempt some sizable bids," Bogey said glumly. "Huddleston won't be the only one bugging me."

He turned off his phone but then lapsed back into dark silence.

Becky studied him out of the corner of her eye. "You can't just dwell on Huddleston. Let's not think about that. Let's not talk about that. Let's talk about me," she said brightly. "I know you're dying to know how I won Judy Patton's fervent love and boundless respect."

"And you're going to tell me."

"Only if you take over the driving."

When they made the change, she leaned back in her seat and launched into the story.

"Judy and I met in elementary school. I liked her, but I liked her pony even more. His name was Bouncer, and I loved him the moment I saw him. I loved Judy for herself, of course, but even more because she shared Bouncer with me. We were with that little rascal every free moment, taking turns riding, grooming him, and talking to him or about him the rest of the time."

She tuned in the seat to glance at him. "Maybe I shouldn't tell you all this, you probably don't want all this information."

"No. I want to hear about it. Actually, it was my friend Fats who got me started on horses. I'll tell you about that some time, but go ahead with your story. It's a lot more interesting than Edmond Huddleston."

She nodded and gathered her thoughts. "I guess for you to really understand I need to tell you a little bit about my family. I don't know how many Jews you know in Baltimore, probably not many with your blueblood gentile roots, but in my family achievement is everything – achievement and reputation. The driving force on that comes from mother. Maybe it's a carry over from how Jews were treated in the wider society, the kind of treatment that has been going on for centuries and was worse for the second wave of immigrants to this country. We had to live in certain areas, weren't welcome in some clubs, you know, all that stuff. It was definitely the case in Baltimore. In any case, my big brother is the joy of my mother's life. Outstanding student, pre-med practically in grade school, doctor now, the ideal son. Now here I come, no real ambition, mediocre grades, playing with ponies when I should have been hitting the books."

"Sounds a little like me," Bogey said. "Does your family have money?"

She laughed. "Not as much as mother wishes we had. Poor dad. He works hard, but he's not the type to climb up the company ladder. Anyway, enough somewhat soiled laundry, the point is that my mother wasn't sure I should be such close friends with a gentile. I never even told her about the pony. If she had known about Bouncer, she would have really flipped out. From her point of view, she should have. After I fell for that pony, I never let myself be away from horseflesh again, and that flew in the face of everything she wanted me to be.

"Mother moved the family to Pikesville. Maybe Judy wasn't the only reason. Mother was concerned that too many black kids were coming to Northwestern. She probably thought she was protecting my brother and me, but I was broken hearted. I didn't drive, couldn't get back to the old neighborhood to see Judy or Bouncer."

"You were sad," Bogey said. His comment sounded dumb to him, but she seemed to accept the support.

"Broken hearted. By the time I could drive, Judy had outgrown Bouncer. She gave him to a younger cousin, lied about her age, and soon was exercising thoroughbreds at Pimlico. She got me on as a hot walker as soon as she could, and my family – at least my mother and brother - all but disowned me when they learned about that. You can't blame mother. When she's at temple and Mrs. Cohen talks about her son the doctor and her daughter the lawyer and asks after mother Friedman's daughter —." Becky shrugged.

"That's why I left a good spot in Maryland and came up here. With me out of town, mother could come up with some face-saving evasion," Becky summed up.

Bogey glanced at her. In the dim glow from the dashboard lights, her eyes were downcast and moist. "Okay. That's the story of Punch and Judy. Tell me about Fats and the – let's see, what did the oaf call you? Oh yeah, the story of Fats and the Shrimp."

Her cheery tone was forced. Bogey swallowed, at a loss for words. He was near tears.

"Come on," she said, her voice almost shrill with false cheer. "Your turn."

"It's getting late. I'm tired. Let's save that for later."

From the corner of his eye he could see her slump against her door. She didn't argue. She seemed lost in her thoughts, wandering sadly down the lane of family regrets. Bogey understood. He had walked that street many times.

* * *

It was two in the morning when they arrived at the barn and put the horses away. Bogey dropped her off in front of the house she directed him to.

"I won't need you until Wednesday," Bogey said when she got out of the car. That sounded cold, but he wasn't sure what else to say.

"I guess we're not great at celebrating, but congratulations. You have a really fine racehorse." She paused and gave him a searching stare. "You're not going to let anyone spoil that, are you?"

"I'll try not to," he said, wishing he could sound more resolute.

After Becky was safely inside the house, he glanced at his watch. Was it worth driving to the farm? By the time he got there it would be time to come back and feed. A nap in the office chair would be heavenly. Of course, that wasn't an option. Sentinel's Cry had to be fed. He turned his car toward the farm.

At least it was Sunday morning. The track was closed to workouts, and Waller wasn't racing that afternoon. He fed the stallion, downed a pot of coffee and drove back to the track. He fed and walked his three horses to give them a brief break from standing in their stalls. Rosie was bouncing around during her walk, apparently none the worse for her race exertion and all the travel. She lightened the blanket of fatigue weighing on him. After a few chores back at the farm, he could tumble into bed for some blessed sleep. That was something to look forward to!

On the ride back to the farm, he remembered to turn his cell phone back on. It immediately chirped, signaling a voicemail. Actually there were several. Two were call back's from the bloodhorse agents. The third was from his father, a warm congratulatory message. The call pleased him, and he found himself wishing Becky would get a similar call from her family. Bogey wondered if they, or Becky for that matter, realized how happy that would make her.

He checked the last message. Huddleston's raspy voice put an end to other thoughts.

"Just wanted you to know I'm watching, and I still plan to buy the horse. We'll talk later."

The bastard! The arrogant bastard.

He drove back to the farm, too riled up to think of sleep. He paced the narrow front room of the house trailer that served as his home. Should he call his father? Even though those calls often turned sour, it might be different this time. His father had sounded happy for him on the voicemail. Surely the wise old lawyer would hear the implied threat in Huddleston's words.

I still *plan* to buy the horse. Plan! Not "hope". Not "still am interested".

Coming after Bogey's adamant rejection of Huddleston's overture, *plan* was a challenge.

Richard Dawson was Bogey's dad and Huddleston's attorney. Maybe he could talk some sense to his client and help his son.

He made the call. As always, his father answered with alacrity and enthusiasm.

"I'm glad you called. I'm so proud of you! Did you get my message?"

"Yes. Thanks a lot. I am really excited about this horse. She's the best I've ever had."

"That's wonderful. If anyone deserved some good luck it's you. What's next for you and your star?"

"I haven't thought about that yet. I'm calling about Edmond Huddleston. I'd like some help in dealing with him."

There was one of those pauses, but not so extended this time. "What has Mr. Huddleston done this time?"

"He came up to Saratoga and cornered me about buying Rosie. I gave him a flat no. So then he leaves me a message saying that he still plans to buy Final Gift."

"Yes. He told me that he still hopes you decide to sell him the filly. It seems reasonable that after this win he will be even more eager to buy her."

"Dad, he didn't say he 'hoped' to buy her or that he 'was eager' to buy her. He said he *plans* to buy her. It's like the fact that I said she wasn't for sale didn't mean anything."

There was a long pause, and Bogey braced himself. In the past, his father had objected to any informal address. Dad, pop, daddy, or poppa – any of those implied a degree of disrespect. Father was the correct word. Bogey was out of line in both style and content.

His father surprised him.

"Son, you may be putting too fine a point on a single word, but in all honesty, I found myself somewhat troubled by Edmond's tone in our last meeting. He seems obsessed with your horse and fixated on convincing you to sell to him."

"That's not going to happen," Bogey said grimly.

"So you have told me. At the risk of offending you, I will repeat my recommendation to you. I believe it would be in your best interest to sell the filly at a good price. I believe Edmond stands ready to make a generous offer."

"Not for sale to him at any price."

"Think this over carefully. What if the filly is injured? What if she isn't as talented as you hope? Are you prepared to rest your entire well being on such a fragile and unpredictable creature?"

"I was hoping that you could change Huddleston's mind, not mine."

"I'm not equal to either task. Both of you are very stubborn men."

"What did Huddleston say in your last meeting that got you upset?"

"Lawyer-client privilege. You know that."

"Just give me a hint. Father-son privilege."

After the pause, Richard Dawson said, "I'm concerned he'll try to pressure you into selling. I have advised him to just wait."

"Sure. He's good at waiting," Bogey said sarcastically. "Let's don't get into what your client said. How would you pressure me?"

"I would find some way to emphasize your precarious fiscal condition."

"He'll do more than that."

"Come now, Humphrey, I'll admit that Edmond is a tough business man, but I don't believe he'll do anything illegal or even unfair."

"After all these years, I can't believe that you don't know him better," Bogey said angrily and clenched his jaws to dam a torrent of resentment based on the simple fact that his father admired people like Huddleston – and yes, brother Dickey – more than he admired weaker people. People like Bogey.

CHAPTER 10

On Monday morning Bogey, found Marshall Herbert waiting for him when he finished feeding and walking Rosie. The banker smiled at him.

"Congratulations on the filly. Did I get here early enough to see my boy on the track?"

Bogey smiled back at him. Herbert was somewhere in his 70's, white-haired and painfully slender. Behind tortoise shell glasses, his blue eyes announced kindness coupled with no nonsense alertness. Bogey had been fortunate to encounter him when he applied for a mortgage loan. The old fellow had read over his application, then looked up at him appraisingly.

"Young man, you're lucky I'm a racing fan. I'll approve this loan purely because of your talents. Let's say that you're getting my cash because of what I read in the *Racing Form.*" He held up the application. "It's certainly not because of what I read here."

Two weeks later, the banker had asked Bogey to meet him at the upcoming horse sale in Maryland. "As long as I'm betting on you I might as well go under completely. I have a couple of thousand to blow on a two-year-old. I've always wanted to own a race horse, and I think you're the guy who might pick me a cheap winner. That is, if you have room for another horse in your barn."

"Now, don't be mean, Mr. Herbert," Bogey laughed.

Bogey had already tacked up Marshall's raw-boned chestnut, the best offering they had been able to buy within the banker's limited budget. He led the colt out for the owner's inspection.

"This big lug is eating me out of house and home," Bogey said, coaxing the big horse to stand square.

"Wrong thing to say to your banker," Herbert quipped. He walked around the big colt, shading his eyes against the slanting morning sun. "He's looking less like a scarecrow. How is he out on the track?"

"I'll show you." Bogey flipped up into the saddle.

"I thought you guys had to have a leg up," Marshall said. "You've got some real spring in those legs."

"People don't realize it, but riding gets you fit. Walk up to the rail, and I'll gallop him around a couple of times. He's coming together. I like the way he strides out."

After the workout, Bogey brought the horse back to the barn and dismounted. The banker walked down the hill and joined him. "Well, what did you think?" Bogey asked.

"I don't know what I'm looking at, but he looks strong. I need to name him. What do you think of Off Shore?"

"Sounds okay. It's up to you. Think about what you want to hear over the public address. You'll get some calls." Bogey slapped the horse on the rump. "See that drive train? It's muscling up more every day." He looked down at the horse's legs, leading him forward a step until his limbs were even. "He's very correct, and now he's getting some meat on him. I think he's going to be useful. Won't know until they pop the gate, though. I try not to get too high on one till they show something in a race."

Marshall Herbert continued to stand in the same place, saying nothing.

"I've got to walk him now and bathe him," Bogey said, wondering why the man just stood there.

"I know. I won't keep you long. It's just...I mean, something has come up. Maybe it's nothing, but I wanted to let you know."

"Okay," Bogey said uncertainly.

"There has been some talk, some rumors going around about the bank."

"I don't listen to rumors. I like the bank. I appreciate you taking a chance on me. The bank is fine."

"You don't understand. The rumors may affect you. A couple of prominent people asked me if there is any truth to the tale that we are carrying some non-performing loans on the books. Two different men at different times. That's the kind of talk that might bring bank examiners around."

"Look, I know I'm behind on the payments. As soon as the Saratoga win clears, I will be able to do some catching up. It usually takes them about a week and then just the mail...."

Marshall shook his head. "I'm not dunning you. I know you'll do what you can. Unfortunately, you're not the only horseman who is behind. If the examiners come in here, they could make me call loans on a bunch of friends. In your case, it would wreck you."

Bogey knew what he was getting at. Everything he owned, not just the farm, but his car, the old horse trailer and, worst of all, Sentinel's Cry, Waller, and Final Gift were on the loan as collateral. If the loan was called, Bogey would have nothing.

"All I'm trying to tell you is this. If there is any way for you to get current on the mortgage, do it." The banker opened his arms as if he wished he could give the trainer a hug. "I don't want to pull the rug out just when you get this nice filly, but it could be taken out of my hands."

Bogey nodded. Then he had a thought that brought a wry grin. "I've got a good name for an honest banker's horse. Don't call him Off Shore. Name him after what I don't have. Call him Substantial Balance," he said.

CHAPTER 11

At that same moment, Becky Friedman slowed as she guided Harry Collins' best runner down the ramp. The dependable mare had worked well and was her usual tractable self, so Becky could ease her and look over at Bogey Dawson. She wanted to say hello and congratulate him once again on Rosie's amazing race. The ride back from Saratoga had turned strange there at the end. Part of the blame was surely hers. Why had she let a cute story about Judy and the pony sour into a bleak tale of family rejection? No wonder the man had clamed up.

Still, she resented him for not somehow rescuing her from the pit she dug herself.

In any case, she needed to normalize things, just get them back to the comfortable working relationship that had existed before she dumped on him. If nothing else was destined between them, she needed at least that much.

But he was talking with his owner and hadn't even seen her. She paused a moment longer, looking at them, ignoring the curious glances of passing riders.

Bogey was standing beside the big chestnut that belonged to the banker. Becky saw the animal was blossoming into a different horse from the gawky skeleton she had seen earlier. Damn him! Dawson saw the quality in a thoroughbred when others could not. She wasn't sure whether she admired him or envied him. Maybe both.

Maybe that was the real reason she had been bummed out since the Saratoga trip. She had come face to face with herself in coming to know Dawson better.

Bogey wasn't running from something. He had beaten a necessary retreat from Maryland, but he wasn't trying to escape, he was simply regrouping. He knew where he was headed.

As she had told her story aloud to Dawson, she realized that was not true of her. She had no real destination. Her withdrawal had no purpose except to put distance between herself and her mother. Her brother was just mother's amplifier, increasing the volume but broadcasting the same message of disappointment and disapproval. She had fled because she didn't want to hear it any longer.

Sure, she could ride any horse that came along. The more ornery the better. She was fearless and loud-mouthed, needing no one, beholden to none. Oh yeah, she was one tough chick.

She was proving things to everyone except herself.

Even the patient old mare was getting tired of puttering along. Becky had to move on. Bogey Dawson was deep in some important and meaningful conversation with Marshall Herbert. He had no time for smartass exercise girls. Once again, he didn't even see her.

CHAPTER 12

Bogey was furious. He knew questions about Marshall's bank originated from Edmond Huddleston. The bastard was increasing the pressure. It was working. Bogey was angry but also terrified. He had nowhere to turn. Of course, his father would loan him the money he needed. He would probably even offer to give it to him. Similar offers had been made in the past and rejected. He couldn't be on his father's dole.

He finished his morning work with the horses, his moves automatic, his mind mired in the struggle to find a solution. Even Rosie's playful nickering as she begged for attention couldn't divert him. Helplessness and a sense of futility settled on him like a cold mist. He managed to drive to the farm without running off the road and to continue building the fence around a newly cleared paddock without driving a nail through his hand.

When he finished the day's tasks, night pushed at the trailer windows, closing him in solitary confinement. He had to talk to a human being. A friendly human being.

He found the card that Fats had given him in Saratoga. A brief calculation told him that it was almost seven p.m. in California. Fats had scribbled his home number on the back of the card, and Bogey dialed it. He got an answering machine. Since he had nothing better to do, he turned the card over and dialed the 800 number there.

"Intercontinental Reach," a cheery female voice answered.

"I was calling for Jim Sheppard," Bogey stammered, caught off guard.

"Mr. Sheppard is in a meeting at the moment. May I ask who is calling?"

"This is Bo— I mean Humphrey Dawson. Nothing important. Just an old friend."

"Oh my God! Humphrey! You are a legend to Jim. He talks about you constantly. By the way, I'm Millie, Millie Ashcraft, Jim's kept woman."

"Oh, hello," he managed to say.

"Listen, hang on. I'll get Jim for you."

"Oh, don't pull him out of a meeting. He can call me later."

"He's only meeting with his computer. I just say the other thing to brush off the money guys; they're always sniffing around these days. Jim would kill me if I let you get off the phone without talking to him."

Bogey heard the phone drop on something solid and then Millie's voice shouting for Jim. In a moment, Jim's exuberant voice came on.

"Humphrey! Thanks for calling. I have to ask you, how's Final Gift? Boy is she well named! She's a gift sure enough. I've never seen a race like that, especially from a first-time starter. That was one to remember. Well?"

The words tumbled out so quickly Bogey forgot the question.

"Well, what?"

"How is the filly? Don't you listen?"

"Oh, she came out of the race fine. I might even take her back to the track tomorrow."

"Terrific! Let me know where and when she runs next. I will be there. One advantage of having your own company is that you can get off anytime you want."

"And you can still be at work at eight o'clock in the evening," Bogey reminded him.

Jim chuckled. "That too."

Bogey was feeling a little better already.

"Fats, I have a question for you. Millie? You mentioned her at Saratoga, but you haven't told me about her."

"She is the absolute greatest, that's who Millie is."

"So she's your receptionist and your girlfriend? Isn't that fraternizing or something?"

Jim laughed. "I'm very happy to say that she is my lady indeed, but she's no receptionist. She is the number one computer hacker in Silicon Valley, maybe in the world."

"Hacker? Isn't that against the law?"

"Hacker, not cracker. Her skills go to understanding and writing software – although if she wanted to go illicit she could crack any firewall that's been invented. Among her many accomplishments, she is my partner. We created Intercontinental together."

In the background, Bogey could hear Millie protesting, and over the phone he heard Jim say, "Take some credit, girl. You're not just another gorgeous lay." Then he could hear Millie clearly. Her face had to be beside Jim's. "Keep up the flattery and I'll let you take me home, but finish talking to your buddy first," she said.

"Damn," Jim said. "I wish I could find me a responsive woman." He laughed. "For some reason I've lost focus here," he told Bogey.

"Look, I'll get off. I don't want to stand in the way of true love."

"Don't worry. You won't. Anticipation just sweetens the reward. Really, seriously. I want to talk a while. What's going on with you? Are you and that little Saratoga beauty together?"

"Not hardly. She likes working horses with me, and that's it."

"I don't know. I saw a glance. I tune in to those since I never saw one before college. Be that as it may, tell me about Charles Town. Did you pick the right place to get back on your feet?"

"I'm surviving. It's difficult, but things are less expensive here. I'll make it."

"You sound strained. What's wrong?"

Bogey wasn't sure whether he was touched or annoyed. Fats had always been able to read him, especially when he was covering up negative thoughts. It wasn't always pleasant to be so well understood.

"Nothing important. I'm just tired. It's been a busy day."

"Bullshit. I'm tired of that "tired" story. Just tell me why you're upset."

Bogey sighed, and as he always ended up doing, told Fats the whole story. When Bogey finally talked himself out, Fats said, "What an asshole! He has a barn full of blue ribbon stock, and he wants your one outstanding prospect. Damn, if this was coming up a year from now, I'd loan you the dough. I haven't told you about it, but people are going nuts to buy companies like mine. The numbers I'm hearing give me a headache."

A female shout. "More like a hard on."

"Don't mind her. Anyway, I don't have the money now, and now is when Huddleston has you over a barrel."

"He has me scared," Bogey said. "I don't know what to do."

"Okay," Fats said. "Remember how we were always bullied? That was because we just took it. We were scared. They knew it, and they just kept sticking it to us. But after that day when we fought back, no more bullying. Remember?"

"I don't really like fighting," Bogey said. "I always go overboard."

"You didn't start it then, and you're not starting it now. You can't let Huddleston put you back on your heels. You need to take the fight to him."

Bogey heard Millie shouting something in the background. Fats laughed. "Millie says if you want she'll have the bastard up on child porn charges. She could do it, too. A little cracking, and then what's on his computer accidentally gets sent to a cop."

Bogey enjoyed the suggestion. Suddenly he felt less helpless. "I don't want to go that way–at least not yet. Tell her I'll get back to her if I change my mind." He paused and then added. "Can you think of a more legal way to fight back?"

"Now you're talking! Let me think a minute." The phone was silent for only a moment. "How about your father? Can he pull some legalese on the bank threat? Maybe he could put some kind of pressure on Huddleston, too."

"I don't want to involve him. After all, he is Huddleston's attorney. Besides he will start coming up with ways to bail me out. He wants to help, but I don't want to go to him. He already thinks I'm a loser."

"Little Dick is the loser. I don't know why your father can't see that." Bogey knew Jim was referring to his brother, using the name he had given him back in middle school. "He sucks up to your dad and to anyone he thinks can boost him. He's an idiot."

"You're being too hard on Dickey. Maybe he wasn't a brilliant student, but he got through law school."

"At your father's alma mater that practically got its endowment from Richard Dawson, Senior. Tell me he didn't trade on that."

"Forget all that. My father is out of this picture."

"Okay. Here's brilliant thought number two. Make Huddleston pay for fucking with you."

"Great idea. Just how would I do that?"

"Why not find a race in his backyard that he plans to win as usual, then take your rocket over there and kick his ass? Show him who knows horseflesh. Embarrass the shit right on his home court."

"In Maryland? I'm not sure I'm welcome there. They talked about revoking my license."

"Welcome, hell, crash the damn party. They can't keep you out."

The notion was appealing. He had never received a formal notice that his Maryland training license had been pulled. Maybe he was still legal there. He could ask his father to check it out. That favor wouldn't come with unwelcome strings attached.

"Do I hear some gears turning? Speak to me," Fats said.

"Yeah. I'm giving your idea some serious thought. I like it."

"Of course you do. You like it, and you're going to do it. Just be sure to let me know the date. I wouldn't miss it."

"Thanks, Fats. I can't even tell you how much I appreciate this."

"Yeah. That's what Millie tells me most every night."

Bogey could hear the lady hooting loudly and screaming, "You wish!"

* * *

Bogey found the prospect of revenge amazingly refreshing. Even Becky noticed the change in his mood and manner over the next week.

"Jeez, Dawson, you're almost human. I didn't know you could look me in the eye, smile, and give me my crap right back. Are you on crack or something?" she asked as they backtracked one Saturday after galloping the horses.

He cocked his head and pursed his lips. "Better," he said. "Much better."

He told her his plan, and she gave a long low whistle.

"You're going to take on Huddleston at Laurel? Ballsy, but I thought they drummed you out of the corps over there."

"Turns out they didn't. I checked."

"So how do you know Huddleston will have horses in the race?"

"It's not a secret. His trainer said they were using this allowance as prep for the Futurity in November. They'll put both of their good colts in as an entry. It's all in the Form." Bogey looked at her with a glint in his eye. "The reporter quotes Huddleston saying 'we plan to run 1-2'. Arrogant son of a bitch."

"Am I going to the lion's den with you?"

"If you will. Same team; you, me, Waller and Rosie."

Becky gave him a long, searching look. "You mean it, don't you? I have to ask you if you've really thought this through. You're going to take your filly to a hostile track to run against colts – very good colts."

"Yes. We're going to shove this down Huddleston's throat."

"Do you want Judy to ride?"

"Of course. Give her a call."

CHAPTER 13

"I can't do that, hon. Not even for you," Judy told her immediately when Becky asked about her availability to ride Rosie on Saturday. "I'm already on five horses here. Two of them are live in stakes races, one actually an even money favorite. My agent would kill me if I even brought up the idea of heading to Maryland."

"I thought you had the man wrapped around your finger."

"I do, but there are limits. I want the guy to propose to me, not drop my contract."

Becky squealed. "You didn't tell me he was your man! How long has this been going on?"

"For me, since I met the guy. It took awhile to plant the notion in his mind."

"But it's growing now?"

"Yeah, but I still have to cultivate. Seriously, the man's livelihood consists of a quarter of my earnings, and we have a chance to make big money Saturday. As much as I'd love to ride your horse, I can't dump two stakes races to ride in an allowance in Maryland. I'm sorry."

"I understand. Bogey has a decent jock here that he can take over."

"You've got to let me back on her when you bring her up here. Don't hold this against me."

"He's not that kind of guy."

"Yeah, I got that vibe. He's kinda cute, too. I thought I detected a little chemistry between you two."

"No, definitely not. He is sweet and cute but about the right size for me to put on my charm bracelet, not date," she lied.

"Aren't we shallow? You're seriously counting out a good looking good guy just because he's not tall enough to dunk a basketball?"

"Come on. It matters. I bet your guy is tall."

"Yeah, he's only an inch shorter than me. Parker is an ex-jockey. He was one of the best before he got hurt."

"Sorry," Becky said. "I didn't know. No offense intended."

"Don't worry about it. You're the one with the height fixation. I gotta go, but do tell Bogey to bring that girl back to the big time in the Big Apple. We have a major two-year-old stakes race here at the end of November, the kind of win that would make her reputation."

"I'll tell him," Becky said humbly, still feeling like a fool.

"And tell your cute little charm that I have to ride her."

"Yes, ma'am. I'll surely tell him that."

"And, by the bye, you might do a little honest self-searching about why you just happened to end up in Charles Town working closely with a trainer you admired in Maryland. Do you really think you're that committed to your charm bracelet?"

CHAPTER 14

Everything went smoothly over the next weeks. Rosie was training forwardly, eager for her daily work and eating everything. She had one period of restlessness and irritability, which was cured magically by another short visit to the farm.

"Maybe she just likes the van ride with her buddy," Becky suggested.

"I think it's just change of scene she craves. Standing in a stall twenty plus hours a day with one exercise period, and two meals served in your cell. Sounds like prison, don't you think?"

Whatever the explanation, Rosie seemed to thrive on the life he had designed for her.

When it was time to enter her in the Laurel allowance race, Bogey felt considerable trepidation about the reception he might face when he called the racing secretary. It could be awkward.

It was not.

"Humphrey!" the racing secretary said. His name was Carl Turner, and Bogey had always considered him good at his job. "How have you been? There is a lot of buzz around here about your two-year-old. When are you going to bring her over here? Taking her to Saratoga! You ought to be ashamed. I need her in a race."

"That's why I'm calling. Enter her for the allowance race on Saturday."

"Not that one, that's a boy's allowance," the secretary objected.

"Haven't you heard of equal opportunity? Put her on the list." Bogey was pleased that lately he occasionally popped out something resembling a quip. Becky's influence.

The other man spoke slowly. He seemed to be choosing his words with care. "Of course, I'll do that if you wish." His tone became hushed, conspiratorial. "Mr. Huddleston has his two best horses in that race. One of them has blinding speed; the other is a powerful closer. They ran first and second in the prep stakes. Fastest six furlongs we've had this year. I mean, even older horses haven't run as fast." The secretary was whispering earnestly.

"Thanks, Carl. I appreciate the warning. Please put her in. Frankly, the only thing I don't like about the race is that it's six furlongs. My girl probably wants to go further."

* * *

Things started going less smoothly when he called to invite Fats to the race. Millie told him his friend was just starting a miserable bout of the flu and couldn't come to Maryland. Things got even worse when Bogey arrived at Laurel on Saturday. He went directly to the racing office to turn in Rosie's registration papers, leaving Becky to see to the horses. He didn't know the young man behind the counter, but the guy looked nervous. He had trouble looking Bogey in the eye. "Er, Mr. Dawson. The boss wants to see you in his office."

Bogey was confused. "I thought this *was* Carl's office."

"Not that boss," the man said, "The big boss, head of the track. Go to Mr. Briarson's office. They're waiting for you."

The CEO's blonde receptionist glanced up at him. "Go on in. They're waiting for you."

Inside the inner office, the same gray-haired man who had told Bogey of his suspension was behind his desk. Two other men flanked him. All three men were staring gravely at Bogey. The man on Bogey's left was Edmond Huddleston. The red-faced, wide-shouldered man on the other side was Sean O'Hannohan, track maintenance supervisor.

Briarson pointed to a chair that faced the three men. "Please sit down, Mr. Dawson," he said stiffly. When Bogey was seated, the CEO continued, "Mr. Dawson, I understand that you have brought your filly, Final Gift, to run in our eighth race today."

"Yes, of course," Bogey said, puzzled. "I just took her papers to the office. She's been officially and properly entered, and my Maryland owner and trainer papers are all in order. What is the purpose of this meeting?"

The CEO's voice was stern. "It is a meeting to determine if I can permit your horse to race here today. I have received alarming allegations that lead me to think your filly may pose a safety hazard to other horses in the race."

"I would assume that these allegations came from Mr. Huddleston," Bogey said evenly.

Huddleston offered a disarming smile. "Look, Mr. Dawson, I hated to bring this up. After all, I'm involved in trying to finalize a business deal with you. It is not in my interest to make you angry, but you must admit that your actions suggest some hidden agenda."

"My agenda isn't hidden. I entered my horse to beat yours and to show you up. A straight forward plan, don't you agree?"

Caleb Briarson was readying an indignant comment, but Huddleston waved him off.

"It's alright, Mr. Briarson. Humphrey lacks basic tact, but if he really was here to contest a fair race, that would be fine. I suggest he has a different plan. He has chosen to enter a filly that has had only one race – in which she ran very greenly, by the way – against two talented and seasoned colts. One of these colts won a stakes race right her, as you know, sir. You may remember the other colt closed rapidly for second. Since one of my horses runs on the front and the other is a closer, there is no reasonable scenario for Mr. Dawson's filly to have any chance to win. I can only conclude that he intends to risk the poor animal in some effort to injure one or both of my colts."

Bogey was incredulous. "What bull! My filly is a very special horse. I didn't bring her here to get hurt."

Huddleston turned to Briarson, apologetic but persistent. "I really hate to bring up Mr. Dawson's painful past, but he did deliberately injure a good horse before. He did it to one of mine."

Bogey was half out of his chair. "You liar! You know who caused that horse to break down," he shouted.

Briarson cut in sharply. "Mr. Dawson. Sit down."

Bogey was so furious that he did not hear the door open behind him, but he couldn't miss the changes in the faces of the men opposite him. Huddleston frowned, puzzled. "Richard? What are you doing here?"

Bogey turned to see his father standing in the doorway.

"Hello, Edmond, Caleb," Richard Dawson, Sr. said in a friendly manner. Nodding to the third man, he added, "Mr. O'Hannahan, isn't it? I'm Richard Dawson."

Edmond Huddleston's surprise turned to suspicion. "Why are you here?"

"I was looking for my son to wish him luck. They told me he was here."

Bogey's father pulled up a chair beside him, leaning over to pat him on the shoulder. "I hope I'm not interrupting an important meeting," he said innocently.

Bogey's breath, trapped in the tension of his chest, escaped in a relaxing sigh. "Nothing too important, Father. Mr. Briarson agrees with Huddleston that I'm here today to cause trouble. I'm actually here to win a horse race, but they don't believe me. This meeting is to decide if I will be permitted to run Final Gift in today's race."

"Son. Why didn't you tell me about the notice you received that this meeting was planned?"

"I didn't get a notice. They just sent me here when I arrived at the track."

"Caleb, I'm sure that was an oversight or clerical error. As you well know, there can be no meeting without notification and cause."

Briarson frowned. "I am within the scope of my authority here."

"Caleb, I would never challenge your authority or good judgment, however your own bylaws clearly delineate the rights of trainers in the state of Maryland. Their right to enter and run horses cannot be abridged without a notification and formal hearing."

Briarson's expression betrayed concern and uncertainty, but he straightened himself and fought to regain control of the proceedings. "You are overlooking one fact, Richard. Threats to public safety widen my emergency powers to bypass the routine hearing requirements."

"Alleged threats raised by a race competitor aren't sufficient reason to block a man's livelihood. Absent any demonstrable danger, I can get an emergency injunction to permit my son to race today. If you wish to contest his future status, send us formal notice, and we will appear as requested."

Briarson's face was hard with suppressed anger. Huddleston was staring at him. "Mr. Briarson, you don't have to listen to this legal claptrap. You are in charge here."

Richard inclined his head and smiled warmly at the CEO. "I know it must be difficult to go against Mr. Huddleston since he fills your races with competitive horses. He has been very loyal to Maryland, hasn't he? He races here whenever he possibly can. A real friend of Maryland racing." He nodded to Huddleston and gave him a smile, too. "Unfortunately Mr. Huddleston does not know the law. Since I handle his legal difficulties, he may not even understand the full extent of risk involved if one does not follow its canons."

Edmond Huddleston's head snapped forward. "Dawson, I may sue you for conflict of interest. You are *my* attorney, not Humphrey's."

"Just a moment!" The old lawyer looked to Briarson. "No one told me that Mr. Huddleston was a principal in this action. I thought he was just advising you. Has he brought legal action against Humphrey?"

"No. It's not a law suit. Mr. Huddleston was just acting in the best interest of the race track, simply offering me information."

The old lawyer shook his head and made a dismissive clucking sound. "Information or conjecture, it doesn't matter. Edmond, you have no legal standing in the matter, so I have no lawyer-client status with you. Come on, now, this whole thing is just a misunderstanding. Let's all go enjoy a day at the races and leave the courts of law out of things."

The three men behind the desk stared at one another in angry confusion. "You may have reason to regret intruding into this, Richard," Huddleston blurted, then quickly caught himself. "I mean if there is an injury or incident in the race."

Outside Bogey clasped his father's hand in both of his. "Thank you. They were going to skin me in there. You were great." He blinked back tears.

His father shook his head. "Don't get the wrong idea. I still think you should sell the horse. I just felt a need to keep things fair. In case you never noticed, that is important to me."

"Excuse me," a voice said. They turned to see O'Hannahan. He spoke to Bogey. "I'm sorry. The boss told me to be there. I didn't know what they were planning. Sorry, Humphrey."

"It's okay, Sean," Bogey said. He shook the proffered hand. "Don't worry about it."

When the track manager walked away, Bogey turned back to his father. "Huddleston doesn't like to be crossed. Are you going to lose your biggest client because of me?"

"I told you I was disturbed by his growing recklessness about this filly. I am more bothered after what I just saw. I'm too old to have a client who could land me in ethical trouble. Maybe I'll take a page from your book and fire him before he can fire me."

"Are you sure?"

"No. Not yet. Just playing with the idea."

"It's wonderful to have you on my side," Bogey said and grabbed his father in a bear hug. His father responded awkwardly, but he was smiling as he walked away to find his seat in the stands.

* * *

When they called the race, Bogey led Rosie out of her stall and headed for the paddock. He was halfway there when he heard a familiar voice behind him.

"How you doing, Shrimp?"

He looked back to see Otey leading a beautiful big chestnut horse. Huddleston's goon was clean shaven, and wearing a blue blazer and tie. His presence annoyed Bogey, but Rosie's reaction was much stronger. At the sound of his voice, her ears flattened and she spun around, trembling and bouncing. She gave a shrill squeal and strained against her shank, almost pulling the leather from Bogey's grasp.

"Keep that crazy animal away from me," Otey shouted. "I'll have them put that killer down. You're on my home grounds now. Keep her under control."

"Why in hell don't you just stay away from us?" Bogey shouted back. "You know you upset this girl."

"She don't own the damn racetrack. I can go wherever I want, and she better not bother me," Otey said, more petulant than threatening. He was holding his place behind them but clearly had a close eye on the filly.

Bogey took a deep breath. "I get it. Huddleston wants you to agitate her. It's not going to work. I'll keep her calm. By the way, how are you staying calm? Huddleston give you a tranquilizer?"

"No, he gave me a well-trained horse, not some psycho."

"This girl will stay calm. Don't waste your energy."

"Gonna sing her a little ditty?" Otey sneered.

"I'll do what it takes," Bogey promised.

"Do you really think that crazy bitch can compete with this champion? You're going home whimpering like a whipped dog. A slinking cur! Do you hear me, Shrimp?"

As Otey spoke, his voice got progressively louder so that the last words were shouted. Rosie reacted with a high- pitched neigh, and a more determined effort to whirl and attack the irritating man walking behind her.

Otey shied away. "You better be careful, Shrimp. If I get hurt, you'll pay big time."

"We all should be very careful," Bogey laughed. He turned his attention to Rosie, speaking quietly and patting her neck. She snorted her annoyance but allowed herself to be led forward, only glancing back occasionally. They passed Waller and Becky waiting at the rail, ready to pony her once she was saddled.

At the paddock entrance, Rosie stopped and calmly allowed the paddock judge to fold back her upper lip and inspect the tattoo inside. Bogey led her into the Laurel paddock, a circular, roofed enclosure with a raised viewing stand in its center and saddling stalls around the outer rim. Normally he saw it as a charming old building, full of glorious history, but today it felt constricted and claustrophobic. When Bogey kept the filly in her stall, she tensed each time Otey passed by. Once the giant deliberately stopped his colt just outside Rosie's stall. She strained forward, ears flat, ready for war.

Things weren't much better when Bogey took her out of the stall to walk. She was hypervigilant, never taking her eyes off Otey and his colt. Bogey could never get her completely settled. Bogey glared at Otey, his eyes burning like the filly's, but the other man just stared back, his lips twisted in a mocking grin.

The Charles Town jockey, Tommy Carmouche, came into the paddock. Bogey smiled at him even though he wished Judy Patton was walking up instead. Carmouche was a good enough jockey, one of the best at Charles Town. He wasn't experienced at the Laurel track, but that also meant that he was immune to any influence Huddleston might bring to bear on a Maryland jock. Tommy was in his thirties but looked a decade older. Hard living in the sun, and the toll of multiple injuries, had aged him. He shook Bogey's hand, his small bony hand surprisingly strong. "Thanks for letting me ride her. She looks great."

Bogey leaned in close to him, talking quietly with a careful eye on anyone who might be listening. "Just watch yourself. There is no telling what may happen out there. This guy Huddleston will stop at nothing to try to beat you. For starters, he has a speed horse in here that is tough. If you let him get away on the front and slow the race down, we're beat. He also has a stakes quality closer that will be running at you in the stretch. Best plan, if you can, is to sit third or fourth, not too far back, then get the jump on the closer around the turn."

The jockey was nodding, and Bogey continued, "But the main thing I have to tell you is this, don't argue with the filly. Don't fight her, and don't bother using the whip. She's one that wants to run her own race. She's a little fired up over the scene here. I don't have any idea how that will affect her."

Tommy nodded. "Yeah, I noticed she was breaking out some."

At that moment, Otey came even with them, stopping his horse and leaning toward them. "That's a bad plan. We'll kick your butt," he jibed although he could not have heard Bogey's instructions.

"Who is that big fucker?" Tommy asked.

"Don't mind him. He works for Huddleston. He's the reason our filly is sweating. She hates him, and he's deliberately agitating her."

"I'll keep her clear of him," the jockey promised.

"And watch out for Huddleston's horses. He may have the jockeys gunning for us."

The rider grinned widely, revealing a missing tooth. "Wouldn't be the first ones try to put me through the rail. Most of them ain't around now. If they fuck with me, they'll be sorry."

Bogey didn't know whether to be reassured or frightened by the little man's bravado. "Well, take care of yourself, but try to take care of the filly too," he said.

"You don't have to tell me that, boss. I take care of my mounts."

They were interrupted by calls from the paddock judge; "Put them in" quickly followed by "Riders up."

When their turn came, Bogey led Rosie out of the stall, grabbed Tommy's leg and flipped him into the saddle.

When Becky took the lead from Bogey, she leaned down and said, "What the hell was Otey doing in there?"

"Being an asshole. Trying to upset Rosie."

"Looks like he succeeded," she said, pointing to the sweat whitening Rosie's coat.

Otey passed his colt to the pony boy and yelled at Becky. "Hello, sweetheart."

She ignored him, turning away to lead Rosie into the post parade, but Bogey turned and stood face to face with him, almost touching him.

"Are you threatening me, Mister?" Otey said loudly.

"No, of course not, sir. I just wanted to shake your hand and wish you luck in the race," Bogey said warmly. He grasped the man's huge hand, moving quickly to encircle his knuckles. As he had hoped, the giant's hand was soft and flabby. Not Bogey's hands. Fingers that tugged at heavy hay bales and feed sacks and hammered nails in stubborn oak wood were ready. He put every ounce of his strength into an effort to crush Otey Musgrove's massive mitt. There was a flash of alarm in Otey's eyes. The big man tried to pull away, grimacing in pain, but Bogey increased the pressure, smiling broadly.

The other grooms, free of their horses, looked on curiously.

"May the best man win," Bogey said sincerely and released his grip. Otey had tears in his eyes.

"Yeah, yeah, you too," he managed to croak.

Bogey made his way to an open spot on the rail and turned his attention to Rosie. Tommy Carmouche was using his whip like a windshield wiper, sweeping the sweat off her coat and flinging it to the ground. She was clearly edgy, looking all around with a wary eye that showed too much white.

One of the other horses, his rider in the brilliant crimson Huddleston colors, darted toward her, cutting across her path. Tommy had to snatch the reins to prevent a collision, forcing Becky and Waller to brake suddenly. Bogey saw Becky fighting to restrain the old gelding, whose ears were flattened in angry aggression.

Bogey felt a rush of guilt and fear. His knees felt weak, and he was light headed. His stomach was tight and bitter with bile.

I shouldn't have put Rosie through this. Damn! What will they do to her once the race starts?

Through a grey haze, he watched Becky give the filly's lead to an assistant starter. She turned to leave but whirled back toward the gate instead of heading off as she should.

Bogey saw why. One of the assistant trainers was approaching behind Rosie, a long whip in his hand. Even across the track he could hear Becky screaming at the man. He ignored her and raised the whip, obviously planning to strike Rosie.

Damn! Who else will turn up on Huddleston's payroll?

Fortunately, Tommy saw the man, too, and moved Rosie forward to avoid the blow, dragging the assistant trainer who was clinging to her lead.

The man with the whip glimpsed Waller advancing on him, ears pinned. Faced with opposition, the whip wielder backed off.

Bogey was relieved Rosie had no gate problems. She loaded quickly. Through his binoculars he could see her standing steady and staring straight down the track.

When the bell rang and the gates opened, Rosie, who had strolled out and studied the scene at Saratoga, flew out of the starting gate like a rocket. In three long strides she was two lengths ahead. She didn't show any signs of slowing, surging ahead of the field by eight lengths as they went the first quarter mile.

Becky came running up behind him. "Oh my God, she's bolting. She's running away with him," she said.

"Damn," Bogey muttered. "I told him not to fight her, but he needs to get her under control."

He glanced up at the tote board. "Twenty one and change," he said, noting the time elapsed for the first quarter. "Way too fast! She can't maintain."

They fell into a shocked silence as Rosie flashed past the half mile pole at an equally suicidal pace. She led the other horses by over ten lengths, but Bogey spotted a rapidly moving horse, detaching himself from the others and cutting into Rosie's lead. She turned into the stretch with a narrowing six length lead.

"Here comes the closer," Bogey groaned.

They watched with mounting alarm as Huddleston's colt roared down the center of the track, relentlessly closing ground. "She's tired, she's shortening stride," Bogey moaned.

"Hold on girl," Becky screamed. "Hold on just a little longer."

The big colt was now on Rosie's flank. The finish line was still a hundred yards away.

"He's got her measured," Bogey said, his voice flat with resignation and with regret. This was his fault. He hadn't protected her. Bogey was no better than Humphrey had been.

"Don't let him get by," Becky yelled.

As though the filly heard her, Rosie gathered herself for one final lunge.

"Too close to call," the public address thundered. "And look at that time. These two horses just tied Northern Wolf's track record."

"Not too close to call," Becky said calmly. "Rosie held him."

"Are you sure?" Bogey asked.

"Of course," she said archly. "In any close contest, the woman always comes out on top, especially if she's challenged by some big lunk of a bully."

The photo proved Becky right. Somehow Rosie had found the strength to hang on for the win. Her number went up on top. When it was official, Becky threw her arms around Bogey.

Then, to his delight and surprise, she kissed him! She kissed him full on the lips, and the world tilted. She pulled away from him, her eyes locked onto his. She was smiling warmly.

"Congratulations," she said softly.

His joy was tempered when Rosie returned to the winner's circle. Her nostrils were flared, showing a wide band of pink tissue within. Her flanks were pumping wildly, great hollows showing behind her ribs with each breath. She was drenched in sweat, and her head and tail were drooping.

Bogey took her rein and led her slowly into the winner's circle. He spoke softly to her and patted her neck. Gradually, her breathing became less labored, and she was able to raise her head for the photo. The jockey jumped off, full of apologies.

"I'm sorry, Mr. Dawson. She just got away from me. I couldn't ride her. She just ran off."

Bogey patted him on the shoulder. "Not your fault, Tommy. I'm the one who has to apologize to her. I put her in the middle of a horror show she had to run away from. That's what horses do. I was showing off and didn't take care of her. Go shower up. You did okay."

Bogey spotted his father at the edge of the crowd. The old man smiled and clasped his hands together over his head in a victory salute. He managed a weak grin and waved acknowledgement as he walked a drained Rosie toward the test barn. After his electric high of the kiss, he was now feeling as tired and dispirited as the filly looked.

CHAPTER 15

Neither Bogey nor Rosie looked or acted any better over the next few days. Rosie picked at her food. Her coat lost its sheen, and she moved in slow motion, her head down, as Bogey dragged her around the shedrow on her daily walk. He watched her with growing gloom. On Wednesday, already four days after the Laurel race, he cringed at her half-full feed bucket. She stared out at him with dry, lifeless eyes. He shook his head dejectedly and once again plodded around the barn with her.

Becky Friedman dropped by daily even though Bogey didn't need her to ride Waller when Rosie was in no shape to go to the track. On Wednesday, after she looked in on Rosie she found Bogey behind the barn bathing Waller. He looked up when he saw her.

"Did you see her? She looks awful doesn't she?" he sighed.

"No, she doesn't look awful. She looks like a champ who left it all on the track and will need time to recharge. She'll be fine."

"She won't be fine," Bogey snapped. "I used her to fight my fight, and I broke her down." He glared at Becky. "Look in her eyes for God's sake." He shook his head in disbelief. "I was her protector, saving her from that evil Edmond Huddleston, who might have used her selfishly." He snorted.

"Aw, come on, Bogey," Becky protested. "You couldn't have foreseen all the stuff that happened. Who could?"

Bogey refused to be comforted. "You tried to warn me how salty the race would be. Even the racing secretary at Laurel told me. I wouldn't listen. Too busy looking forward to slapping the rich guy around. I used that grand, honest filly." He was on the verge of tears.

Becky's eyes suddenly became hard, her face set. "We'll talk again when you leave your pity party. Get a grip on yourself. Rosie is actually getting better, a little at a time. You need to think like her trainer, not wallow in guilt." She stalked away. After a few steps, she turned on her heel and nailed him with another steely glance. "You need to also remember that Waller has a big race Sunday afternoon. You need to stop whining and think about him. He was your meal ticket before little sister stood and nursed."

Bogey watched her walk away, her back stiff, her strides long and angry. He felt curiously heartened by her outburst. The girl cared enough about him to get mad at him. Maybe that impulsive kiss after the race meant something after all.

She's concerned about the horses, not you, fool.

But, after all, they were *his* horses. Wasn't that a good sign?

* * *

Over the next few days, Rosie did improve. Each day she showed a little more interest in her food and looked less wilted and bedraggled, but the filly was still not herself – not by a long shot. Her eye was still dull, her coat did not glisten, and she was docile and subdued. Rosie seemed to be going through the motions. He arranged for Becky to ride Waller so that he could take Rosie to the track, hoping that would spark her interest.

She galloped lazily, without interest, never getting on the bit. Going through the motions.

As they backtracked toward the ramp, Becky spoke. "She's still not herself. What are you going to do, Mr. Trainer?"

"After Waller's race Sunday, I thought I might take them to the farm. He doesn't like leaving the track, but he'll do it with her. It may not do any good. It's helped before, but then she was just sour. Now she's spirit broke, she's really bad."

Becky turned in the saddle and yelled at him. "Damn you! Stop it. She can read your mood, you know. How can she have hope when you keep predicting doom?"

"It's not my predictions. Look at her," he said miserably.

"I'm looking at her. She's not herself, but she's better. Let's see how she reacts to the farm. That may be just the thing. But you have to stop singing the blues to her. Go back to your lullabies."

That evening, Bogey sat alone in his tiny living room. The trailer was pitch black. With lights on, he might glimpse himself in a mirror. He didn't want to even look at that guy.

Things were hard to sort out. There was no escaping the fact that he had taken a talented but green young horse into a hornet's nest, where she was cruelly stung. Her victory in the face of adversity was proof of her class and heart, but the price she paid for that triumph was painfully evident. She had generously sacrificed herself to master the task he had assigned. A task based on his vindictiveness.

His burden of guilt was richly deserved.

Still, there was truth in Rebecca Friedman's rebukes. Rosie was beginning to turn around; at least she was cleaning up her feed now. But he remained in total despair.

Was that realistic? Was he continuing to damage her with his pessimism? What about the accusation that his doom and gloom was a bad influence on the filly? He thought about it.

The fact that he rode the filly every day and cared for her basic needs gave credence to the notion. Bogey knew that horses had an uncanny ability to sense a rider's emotions; fear, tension, uncertainty or anger was clearly read and sure to strongly influence the animal's behavior. Maybe pessimism and depression could be a drag on Rosie's recuperative effort. It was possible.

That said, he didn't see how he could change his outlook. Telling himself he needed to cheer up just made him feel more guilty and inadequate since he wasn't able to flip his mood.

I will try. I will really try. I will concentrate on the positive. Rosie is better. She is better. Waller will run well. Things will come around.

Bogey tried to hold the good thoughts when he turned in to get some rest for the busy Sunday ahead. Despite his efforts, a sad-eyed, depleted Rosie kept flashing onto his mind's eye, visions that rekindled guilt and smothered any spark of cheer or hope of sleep.

* * *

Becky Friedman appeared at the barn soon after racing began the next afternoon.

"Hi," she said cheerily. "You look like a zombie. Ever heard of Visine? Gets the red out."

"I'm okay," he muttered to the floor.

"Right," she said, raising an eyebrow. "Still I thought I'd let you act like a real trainer today. Why don't I take Waller over and handle him in the paddock for you? You can stand at the stall looking important. Okay, deal," she said without waiting for his answer. She turned and walked away, talking over her shoulder. "I'll be back before they call his race." She stopped and took a couple of steps back toward him. Bogey noticed that this time she was having a little trouble meeting his gaze. "By the way," she said softly. "That kiss, the other day at Laurel? It didn't feel so bad."

Bogey was sleep-walking but her words awakened him. He started toward her but she walked quickly away.

She was watching out for him. He was in no condition to handle Waller, and she knew it. And the kiss! She had liked the kiss!

Careful! Go slow. Don't say too much and run her off again.

There was another advantage in having her handle Waller today. He could use the free time to make a bet on the old campaigner. In Maryland, Bogey never gambled on races. He didn't have time to handicap races his horses weren't running in, and in his opinion, betting his entries could interfere with objectivity and lead to training errors. But since coming to Charles Town, he needed to use shrewd wagers to boost income. Occasionally, he had entered Waller in races that didn't really suit his distance preferences with the deliberate intent of getting him beat. By darkening his form in this way, he could get better odds the next time the old boy ran.

Such maneuvers were unnecessary today. The race was a starter's allowance race for horses that had run in a five thousand dollar claimer. Normally, these came up easy for Waller, but today's version had attracted a Penn National invader that had won three of these in a row – a record that would attract a lot of money. Waller should get decent odds, and since Bogey had cash from Rosie's recent win, he intended to make a worthwhile profit at the betting window.

Becky returned as promised and led Waller from his stall. Rosie protested as she always did when separated from her buddy, and Waller seemed unusually aroused. The gelding was prancing, snorting and straining at the lead.

"Wow, I've never seen him like this on race day," Becky said. "Stay here a minute and calm Rosie down. I've got this one." She was able to maneuver the old campaigner out of the barn.

Bogey stayed behind a moment to soothe Rosie, then headed up to the paddock.

Waller was still on the muscle, but with Becky's help he got him saddled. The jockeys came in, and Tommy Caramouche told Bogey, "You don't need to worry about this one running off with me."

Bogey patted him on the back. "I hope not. He's pretty pumped up. Forget the Maryland race, Tommy. Just ride this guy like always. The favorite will go to the front. Don't worry about that. Our boy will catch him at the wire."

Bogey hurried up to the betting window after glancing at the TV screen over the indoor saddling area. Waller was thirteen to one. Becky had told him to bet five dollars for her.

"If he doesn't win, I won't charge you the next time he goes to the track," she said.

He hung around the window as long as possible, feeding his bets in slowly. These days the bet pools were small, and it was easy to spoil good odds with small amounts of cash. Bogey made his bets in tiny increments, using some of the money to bet an exacta with Waller on top of the favorite. With a minute left till post time, he headed for the rail with Waller still ten to one. He saw Becky there and joined her. She gave him a confident 'thumbs up'.

The race distance was seven furlongs with the starting gate to his left, at the end of a chute. The horses would run down the chute to the main track, pass the grandstand and then circle the half mile track, returning to the finish line in front of the stands. Waller seemed to be more settled but definitely on his toes. Bogey turned his attention to the invader. The colt looked terrific. He was a big grey, his silver coat glowing in the afternoon sun and his movements full of grace and energy. Waller and Tommy had their work cut out for them. Bogey's hopes were based not just on Waller's ability but on the fact that the invader faced two disadvantages: the colt had never raced further than six furlongs, and he had never run at Charles Town.

The race began as scripted. The grey bounded out of the gate with electric energy and opened a four length lead on the field. Waller, as usual, galloped along at the back of the pack, apparently disinterested in the whole proceeding. One of the local jockeys recognized that the leader couldn't be allowed to coast along on the front. He hustled his mount forward, and on the first turn was able to reach the grey's flank. The favorite responded, quickening pace and pulling away with ease. As they proceeded down the backstretch, he drew away again, putting five lengths of daylight between himself and his closest pursuer.

Bogey turned his attention to Waller. Tommy had him on the rail, saving ground. He had passed two horses but still was seven or eight lengths off the lead and blocked by a wall of other runners. The big grey was into the turn for home.

"Cut him loose," Becky yelled.

Bogey said nothing. Waller was pinned in. Tommy had nowhere to go. Frequently the rail opened up when horses turned into the stretch. Fatigue, coupled with centripetal force, pushed horses out toward the center of the track. Not today.

Bogey could see Waller quickening, pulling against the rein, closing ground on the group of horses just ahead.

"Oh no," Becky shouted. "He's going to clip heels."

Indeed it appeared that Waller was going to run right up the back of the horse in front of him. Bogey held his breath, then watched as Waller stuck his head between the flanks of two of the horses. For a few steps, the three horses ran in a tight pack, the two in front squeezing Waller's head between them. The old gelding was trying to force his way through but there was no opening.

Then, suddenly, as though bending to the old devil's indomitable will, the outside horse drifted outward, and Waller bulled his way through. He was flying now, but the grey still had four lengths on him. Bogey turned his attention to the front runner. Was he shortening his stride? He glanced at Becky. She was laughing and crying out happily.

"You got him measured boy. You got him!"

The old campaigner was gaining rapidly, but the finish line was coming up.

The two horses flashed by the finish together. From their spot on the rail it was impossible to say who had won. The photo finish sign came up immediately. Bogey's heart was in his throat. He needed money.

Becky looked at his stricken face and laughed. "Loosen up, Dawson. Waller got him by a long nose. Not even close."

He ignored her, watching the tote board, waiting for the order of finish. If Waller was second, none of his bets would pay. He would get twenty percent of the miniscule purse, scant consolation.

Becky was really having her fun now. She placed herself between Bogey and his line of sight to the board, bouncing up and down, and shaking her finger at him. "Do you dare to question my word? Waller won. Head on up to the window and get our cash. No, wait. You need to be in the picture."

She prattled on, jumping from side to side as he tried to look around her at the tote board. He could see Waller trotting back. "You need to take care of the horse," he said gruffly.

She smiled at him. He was completely confused now. The smile was warm, even affectionate. "I was just trying to help you pass the time. Didn't want a heart attack."

She turned toward the track, and both of them saw Waller's number go up on top. She winked at him. "Told you," she said and went to lead Waller and Tommy into the winner's circle. The old horse was prancing, pawing the dirt and shaking his head as if to say, "Take a look at me!"

Tommy leaned down to Bogey. "You said catch him at the wire, right?"

* * *

Bogey enjoyed his walk back to the window, winning tickets in hand, and took even greater pleasure in the stack of greenbacks that he took away. Stuffing the wad of cash into his pocket, he felt prosperous for the first time in years. It wasn't the kind of money that would pay the mortgage, but a bundle like this was psychologically powerful. He wasn't entirely sure why it made him so buoyant until he was halfway along in his walk back to the barn to check on Waller.

He was flush enough to ask Rebecca Friedman out.

The idea filled him with anxiety mingled with anticipation.

Bogey can do it! Bogey can ask her for a date. She can't say no to Bogey.

After all, what was the worse thing that could happen?

She could say no. She could laugh at him. She could deride him for even entertaining such a foolish thought.

Bogey can do it! Bogey has no fear.

He wanted to ask her right away, before he weakened, but he couldn't ask her in the test barn with lots of people around. He treated himself to a hotdog with all the trimmings and then wandered down to the grandstand boxes and accepted congratulations. He made absent-minded small talk with Harry Collins until he'd killed enough time for Becky to finish up with testing, and then he walked slowly toward his barn.

He was pumping up his courage when everything changed.

Inside the barn, Becky began to scream.

The screaming startled and confused him. For a moment his mind rejected the foreign sound, something that had no place in this sunlit happy afternoon. Finally his brain had to accept reality, and Bogey ran toward the barn.

The narrow aisle of the shedrow was blocked by a large mass. In the muted light within the barn, it took Bogey a moment to realize the mass was a fallen horse. Becky was on her knees beside it. Her dark hair fell over the horse's face. Her arms were locked around the animal's neck. She was no longer screaming. She was wailing softly and weeping.

"No, no, no," she kept moaning. "Not Waller, no, no. This can't be happening. No, no."

Bogey sat beside her. "What happened?"

Her face was clouded, her voice choked. "He just fell down. He fell down. We were walking...."

He felt no pulse in Waller's neck. He touched the horse's open eye. Waller showed no reaction. Bogey stood slowly. "He's dead. Must have had a heart attack," he said mechanically. He looked around the barn as though hoping to see someone who could help. He was numb. The loss he felt was beyond expression, too deep and personal for words. Waller was part of his life, part of who he was, part of him.

And suddenly he was gone.

Finally he realized that Becky was still draped over Waller's neck, and he reached down to help her up. She still looked to be in shock.

"I was just walking him. He just suddenly crashed down to the ground. I was just walking him," she muttered.

"I know. It just happens. Come on. I'll take care of this. You should go now." He tried to lead her toward the door, but she hung back looking at Waller, her damp eyes pleading.

She looked at Bogey, trying to focus. "I'm acting crazy, aren't I? Waller is – was – just an animal. I'm making way too much of this." She began to weep silently. Bogey knew there was nothing to say. He moved closer and held her.

After a while, she used the handkerchief he offered. "Can you understand? It was just so sudden. One moment he was my old brave, cranky Waller, and then he was gone. I had no chance to say goodbye." She started the silent weeping again, shaking her head. "Maybe he was just a horse, but I still wanted to say goodbye. Just goodbye," she whispered.

"I understand," Bogey said softly, trying to hold back his own tears.

She cried for awhile longer in his arms but then suddenly pushed him away. Her tearful face hardened, and her voice turned tense and angry. "You know what pisses me off? Waller took care of you. You've had him since he was born. He kept you afloat when you hit bottom. The horse earned you over a hundred thousand dollars."

Her dark eyes bore into him. "Don't you owe him some respect? Damn right you do."

"Yes, sure I do," Bogey agreed, totally bewildered by the sudden change in her manner.

"So does he get a decent burial out at your farm? A graveside eulogy?"

He stared at her, his eyes begging for understanding. "You know I can't do that. It's against the law."

"Don't they have pet cemeteries?" she demanded.

"You know I can't afford that," he said miserably.

"Okay. I get it. When I leave here, you'll get a forklift and carry my dear friend, who has done so much for you, across the street for the rendering plant to pick up. I know the drill. Then Waller will get to be dog food. That's what the tough old bastard gets." Her lips curled with disgust. "He gets to be fed to Fido."

Bogey could only hang his head. What she said was true. State law did not allow for burying horses on your land. The decaying mass of a horse posed dangers to the groundwater and other potential environmental hazards. Pet cemeteries were available but not really practical for a huge animal like Waller owned by a financially strapped person like him.

Becky glared at him. He glanced up and saw pain in her eyes even as her jaws clamped in anger. She suddenly threw up her hands in surrender. "Do what you have to do."

"Can I take you home?" he asked timidly.

"No," she said, but her voice was not as hard. "You need to take care of Rosie. She's going to go crazy without Waller." She walked away, her shoulders slumped.

* * *

Bogey had tears in his eyes when he returned to the barn after getting Waller to the prescribed pickup area behind the huge pile of dirt across the street. He was grieving his beloved scallywag, but his mind kept straying to the likelihood that he had also lost Becky. He could feel himself sinking, his spirit shriveling within him.

When he walked through the barn door he could hear Rosie. She was bleating and walking her stall from one side to the other. Her head was out in the aisle. She looked toward Waller's old stall and whinnied anxiously for him. When he did not appear, she repeated her stereotyped behavior, weaving wildly from one side of her space to the other and then calling out again. She was already lathered.

Bogey walked closer to the stall. Rosie glanced at him but then went back to her patterned dance of distress. He wasn't sure of what to do for her, but nothing could be worse than this exhausting display of anxiety and frustration.

He reached for her shank and opened the stall. "Here goes nothing," he said under his breath.

Rosie lurched out of the stall, dragging Bogey with her. He hung on, scared that the distressed filly might bolt. Instead she went to the door of Waller's stall, sniffing and looking inside. After a few minutes of this futile effort, she pulled Bogey further down the shedrow, looking carefully at every stall they passed. On the back side of the barn, she came upon the spot where Waller had fallen. Rosie stopped dead still, sniffing the air. Then she craned her neck down and explored the area carefully. Finally she raised her head. She looked at Bogey, who spoke with her softly.

"He's gone, girl. He's gone. You'll be okay."

The horse shuddered and the fierce shaking took control of her body. Bogey stroked her neck and patted her shoulder. Then she started to pull him forward again.

"I know, Rosie. You want to look everywhere. You want to be sure. Lead the way," he said soothingly, and then he began to sing to her. He continued his serenade even when he returned her to the stall and sat down on the straw beside her.

CHAPTER 16

Both of them must have succumbed to exhaustion and dozed off. When Bogey awakened as dawn broke, he saw that the filly was calmer but subdued. He blinked the sleep from his eyes and stood stiffly, stretching to ease the ache in his back.

When he brought her oats and sweet feed, she showed no interest.

Just what she needed. More trauma.

At least this time he didn't feel guilty. As terrible as he felt about Waller's heart attack, he knew that it wasn't his fault. There was no way that he could have predicted the gelding's death. The horse went into his last race radiating vibrant good health, in fact more on the muscle than usual. Rosie was standing calmly now, no longer agitated. He hugged her and stroked her silky coat, straightening her mane and talking to her. "We'll miss him, won't we girl? But we'll be okay. We'll stick together." He kept up the chatter as he groomed her and picked her feet clean. After he fed Substantial Balance, he cleaned up and came back to give her a few departing pats. "I have to go," he told her. She looked at him with big sad brown eyes but did not protest as he walked away.

To his surprise Becky Friedman was waiting for him outside the barn. "I've been waiting to hear about Rosie," she said.

"Better now," he said. "She was pretty upset last night."

"Makes two of us. I'm sorry about how I acted. I shouldn't have dumped on you like I did."

The cloud of foreboding pressing on Bogey burned off.

She doesn't hate me after all!

He was quiet, not trusting himself to say anything.

"If I bought you breakfast, would that help?" she asked, misinterpreting his silence.

He was suddenly ravenous, remembering that he had eaten nothing since yesterday's hurried lunch. He smiled.

"Breakfast sounds great, but I'm buying." He patted his side pocket. "Actually, we have Waller to thank this one last time. His treat."

Her eyes dampened but she managed a grin. "Good ole Waller," she said. "I'll lift a mug of coffee to that old devil anytime. And by the way," she added with a touch of her old mischievousness, "You owe me my winnings. My landlady is waiting."

They met at the Turf. Becky's friend and benefactor, Sarah, brought them steaming plates of ham and eggs served with a smile for Becky and careful scrutiny of Bogey. He smiled nervously at Becky, not sure what conversational track would be appropriate. Small talk might trivialize her intense reaction to Waller's death. If he talked about his own sadness, that might add to her pain. He stared at his plate, less hungry than he thought.

Becky finally spoke. "I don't blame you, but I am still angry about what will happen to Waller."

He forced himself to look at her. She looked more sad than angry as she continued. "This morning when I came in, I was tempted to look behind the mound and see if he was still there. I wanted to go stay with him till they came to pick him up." Tears broke through. "How dumb is that? A wake for a horse. I shouldn't be in this game. I'm too silly. Everyone else is tough. I'm a soft-headed ninny."

Bogey offered her his handkerchief, and she accepted. He used a napkin to dab hastily at his own eyes.

He spoke, fearing the lump in his throat would betray him. "Not soft headed," he muttered.

"What?"

He swallowed and took the risk. "You're not soft headed. Soft hearted maybe, and we need more like you in racing."

She dried her eyes and handed him his handkerchief. As he reached to receive it, she covered his hand with hers. Her touch was soft and warm. "Thank you," she said.

He had to say something. The moment was drifting away, victim to his tongue-tied shyness.

Something! For goodness sakes, say something!!

"How do you keep your hands so soft?" he stuttered.

Becky broke into peals of laughter.

Bogey was humiliated. "I'm sorry. I'm sorry. I just meant you handle all those horses, the reins, the weather —"

He started to withdraw his hand, but she gripped it more tightly. "You didn't say anything wrong. It was sweet. I was laughing about what you would think of my answer."

"Your answer?" he asked in confusion.

"Yes," she said. "I keep my hands soft with Bag Balm. Dairymen use it on milk cow teats to keep them from getting irritated and cracked. Works good for me, too."

Of course, Bogey responded with a crimson blush. "Oh," was all he managed with a nod.

"I only use it on my *hands*," she assured him.

This girl is laughing at me again.

Strangely, he didn't feel all that embarrassed. He felt excited. He put his other hand over hers.

"I'm not a good talker," he said, "but I'm glad you're my friend."

He was pleased to see coloring in her face.

* * *

Bogey had work to do, including serving a belated breakfast to a very angry Sentinel's Cry. The stallion had vented his rage on his empty feed bucket, which was in shreds outside the door of his stall. He ranted and raved at his owner, who hurried to find another bucket and fill it with oats. Even when he was served, the horse contained his appetite long enough to glare at Bogey and trumpet one final snort of outrage.

"Sorry big guy," Bogey said, but the stallion ignored him.

As he tackled his other daily chores, his mind wandered between gray thoughts of Waller and Technicolor replays of breakfast. For someone who had spent an emotionally draining and physically uncomfortable afternoon and night, he felt amazingly energetic. Sometime in the late afternoon, both trains of thought converged, and Bogey Dawson came up with a daring plan. The idea thrilled and terrified him, but he was determined.

Bogey can do it!

He took the first steps, the ones he had to do at the farm.

CHAPTER 17

Rosie was a little better the next morning. She nosed at her feed and ate a little. Bogey had hooked his dilapidated horse trailer behind the Mustang, ready to follow through with his plan to take her to the farm. The late September morning was unusually crisp. The lacy fog, still lying soft on low spots in the road as he drove in, was burning off. Bogey took that as an encouraging omen.

First he had to gallop the banker's horse, a task which reminded him that he needed to do something about his delinquent mortgage payments. The purse money from Laurel had finally cleared, and he would get it to Marshall the moment the check came. He put it out of mind. There was nothing to do about it until then. For the moment, he had other priorities.

After he hot walked and bathed Substantial Balance, he stopped to groom Rosie. He talked with her and hugged her until he had to admit to himself that he was stalling. Leaving her, he walked up the hill to the track looking for Becky. She was astride a stocky bay. As he watched, she galloped around the turn and down the backstretch before breaking the horse off for a serious work. He watched her ride, low and motionless over the horse's neck.

He saw Harry timing the work, so he headed back down to his barn to wait. She would have to pass him as she took the bay back to the Collins barn.

He waved to her as she passed. She smiled and waved back, and he fell in behind her.

"Good morning," he said after she dismounted. He hoped his voice sounded casually cheerful.

She looked toward him, a little surprised, tilting her head in the way that always caused him alarming knee weakness. "Good morning to you. I was about to drop by and ask about Rosie. How's she doing?"

"Better. She is missing big brother but coming around. I think she might like some time at the farm. That's why I was looking for you. If you're not too busy, I wondered if you might come with me and help her settle in there. She may be a little tough to manage without Waller."

Becky's forehead wrinkled in a thoughtful way. Bogey, as usual, interpreted that in the most negative possible way.

"If you're tied up, that's fine. I mean I had no right to bother you. It's fine."

She shook her head. "No, no. I'd like that. I've been curious to see this farm of yours anyway. I was just running my schedule through my head, but this is the last one I need to get on. I'm through." She paused and then raised an eyebrow. "Now this does include some food after we get her settled, doesn't it."

"Sure. Sure. And I'll pay you for your time."

She waved him off. "Nonsense. I'm just kidding around. Are you ready to go? Let me put my helmet and stuff in the trunk of the car, and we can roll."

Amazing.

Harry Collins called to him. Bogey saw the trainer walking down the hill.

Please don't have another horse for her to gallop. Please, Harry, please.

Harry looked uncomfortable, his lips pressed tight, his square face hard beneath his Baltimore Oriole baseball cap bill.

"I've got to tell you something, Bogey."

He pulled Bogey to the side, and Becky backed away, giving them privacy.

"I saw something Saturday night that I should have mentioned to you."

Bogey looked intently at Harry. The man looked miserable. He was gazing at the ground and forcing out his words as though they were choking him.

"See, I didn't think anything of it at the time. I mean, I thought you knew."

"I knew what?"

"That they were at your barn."

"Who was at my barn?"

"The big guy for sure. He's the only one I saw. He was getting into that big black car."

Bogey couldn't catch his breath. His mind fought against the chilling understanding that flooded him.

"You saw Otey at my barn Saturday night?"

"I'm pretty sure. I didn't see his face, but not many men are that big."

"Why didn't you tell me Sunday?"

"I didn't think it was important. They've been at your barn before, I mean with you there. Otey was with the rich guy then, and you were talking to them. I thought they came to see you again."

"I wasn't at the barn Saturday night."

"I didn't think much about it. Then Waller died. Made me wonder."

Bogey stared at the man. "Yeah. Makes me wonder, too."

Without another word, he pivoted and walked swiftly toward his car. Becky hurried after him and jumped into the passenger seat.

Bogey's thoughts were a swirl. He started the engine. Becky spoke sharply.

"Hey! Slow down. Turn off the ignition."

He looked at her, dazed and disoriented, but he obeyed.

She indicated the helmet and tack piled in a jumble on her lap. "The trunk, remember? And while we're at it, shouldn't we load up the horse, too?"

* * *

He drove along, stewing silently. When they were passing the Fair Grounds, headed toward Middleway, she spoke to him.

"Had a hell of a county fair here in August. Did you get by?"

"What?" he asked irritably.

"Ah, it speaks. Just seeing if there was anyone in that steam bath."

"Sorry. Just thinking." He considered a moment, but then he told her what Collins had reported.

Her eyes flashed. "Now *I'm* thinking. I'm thinking that murder would be too good for the son of a bitch. He killed Waller."

"He must have put something in the vitamin jug I gave him before the race."

"No wonder Waller was unusually hyper."

"I suspected Huddleston of juicing some of the horses we ran. After what that vet did to Sentinel's Cry, I know he would do anything Huddleston told him to do."

"What could he have given Waller?"

"Lots of things. People used to use epinephrine and other stuff like that to stimulate horses. Lately they use adrenal cortex extract. It stimulates the brain, but it also stimulates the heart. He could have overdosed him on that."

"Wouldn't they have found it in the drug test after he won?"

"No. It's a natural body hormone. They don't test for it."

She was quiet for a while. Bogey assumed she was absorbing what he said.

"I've got one more question," she said after a few more miles. "Why was Harry Collins lying? And what was he lying about?"

He glanced at her. She continued to astonish him. "You saw that, too?"

"That's pretty easy with Harry. He always looks that way when he's stretching the truth."

"I don't think he was lying about Otey being there. It was more like he wasn't telling everything, holding back," Bogey said.

Becky looked puzzled. He agreed. It was strange.

CHAPTER 18

He turned off Old Leetown and drove down the gravel side road leading to his farm. As they passed the nursery on the right, she sighed.

"What's wrong?" he asked.

"Nothing. Looking at this nursery reminds me of our garden at home. When I was little, I worked in it with mother and we shopped for plantings at places like that. Those were our best times." She made a dismissive gesture. "The garden is the main thing I miss. In my humble rented room, there's not even enough sun for a house plant."

Plan going off course. I'm too preoccupied with Huddleston. She's too pensive.

They came to the boundary of his farm.

How would she view his work in progress? Trying to look with fresh eyes, he decided he could be proud of his efforts. His pastures were still richly green under the autumn sun, and his black fences were in immaculate condition. Sure, she would see a modest place, but it looked well tended.

"One of these days I want to see a lot of mares and babies out there," he said, pointing at the pasture.

"Are you sure? They grab your heart. Then they die. Think about it. A twenty-year-old horse is old. Most of them don't get that old. Waller was what? Six? Think of how many times your heart will be broken by the time you're seventy."

"That's true," Bogey said, disappointed that she had turned glum again.

He pulled up at the small, unpainted barn that he was building when he had free time. Now it looked raw and unfinished to him.

They unloaded Rosie, who stopped and looked around. She whinnied happily and pulled Becky toward the pasture gate. Bogey rushed ahead and opened the gate, and, once free of the lead shank, the filly bounded away across the grass.

"Whoa," Becky said. "This may work. She looks like a different horse."

"I hope it does the trick," Bogey said, unable to suppress a wide grin.

Becky turned to him. "You got any food in that double wide over there?" she asked, pointing to his trailer. "I want to look around, especially to see Rosie's poppa, but first you have to feed me."

Plan looking a little better.

One reason for his optimism, his hash brown potatoes were the best. When you live on paupers' funds, you learn the value of the humble potato and a thousand ways to make it tasty. He opened the door for Becky, and she stopped inside the door to look around.

The interior was almost bare. There was nothing on the walls of the trailer save multiple pictures of Bogey with horses in the winners circle, all framed in cheap black plastic. A threadbare brown sofa and a stained purple chair faced a small TV perched on a white table. A huge rabbit ear antenna towered over the set.

"Looks like you got to Goodwill after my landlady had already picked over the good stuff," Becky said. "But I'll say one thing for you," she said. "You're not a slob."

"Thanks for the kind words," he said. "Let me get to work on some breakfast. Make yourself comfortable."

"Mind if I look at your books?" she asked, pointing to the hodgepodge of mismatched bookcases which covered one wall of the trailer.

"Go to it," he said, moving to his small galley.

He assembled ingredients, willing himself to focus on the food preparation. It wasn't easy with her standing only a few feet away.

"Do you have every book ever written on the subject of breeding race horses?"

"I have a lot," he admitted.

"The granddaddy of them all, Frederico Tessio," she exclaimed.

"No one has ever done it as well," he said over his shoulder. "He bred twenty-two winners of the Italian Derby. Twenty-two! And he trained sixteen of them. Can you imagine anyone winning the Kentucky Derby sixteen times?"

"Here's one I want to read: *Joe Taylor's Complete Guide to Breeding and Raising Racehorses.* If he does as well with the horses as he did with his kids, it'll be good. Have you met those boys from Taylor Made?"

"Sure. At the sales. Good guys."

"Now here is one I *have* read: *Wonder's Victory.* Serious stuff. I loved the Joanna Campbell books, must have read ten of them. I hid them from mother under my mattress like boys hide Playboy. How come you were reading these little girl books? Have a crush on Ashley?"

He was glad he was bending over the stove flipping the potatoes.

"Ashley loved horses. That's a good thing," he said lamely.

"Sure," she scoffed. "You probably had the hots for her. What about all those breeding books? Are you seeing a future as a breeder?"

"To tell the truth, I have to thank Huddleston for getting me into that. It's the only thing good I took away from that train wreck."

"He asked you to study up on breeding?"

"No, but he knew breeding. I didn't want to be shown up when we studied sales catalogues together."

"Hum, a little competitive are we?"

When he called her to the table, she dug into breakfast with abandon, annihilating every morsel, and sat back from the narrow drop-down table with a satisfied sigh.

"Best I ever had," she said.

Bogey felt ridiculously pleased with himself.

"Glad you enjoyed it," he said, trying for suitable modesty.

"Are you going to give me the recipe for those hash browns?"

He hesitated, not wanting to say no but reluctant to surrender the secret ingredient he had discovered by accident. The addition of this special, unexpected touch led everyone to wax enthusiastic about this one dish, his only culinary claim to fame.

"I'll fix them for you whenever you want," he said.

"I get it. You know a girl would do anything for food like this. What a flagrant effort to seduce this poor maiden."

She laughed and watched Bogey blush right on schedule.

"If I can identify what's in it, will you admit it?" she asked.

He thought only a moment. She would never guess his secret. "Sure."

"Paprika, of course. I think I taste a touch of cumin, pepper – how am I doing?"

"All correct," he acknowledged.

"What else?"

"I'll make them for you again. Maybe with a second test you'll pick up the others."

"You're a tease! Pulling me into your web. Okay, have it your way. Let's go see your stallion."

When they went outside, he directed her to the barn.

He brought Sentinel's Cry out and paraded him back and forth in front of her. She was wide eyed. When he stood the stallion, she came closer, studying his legs and stroking the arch of his neck. He rippled with contained energy, occasionally twitching his neck, setting off flowing waves in his long ebony mane.

Becky stepped back. "What a brute!" she exclaimed. "He's magnificent. How many mares did you breed him to?"

"None this year. Final Gift is his only foal. I just had the one mare," he explained.

"That's a shame. I can sure see where Rosie gets her looks."

Sentinel's Cry, unable to stay in one spot so long, flung himself backward and reared upward, pawing the air.

Becky backed away, startled. Bogey calmly gave the stallion slack and walked with him as the horse danced backward on his hind legs.

"I can also see where she gets her attitude," Becky said.

Bogey got the stallion under control and led him back to his paddock. When he returned, he said, "He could have been great. I will never forgive myself for not taking better care of him."

"Too late for all that, but you do need to give him a chance at stud."

"I know. That was the only tempting part of Huddleston's offer. He could get a lot of good mares to Sentinel's Cry."

"If he didn't figure out some way to kill him first," she said sarcastically. "No, there has to be some other way to get him out there."

Bogey shrugged. "We'll see. Not in West Virginia. No one has money for stud fees these days, and if I offer him free, what kind of mares would I get? Even a good sire can't work miracles."

"I'll think about it. Maybe Judy would have some ideas."

"In the meanwhile, I want to show you something else." He led her to the back side of the trailer. There was a tended garden there and a tall weeping willow tree. It was a little jewel of backyard tucked in between the trailer and a paddock.

"Your farm is really nice by the way," Becky said.

"Thanks," he said. "It's nice land. Just needs lots of work. I have plans." He pointed toward the willow. "I love that tree. That next paddock was built for Waller so he could be close to the house. Only trouble was, he wouldn't take a vacation except that one with Final Gift. Before she came along, I vanned him out here and put him in there. I wasn't even inside the house before he jumped the fence and ran up to the trailer, waiting to get in and go back to the track. I put him in the paddock again, and the same thing happened. Waller wanted to be racing."

He walked a few feet to the side and beckoned to her. When she joined him, he pointed to a spot between the tree and the fence. "This was the best I could do."

Just beyond the draping yellow leaves of the willow was a slab of concrete, embedded in the ground so that it stood on edge. As she came closer she could see that the concrete was decorated with an etched outline of a horse's head. Below the picture was painted a single word: Waller.

Becky looked at the monument for a long time. She walked slowly toward it and leaned down to touch it softly. When she turned back to Bogey, there were tears in her eyes. She came to him and took his hand.

"That's the ugliest damn memorial I ever saw," she said and smiled.

"I guess I'm not much of an artist."

She hugged him warmly. "No," she said. "You're not. But you are a really good man."

She leaned back, her arms still around him.

He gathered his courage, pulled her to him and kissed her gently. A bolt of electric excitement coursed through his heart and set his loins on fire. She wasn't pulling away, so he kissed her with passion and she responded, wrapping him in a strong embrace. Her mouth opened, and her tongue moved in his mouth. He crushed her to him, kissing her eyes, neck, whatever part of her he could reach. Their breathing became rhythmic, deep and harsh.

She stepped back and looked at him intently. "Should we be doing this?"

"I really want you."

"Look, I was on five horses this morning. You're a bit grimy, too. Okay with you if we both have showers?"

"Sure," he mumbled into her neck. "You can go first."

"How big is the shower stall in that tin box of yours?" she asked.

* * *

As a matter of fact, the stall wasn't very large, but they squeezed in together anyway. Bogey was a little embarrassed at first because the erection that followed the first gentle kiss had only grown and tightened. Becky didn't seem offended. As a matter of fact, once or twice Bogey thought she was stealing glances.

Under the steamy spray, she set in soaping his body, beginning with his back and buttocks and then spinning him to do shoulders and chest. When her hands dipped toward his penis, he grabbed them.

"Better not."

"Okay," she said, handing him the soap and turning her back. "Do me."

Her back was beautiful. Her shoulders, wide for a girl, tapered gracefully toward a tightly muscled torso that narrowed further to her slender waist. He slid his hands, slick with the suds, over her, feeling grateful and amazed that this was happening.

She sighed contentedly and leaned back into him. "Do the front now," she said softly. Since she was the same height as he, her firm butt pressed against his erection as he pressed forward, encircling her with his arms. He soaped her flat belly first, aware of the tight musculature under her silken skin. Gently, he slid upward to caress her small, round breasts.

"Should I use the Bag Balm there, too?" she joked, but her voice was thick in her throat.

They dried each other using the luxurious thick towels that were another remnant of the high life in Maryland. She stood in front of him, completely relaxed in her nakedness. Bogey drank in her beauty. Her thick, dark hair was wet from the shower. Freed from her signature pony tail, it clung to her head, sweeping away from a black diamond widow's peak and falling down her back. In its frame, her small, delicate face was exotic, other worldly. He was reminded of the goddesses and heroines in the science fiction books he read as an adolescent.

"I never thought I had a chance with you," he said, almost reverently.

"You didn't," she said. "But you nailed me anyway."

"Don't put it that way," he said. "I really care about you."

"Yeah, that's what they all say." Her wide eyes with the dilated pupils told him her mind wasn't really on the words.

She walked into his arms. He lifted her and carried her to his bed, just a mattress on a bare frame, but with her lying there, it was the most beautiful boudoir in the world. She folded down the blue bedspread on the other side and slid over. She repeated the move on the side where she had been and then patted the bed. He joined her and began to kiss her again.

"Just a minute," she murmured, pulling back. "I've just got to tell you. You have a hell of a bod. I like it." Then she hurried back into his embrace.

"Feeling very mutual," he managed, and they both stopped talking.

* * *

After an extended vigorous and very passionate time, Becky spoke. "Now look what you've done. I'm all sweaty again. Back to the shower."

CHAPTER 19

When they were finally satiated, the afternoon sun was slanting through the window over them. Becky raised herself on an elbow. "Now you have to tell me the story," she said.

"What story?"

"The one about how you fell in love with horses. You promised to tell me later when we were driving back from Saratoga."

He scowled. "I hate to tell you that. Makes me sound like a dork."

"You probably were a dork. You act dorky sometimes, like right now for example. Tell me, you coward."

He sighed. "It happened on the night of my senior prom. My father sent me to a fancy boy's school, and frankly I didn't fit in. Fats was my only friend. Both our families said we had to go to the stupid dance, so we did."

"So what happened?"

"It was awful. All the guys except for Fats and me had dates from fancy girl's schools. I felt totally out of place, and poor Fats was catching a lot of nasty teasing as usual."

"So he was really fat back then?"

"Oh yeah, big and fat and soft but mentally tough. Not me. I couldn't stand it. I had to get out of there. Fats suggested we drive to Charles Town for the races. I didn't know anything about them, but he had gone with his uncle once or twice. I would have accepted an invitation to hell to get out of there, so off we went.

"Fats had a bottle of vodka he had sneaked into the dance, so we had a nip or two on the drive. Charles Town was different then. It was Saturday night, and there was a good crowd, a good mood. I liked it right away, and then we went down to watch the horses saddle up for the next race. Man, the sight of those thoroughbreds up close hit me like a punch in the belly. They took my breath away. One of them caught my eye, something about the way he carried himself and the look in his eye. I told Fats, but he laughed at me.

'That horse is twenty five to one.'

"But I wouldn't stop blabbing about him, so Fats said he'd bet two dollars on him for me. When he won, Fats was all excited. I was excited, too, but not about the bet. I wanted to go with the horse when he left the winner's circle. Fats had to explain they wouldn't let me into the barn area unless I worked there. I was broken hearted. I couldn't drive from Baltimore to Charles Town every day in my parents' car, but I knew I had to be around these animals.

"I didn't even know there was a track in Baltimore. Fats had to tell me about Pimlico."

Becky laughed. "A new world, eh?"

"Yeah. Long story short, I managed to get a summer job hot walking there, and it was as great as I expected. I never wanted to leave. Father insisted I go to college that fall. I lasted three months, and I missed the horses every day. So I came back, and I haven't left the track since – much to my father's disapproval."

Becky looked at him musingly. "So you had that damn eye of yours from day one," she said. "Lucky son of a bitch."

"I don't know about that," he laughed. "It hasn't exactly brought fame and fortune."

"It's one of the things that brought you this." She indicated the length of her body with a backhanded wave.

"I take it back. It has brought me fortune, great fortune," he said.

"Damn well better say that."

* * *

Later as they started back to town. Becky stared out the window. "I'm not sure what just happened," she said, "but I feel okay about it."

"I feel better than okay. I feel great."

"Another notch on the gun, eh? I saw those women falling all over you in Maryland, and your pal Huddleston let the cat out of the bag about your groupies on the private jet. How many times into the mile high club? Didn't he also mention a niece? What was that about?"

"This was different. I didn't even know those women. I know you. I admire you," he protested.

She looked at him tenderly. "I know. It scares me. What if it goes away?"

"I'll never go away."

"You mean that now, but everything beautiful and great is fragile," she said quietly. "But then maybe it's our duty to enjoy it and protect it as much as we can."

She reached over and squeezed his shoulder. "You do need to fill those pastures of yours with mommas and babies. You need to raise more Rosies and Wallers."

He glanced over and saw she was smiling warmly at him. "By the way, thanks for pulling me through after Waller. Good thing one of us has balls when the going gets tough," she said.

Bogey took her hand and squeezed it, not trusting himself to say anything through the lump in his throat. After all, tough, protective he-men shouldn't get all misty eyed.

CHAPTER 20

When the phone in her boarding house rang that night, Becky ran to answer. She hadn't given the number to Bogey, but she still hoped it might be him. It wasn't, but she was happy to talk to Judy Patton.

"I got a look at the video of that Laurel race. Rosie needed me. She got a weird ride," Judy said.

"I wish you had been there, but it probably wasn't the jockey's fault." She told Judy about the day's harrowing events. "The whole thing wilted Rosie. She's just now beginning to bounce back."

"That guy Huddleston is a real asshole."

"Yeah, he is truly psychopathic, just like you read about in freshman psychology."

"Does this mean Rosie won't be able to come up here for the big one?"

"Probably, but Bogey and I took her out to his farm yesterday. That seemed to brighten her up."

"*You* and the Bogey Boy? He had to have help? Or did you just want to go?"

"It turned into an interesting trip," Becky said coyly.

"Tell! Talk! What was so interesting?"

"I slept with him," Becky blurted.

"Oh, I see. Your ole sis *did* see what I thought I saw. Sis is never wrong," Judy gloated. "So you took him off the charm bracelet and threw the little cutie in bed."

"Actually, he threw me, very gently, on the bed. The man has muscles on his muscles. He picked me up like a bag of potato chips."

"So the little man is strong."

"He's a small package, but when you take off the wrapping...."

"Tell sis all."

"I'm only saying that he is all man. All man. This phone is in a hallway."

"No need to say more. I take it you found the gift within the wrapping satisfying."

"Very. Very satisfying indeed," Becky said, sighing contentedly. They talked on for a while. Becky told her about losing Waller, and Judy gave an update on her romance. Becky hung up, glad to have such a good girl friend, one you could tell everything, well, almost everything.

CHAPTER 21

Bogey was whistling on his way to the track on Monday morning even though the day was grey with the threat of an early fall cold front. Of course Becky was the main reason, but there were more reasons to rejoice. Rosie had trotted up to greet him earlier, looking more like her old self and attacking her feed happily. In addition, his cell phone finally yielded a new owner – actually the return of an old owner from Maryland days. The man expressed delight that Bogey was training again and asked if he could send three of his horses that weren't quite good enough to compete in Maryland.

Things were looking up.

He tacked up Substantial Balance and took the colt out for a spirited gallop. The horse was coming to hand, probably ready to breeze an easy three eighths. He kept an eager eye out for Becky, but she didn't seem to be on the track while he was there.

After he bathed the colt and took him back to his stall, it was time to take care of some paper work and to call Marshall. He intended to report on the banker's horse but also to tell the man that money from the Maryland purse would be on its way for application to his mortgage debt.

Marshall was pleased to hear of his colt's progress and promised to come by to watch the first work. When Bogey went on to the subject of the mortgage, there was a long pause.

"Bogey, you're current on the loan. Don't send more money right now," the banker said.

"What? How could that be?"

"The money you wired in brought you up to date."

"I didn't wire any money."

"Well, your business manager did. That's the same thing. I left the rest of it in your account."

"The rest of it," Bogey repeated dully.

"Yes. There was only a little left over. I have another call here I need to take. Let me know when you plan to work the colt."

The line went dead. Bogey first thought that his father might have sent the money. On reflection, he knew his father wouldn't operate that way. He might try endlessly to convince him, but he wouldn't act behind his back. That left only one "business manager". A quick calculation told him that it was not even seven a.m. in California. The call to Fats would have to wait till later.

He had turned his attention to a stack of condition books on the desk when the track siren shrieked, followed by the recorded loudspeaker message, "Attention horsemen. There is a loose horse on the track." The warning was repeated again and again as the alarm continued to shriek.

Bogey paid little attention. It was a relatively common occurrence this time of the year. Some of the young horses had not been properly broken, and not all riders were equally skilled. An agitated horse with no rider running around the track as an uncontrolled threat was all too frequent.

Then a groom rushed through the barn door calling Bogey's name. "Come quick, Harry wants you," he shouted when he spotted Bogey.

"Where?" Bogey asked, wondering why Harry Collins had sent his groom to get him.

The kid pointed. "Up on the track. It's that girl. The exercise rider. The loose horse ran into her."

Bogey stood rooted, not understanding, not wanting to understand. "Becky? You mean Becky?" he asked woodenly.

"Yeah. The exercise girl. Harry wants you up there."

Bogey felt a wave of panic. His legs felt icy and leaden as he ran up the ramp toward the blaring siren.

At the top of the hill, he looked both ways and saw the crowd of people to his right, in front of the stands. A horse was down, sprawled across the track, not moving. He sprinted toward the scene. He saw people lifting a stretcher onto the track ambulance, and cold sweat drenched him. The ambulance sped past him and headed through the chute, siren wailing. Bogey stood frozen on the track, unsure what to do. Harry Collins came trotting toward him. One look at the trainer's face told Bogey that he carried bad news.

"They're taking her to Jefferson. You two are friends, right? Maybe you ought to go over there."

Bogey was frozen with fear. His stomach clutched and he choked back sour bile.

"What happened? Is Becky okay?" he asked foolishly as though he hadn't just seen the ambulance and heard Harry tell him to go to the hospital.

"No," Harry shouted, frowning at him. "The loose horse plowed right into her and her mount. She's busted up pretty bad."

* * *

The ambulance beat Bogey to the hospital. He rushed into the emergency room waiting area. A grey-haired receptionist sat behind a desk.

"Where is the girl who was hurt at the track," he stammered.

She didn't even glance down at her records. "They took her right in," she said, pointing to the double doors to Bogey's right. When she saw him lean toward the entrance to the patient area she added, "No one can go in. She's high triage, and half the staff is with her."

"High triage? Is that serious?" Bogey asked anxiously.

"Please have a seat. I'll let you know when one of the doctors can speak with you." Reluctantly he started toward the hard back brown chairs lining the institutional green wall but she called him back. "By the way, are you family? We do have some paperwork here."

"No, I'm not family. We're friends. I work with her at the track."

"Can you tell me how to reach her family?"

"No. I can't. I don't know the family."

"Do you think you could get the number for me?" the woman asked in an exasperated tone.

Bogey shook his head, trying to clear it so he could think sensibly. He came out of the fog and told her he thought he could get the information. After some difficulty, the helpful track operator was able to run down someone in the licensing office, who gave him the contact information.

He wrote it down for the receptionist. She motioned him back to his chair and made the call.

She spoke softly into the phone. She listened for a moment and then stiffened, her expression angry. Her voice rose, and Bogey could hear her clearly. "Just a moment, madam. I am calling to give you information, not to be insulted." She listened again and then said coldly, "Yes, I'll tell the doctor you wish to talk with him, just as soon as he has a moment off from trying to save your daughter's life." She seemed to listen briefly, then shouted at the phone. "Madam, you are very rude," and slammed it down. Her face was red.

After a moment, the phone rang and she answered it, nodding. When she hung up and called another number, Bogey heard her mention the words "extreme emergency", and his entire body was gripped by an icy spasm. He couldn't stand this. He went to the desk and pleaded with the grey- haired woman.

"I'm sorry, but I'm very worried. Can you tell me anything? What's happening?"

She leaned forward. "Technically, I shouldn't say anything, but since I can see you really care about this woman, I will tell you what little I know. She's hurt pretty badly and the family is requesting that she be transferred to Johns Hopkins Hospital in Baltimore. The doctors here are working to get her stable enough for the trip." She gave Bogey a kind, sad smile. "That's all I can tell you. Maybe you should go home and talk to the family after she is settled in at the new hospital. Right now she is in no condition for visitors; you'd just be in the doctors' way."

Bogey shook his head. "I can't go. Maybe I will see her on the way out. I'll just wait here if that's all right."

"You can wait if you like, but she's going by helicopter. You won't be able to see her," she said. Her gaze was kind and caring. "Frankly, I'm sorry you aren't the one taking care of her. I think she'd be better off with you."

"What do you mean?" Bogey asked in confusion.

"Never mind. I'm a silly old lady who all ready said too much."

"No. No. Thanks for talking to me. I was going crazy. I still am, but at least I know what's happening."

Bogey sat down again. Time dragged slowly by.

If I could just see her. If I could see that's she's okay. She's got to be okay.

The tortured thoughts circled his mind like a monotonous recorded loop of doom. He heard the loud descending clatter of copter blades. Their whooshing beat seemed to compress the air in the room, further squeezing his heart. His drained face must have been visible across the room. The grey-haired lady looked at him sympathetically.

"If you go out that door you may be able to watch them take her to the helicopter," she said.

He nodded silent thanks and went outside. Two men were running from the copter through a back door into the emergency room. In moments, the door opened again, and the two men came out carrying a stretcher between them. A third man walked beside the stretcher holding up an IV bottle which clearly contained blood. They moved briskly, ducking the downdraft of the whirling blades, and loaded the stretcher into the helicopter. The door closed, the third man ran back toward the hospital, and Bogey watched Becky lift into the air and nose east into the afternoon sky. When the helicopter was out of sight, he dragged himself to his car. There was nothing to do but to drive away.

Even in his state of emotional collapse, he remembered his duty to the horses. He headed to the track first to feed Marshall Berman's horse. As he was headed back to the car, Harry Collins approached.

"How is she doing?" he asked.

Bogey shook his head. "Not good. They flew her to Johns Hopkins."

Harry clapped a hand on his shoulder. "I got to ask. People say you two are close. That true?"

Bogey looked him in the eye. "Yes."

"I just want you to know that if you want to see about her, I'll cover for you here. She's a good person."

"Thanks. I may take you up on that," Bogey said. He felt surprised and grateful. Collins was becoming a regular source of unexpected messages.

"Just holler," Collins said and walked away.

* * *

In the trailer, Bogey felt lonely and afraid. He looked at the phone number for Becky's family that he had written down. There was no point in calling. They would be at the hospital. He paced restlessly, full of fearful imaginings. There was no release from the cold aching within.

The phone rang, and he jumped to it, answering breathlessly.

It was Fats. Bogey tried to keep the disappointment out of his voice, but the perceptive friend caught it.

"Whoa," he said. "So you know and you're mad. Let me explain."

"I'm not mad."

"Don't lie to Fats. You're upset. Here's the deal. When I told Millie about your problems, she reminded me that the bank out here is drooling over the sale of Intercontinental Reach. They fell all over themselves to give me a sweetheart loan. It's basically free money till the company sale goes through. No skin off me. It's no big deal. You can pay me back when the filly makes some big dough."

"I'm not mad at you, Fats. I appreciate what you did. Something else has happened. Something horrible."

He explained, and Fats listened.

"So I want to get off the phone now. I'm hoping she can give me a call. Maybe it's not as bad as it looked."

"I understand," Fats said quickly. "One word of advice. Call your dad. I bet he can get information from Hopkins. He's connected everywhere."

After Fats hung up, Bogey paced again, trying to decide what to do. He didn't actually decide to call his father. He just found himself dialing the number.

"I'm glad you called," his father said immediately. "I've been toying with an idea that I wanted to discuss with you."

"Dad, er Father," he corrected. "Right now I just need some advice. My girlfriend, her name is Becky, Rebecca Friedman, was seriously injured at the track this morning. She's being admitted to Johns Hopkins. I don't know what to do. I've never met any of her family, but I've got to see her. I'm scared to death." The words flew out in a tumbling torrent. "I'm going crazy. What should I do? Is there anything I *can* do?"

His father's voice was calm and reassuring. "Miss Friedman is either in Johns Hopkins or on the way here, is that correct?"

"Yes. Right," Bogey said quickly.

There was a slight pause, and the soothing voice continued. "Then what you must do is to come here. Meet me at the house. I'll make some phone calls, and we'll decide on the best course of action. Do you understand?"

"Yes. I'll leave right away."

"And Humphrey – Bogey - drive very cautiously. Don't speed. Keep your mind on the road. You won't help your friend if you have a wreck. Promise me you will get yourself under control." These were orders, but they were not stern. They were caring and filled with concern.

"I promise," Bogey said. In fact he did feel calmer. "And Dad, thanks a lot."

"You're welcome, son," his dad said. "And just one more thought. You might want to bring some nice clothes to wear if we can get you into the hospital."

* * *

Night was falling when Bogey pulled into the driveway of his childhood home. His father met him at the door and led Bogey into the living room. "Do you need any food or something to drink? I doubt that you've thought about that."

Bogey shook his head impatiently. "No, no. Just tell me what we can do about Becky."

"I made a few phone calls. First, I should tell you that I know the Friedman family, not well, but I've had some contact. The father and I have had professional dealings. He's a fine man. His wife, your friend's mother, is a different matter. I'm afraid she won't be helpful in this situation."

"What about Becky?" Bogey asked impatiently.

"She is in the ICU. Visiting is limited to family members with strict time limits even on them. You will not be permitted to visit unless the family authorizes it, and even then medical restrictions may interfere."

"Should I talk to the family? They'd understand how badly I need to see her, wouldn't they?" Bogey pleaded.

"Sarah Friedman won't look kindly on anyone from the race track, not to even mention you aren't Jewish. I hate to discourage you, but these are facts," Richard Dawson explained gently.

"What can I do then?" Bogey asked. "I can't just sit here."

"I know. Here's my suggestion. Your friend was admitted only an hour or so ago. You should take a deep breath, try to eat and drink something to keep yourself together. Clean up and put on your best outfit. Then we'll go to the Critical Care waiting area, and I will introduce you to the Friedmans. Maybe Hiram Friedman will at least give you a hearing."

"Okay," Bogey said. "I'll do what you say, but I'm not sure I can eat."

"That's what everyone thinks till they sit down to some food," his father said calmly.

* * *

Richard Dawson had obviously been to the Hopkins Critical Care Center before. He stationed them just inside the waiting room door and looked around at the people there. The illumination in the room was muted, and tension and fear hung in the air like a dark shadow. Family members huddled together, speaking in anxious, secretive whispers as though disaster could be averted by not mentioning it aloud.

Finally, the elder Dawson took his son's arm and nodded toward a couple in the corner of the room. Bogey saw a slight, grey-haired man and a much sturdier woman with flowing black hair that shone even in the dim light of the room. Bogey could see the origins of Becky's beauty in the older woman's face. However, in the mother's case the good looks were spoiled – not by time but by an angry hardness. Sarah Friedman looked as fierce as advertised.

As Bogey watched, her husband reached to take her hand. Without even looking at him, she snatched it away.

Bogey's father squeezed his arm and leaned close. "Are you ready?" he asked.

Bogey nodded uncertainly and allowed his father to lead him toward the Friedmans.

They stopped in front of Hiram Friedman, who looked up uncertainly and then smiled in recognition.

"Richard. Do you have someone here, too? Our daughter was in an accident."

Sarah Friedman just glared angrily at Dawson, apparently resenting the interruption or her husband's friendly greeting or life in general.

"Yes, Hiram, I know about your daughter's accident. Actually, that's why I'm here – why we're here. This is my son, Humphrey Dawson. He's a friend of your daughter."

Bogey stepped forward and shook hands with Hiram Friedman. "How is she, Mr. Friedman? Is she going to be okay?"

Hiram started to answer, but his wife broke in. "Who are you young man? I don't recall you as one of Rebecca's friends."

"I – I work with her. We're really good friends," Bogey offered eagerly.

Sarah Friedman's forbidding countenance darkened even more. "You work with her? Do you mean at that race track?"

"Yes ma'am, at Charles Town Races."

"Get out of here! Your race track, your barn, whatever you call it, has just about killed my only daughter. She should never have gone there. If her father had had any backbone, she would be healthy and happy instead of fighting for her life inside those doors." She pointed to the ICU entrance, growing more enraged as she spoke. Her voice was cold, her words biting. "Get out of my sight. I don't want to be reminded of that decadent and despicable life. My daughter will never go back there. She will not associate with any of you track people." Sarah Friedman's scowl made "track people" a vile explicative spat contemptuously into the room.

"Sarah, please," Hiram beseeched.

"Don't speak to me," Sarah told him. "I blame you for what happened. You never backed me up, stood up to your daughter. Now you may have killed her."

The other people in the room were staring at them in alarm. Richard Dawson took his son's arm once again. "I can see this is not a good time. We'll just wish you our best and go now." He nodded respectfully to the Friedmans. "Sarah, Hiram."

Bogey looked back imploringly as his father led him away. He saw only the mother's stone-faced hatred and the father's sad and helpless eyes. Bogey felt at one with the man. He could understand sad and helpless.

Back at the house, Bogey called Harry Collins and explained the situation. He apologized for calling so late and asked if it would be all right for him to stay in Baltimore for a day or two.

"Sure. Everything's under control here. Just get Becky well. I'll see you when I see you."

It was a strange experience to spend the night in his childhood room. He had thought his father would redecorate and put the space to some practical use, but the Star Trek posters were still on the light blue walls, and the bookcases filled with science fiction novels were as he had left them.

He was suddenly blindsided by a longing for his mother. The dam holding these thoughts safe was breached by a surge of yearning. He was flooded with tender memories of her love and resentment of her early death.

The painful feelings merged with his despair over Becky, and he wept.

He was exhausted. He had slept little the previous night, and the unrelieved anxiety of the day had been draining. He knew he couldn't sleep, but he was too tired to stay upright. He lay down on his bed to rest a moment and fell into a deep sleep.

He wakened early, thoughts of Becky shocking him into total alertness. Downstairs, he found his father already impeccably dressed in a grey suit and muted tie. He looked up when Bogey entered the room. "Good morning, son. Have some coffee and toast."

"Good morning, Father. Have you talked to the hospital this morning?"

"No. I was waiting for you. We should talk about the best approach. I'm not sure how to proceed in such a way that we don't make things worse. Rumor has it that Sarah gets even more difficult when challenged."

Bogey sat down and accepted the cup of coffee. He nibbled at a piece of toast, but his stomach was in knots. "Yeah," he said. "I saw her face. How could someone as sweet as Becky have a mother like that?"

His father's smile was sad, self-mocking. "Some people probably wonder how a nice guy like you could have such a rigid, tight-assed father."

Bogey was shocked. For one thing, he had never heard Richard Dawson curse or even use slang. His father went on calmly, "The answer in both cases probably has something to do with the other parent. Hiram and Madeline brought the love. Sarah and I think we need to bring the discipline. Maybe both are good, but maybe more love and less discipline would be better."

Bogey looked at his father. He spoke sincerely, very sure of what he wanted to say. "Father, I have never doubted your love. I never doubted you were trying to do what was best for me. I didn't always agree with the lessons you were trying to teach me, but I never doubted your intentions."

"That's kind of you son, but though I did try to do the right thing, I failed Madeline, and I failed you. My definition of strength was flawed. I saw the two of you as weak people. In fact, you're not weak at all. Madeline, though she finally surrendered, had a quiet strength that I didn't see."

Bogey was dumbfounded. He struggled to sort out his chaotic thoughts. Richard Dawson, Sr. never admitted weakness, never confessed to mistakes.

"I can't talk about Mother. I don't even like to think about her, but I don't see any problems in how you treated me," he finally said.

"I didn't stand up for you against your brother. I thought he teased you to make you stronger. I now see his goal was to keep you down. I failed you again when I didn't protect you from Edmond Huddleston. I thought he was a realistic man who understood the thoroughbred business, and you were a foolish idealist. I should have known better." His father's tone was factual, simply recounting facts.

"But Dad, you did many good things for me. You tried to understand me even though I was so different from you. You're a good father," Bogey protested.

His father smiled. "I didn't say that I was always wrong. Just that sometimes I was very wrong. For another example, I always wanted you to call me Father, and I now learn that I really like to be called Dad." The old man suddenly changed gears. "Now that's enough of the past. Let's think about what we can do to improve the present." He paused a moment, collecting his thoughts. "I'll call my hospital contacts. They'll want to help within ethical constraints. I believe they are allowed to say whether she is still in ICU and, perhaps, her official status, you know, stable, critical and the like."

"That's better than nothing. Please call."

Richard hung up the phone and turned to Bogey. "The news is somewhat encouraging. She was bleeding internally, and they determined she had a ruptured spleen. She had surgery early last evening to remove the spleen. It went well, and she has had two transfusions. She is still in the ICU and listed as critical, but the expectation is that her status will soon be changed to stable. She is definitely much improved."

"They took out her spleen?" Bogey asked in alarm.

"They assured me that the spleen is not an essential organ. She won't even miss it."

"God, I wish I could see her. I should be sitting by her bed."

"This is the time you should remember one of the good lessons I tried to teach you. Patience. Logic should tell you that a visit is not possible."

Bogey managed a slight grin. "You and your logic. You're right, but that doesn't matter."

His father actually chuckled. "Okay. Trust your emotions but – as we say in racing – try to rein them in."

"I can't believe you're joking with me."

"Enjoy it. It won't happen often."

The phone rang. The elder Dawson answered and then held the phone out to Bogey. "Hiram Friedman needs to talk with you."

He grabbed the receiver eagerly. Becky's father's voice was thin and low. He sounded tired. "Mr. Dawson, Bogey, I have to tell you that my daughter is asking to see you. She is quite insistent. Of course, my wife wouldn't hear of it."

"Yes sir, she was quite clear on that point."

"Don't judge her too harshly. Sarah is a good woman. She loves all of us very much. In some ways, I think she loves Becky most of all. She is just trying in her own way to take care of her baby girl."

"I believe that. Becky believes that. I just want to see Becky. To hold her hand. Can I please do that?"

"Yes, and without the distress it would cause my wife. My son has insisted that Sarah keep her own medical appointment this afternoon. He will be driving her there. My son is like my wife. He doesn't take 'no' for an answer. The point is, Mr. Dawson, I will take you in to see my daughter this afternoon between 2 and 3."

* * *

When Bogey arrived at the Critical Care waiting area promptly at two, he saw a smiling Hiram. "They took her off the critical list and moved her down to the surgery wing. She's much better, has some color in her cheeks. Come on, seeing you will make her even better. You're the only subject of conversation – with me anyway."

When Bogey peeked around the door frame of her room, Becky was propped up in the hospital bed. The side rails were up, and a tangle of tubes snaked away from her. She was very pale. If her earlier color had been worse than this ashen hue, she must have resembled a ghost. She looked small and frail but still gorgeous. He broke into a wide smile. "Hello, beautiful," he said softly.

She rolled her eyes. "I don't feel very beautiful," she said weakly. "I'm really glad you came. Daddy told me he had to slip you by mother. Sorry."

He went to her side and took her free hand in his. "No apology. I'm just so glad to see you."

Her voice was weak, but her words were emphatic. "I had to tell you face to face. I like you very much, but I won't be coming back to Charles Town."

He shook his head. "Don't say that," he said.

"Mother was right all along. I don't belong at the race track. I've been faking it, and I almost got myself killed."

"That wasn't your fault," Bogey protested. "You're great at the track. This was a freak accident."

"I'm scared, Bogey. What happened between us scares me. The very idea of getting back on a horse scares me. I'm saying goodbye. Give me a kiss. Right here under the oxygen. Don't knock it out."

He did as he was told. Her lips were cool and soft and wonderful. He fought to hold back tears.

She spoke again in her threadbare whisper. "How is Rosie? I picked an awful time to get myself hurt."

"Rosie is fine. You need to rest. The nurse said I could come in but only for a minute. We can talk about future plans when you're better. I'll come back when I can."

She smiled tiredly. "No. Don't come back. Seeing you hurts too much. I'm very tired. You need to go."

He backed away from the bed in shock, addled by the numbing sense that his world just ended.

"I wish I could have one of your lullabies," she murmured, but her eyes were already closing, pushing out tears that rolled slowly down her alabaster skin.

CHAPTER 22

"I don't know what to do," Bogey told his father. He had been saying that a lot lately, but now, sitting on his father's fine leather couch, his dejection had reached a new low.

"It's a difficult situation."

"I don't want to create a big family squabble for Becky. She needs peace and quiet. She doesn't want to see me anyway."

"Becky doesn't want to see you? I thought her father said she was demanding to talk with you."

"Yeah, to tell me goodbye."

"But why?" his father insisted.

"She says she is afraid of horses and afraid of me. I don't think Becky even knows how the accident happened. She seems to think she got hurt because she made some kind of mistake on the horse. She didn't do anything wrong."

"Victims do that. They blame themselves."

"I just don't know what to do," Bogey said again. He put his head in his hands and cried quietly." His father sat beside him on the couch and squeezed his shoulder.

Finally Bogey said, "Any suggestions? I won't be bullheaded this time."

His father chuckled. "Very well. Here's my advice. Your key here is Hiram Friedman. I admire him for understanding Sarah and trying to protect her from herself. I regret I didn't do more to protect your mother from her demons." He was lost in his thoughts for a moment and then pressed on.

"In any case, Hiram loves his family. He'll try to keep Sarah happy, but he'll take care of Becky, and even you. He's a caretaker."

"So how can he help me?"

"I can't say. I can say that you'll hear from him. He'll tell you the truth as he sees it. You should go back to Charles Town. I'll be sure Hiram knows how to reach you."

"I do need to get back. There's work to do, but it'll be hard without her there."

His father patted his shoulder. "You underestimate yourself. I'm sure you're stubborn enough to do anything you decide to do."

Bogey looked sideways at him. There was a sly grin on the old man's aristocratic face.

"Yeah, I guess you would know," Bogey admitted.

"Take care of business. Give Becky time to heal, body and spirit. Hiram will keep you informed, I'm sure of it."

Bogey met his father's level gaze. "I guess you're right. I'm not accomplishing anything here. If anything goes wrong, you'll call me right away, right?"

"I'll stay in touch with Hiram. He'll update me if anything changes. I believe, however, that soon he'll be calling you."

Bogey packed quickly and came downstairs. He stopped in front of his father. "Thank you. You don't know how much you've helped."

His father's customary steely composure was in place. "You're very welcome. It's time I was helpful to you." He reached to shake hands, but Bogey took the proffered hand and used it to pull his father to him. He hugged the old man tightly. "I love you, Dad," he said quietly and turned to walk away.

"I love you too, son." Bogey didn't trust himself to look back. His father had never encouraged maudlin shows of emotion.

CHAPTER 23

Rosie was getting better. And Bogey had horses from two new clients – new to West Virginia at least. He tried to cling to those facts each morning when he fed his star before going to the track, every evening when he came home and cared for her, and every night when he was trying to relax into sleep. In spite of accentuating the positive, time dragged and his mind was never free of worry.

Hiram Friedman called him every few days. There was nothing alarming in his reports, but Becky's progress was slow. She was home but still weak and still taking pain medication. Bogey longed to know if she ever mentioned him, but he thought that asking about it would seem selfish and insensitive. He just thanked her father for the calls and waited anxiously for the next one.

He talked with his father twice. The old man continued to counsel patience. He called Fats only once. He knew his friend was in the middle of a crucial business deal and refused to burden him with his bleak mood. Fats was sympathetic but strangely noncommittal when Bogey told him of Becky's slow progress and her rejection of him.

A jubilant Fats called on the last day of October.

"It's a done deal!" he shouted. "Can you believe it? Your old pal Fats is a rich man. I just signed a hell of a deal."

Bogey was happy for his friend. He tried to get that excitement into his voice. "That is great, Fats. You really deserve it. You are one smart son of a gun!"

"Of course I am. However, since she's sitting right here, I have to admit I couldn't have pulled this off without Millie. She's the real brains here."

"This is so great, Fats. You guys worked hard for it. Congratulate Millie for me."

"Actually, she wants to talk to you. I'll put her on."

"Bogey," she said. "We haven't met, but Fats has talked about you so much that I think I know you. Up front, I'm a pushy broad. I'm gonna shoot my mouth off. That's what I do." Her voice was deep and musical. Her words bounced ahead of her as though she couldn't quite keep up with her thoughts. "Here's the deal. You need a woman's advice. Obviously you and Fats don't have the least notion of how we think. I'm sure you agree."

She didn't wait for an answer. "So it falls on me to tell you what to do about your Becky. Fats tells me she's a smartass loud-mouthed dame like me. He met her at Saratoga, remember, and, of course, he's got to brag about how she's impressed with his body. See, that means one thing to him and another thing to me. Want to know what it means to me, which is what it really means?"

Bogey was rendered almost speechless by her. "Yeah, I mean sure," he managed to say.

"Okay. What it means is that she's got a thing for you, probably has had for a while. Since you're as clueless as my Fats, I'll tell you she was trying to make you jealous. She was trying to flush you out of the brush, man. I bet it worked, didn't it? Made you jealous, didn't it? Don't lie."

Even at her windiest, Becky was a gentle breeze compared to this hurricane. Bogey would have been afraid to lie even if he had been tempted.

"Yes. I was jealous."

"Of course you were. That's settled. Now, let's get to the present. I understand from Jim that she finally got you to make a move. You two got it on, right?" Again, no need for confirmation. "Now she's sick, and she says she doesn't want to see you. Okay, now you have to tell me exactly what she said. Not what you thought she meant. Tell me the reason she gave for not wanting to see you."

"She said she was scared. She doesn't want to ride again because she's scared, and she's scared about our relationship."

"That's not it. *Why did she say she didn't want you to visit?* Exact words only, please."

Bogey made himself think back; to remember the precise reason she gave for carving his heart out. "She said it hurt too much to see me."

"And you stopped going? Because of that?"

"She said she didn't want to see me," Bogey said. "She was very definite."

"For goodness sakes, Bogey! Girls say lots of things. You have to try to understand us. Use your head. Even if she hurt your feelings, try to think. She said that it hurt too much to see you. That means you are really important to her. If you're that important she *needs* to see you. Doesn't matter what she says she wants."

"Her mother doesn't want me to see her either."

"You can't report to both of them. Look, I've said all I have to say. Just go see her. Help her through the hurt. If she really isn't interested, okay, walk away. Just don't drop her when she's so confused she can't decide anything. That's my take."

"I do thank you," he said hesitantly.

"Don't give me that. You don't have to listen to me. Here's my final advice. Jim tells me she has a best friend who is a jockey in New York. True?"

"Yes. Judy Patton."

"At least call her. Get another woman's take on the situation, a woman who knows Becky well. This situation is so far beyond male understanding. Sorry, but it's true. Goodbye."

The connection broke. Bogey put the phone down and stared at it.

Fats had his hands full.

CHAPTER 24

Edmond Huddleston had given this phone call a lot of thought. It was an important call and one he looked forward to. He lounged back in his plush swivel chair and waited for Richard Dawson, Sr. to answer.

"Hello Edmond," the old attorney said. "What can I do for you today?"

"We haven't talked since our meeting in Briarson's office. I thought we should."

"I hope you understood my position that day."

"Yes. I did. You felt you had to represent your son's interests. Admirable, I'd say."

"I'm glad you understand."

"I do. I understand you will continue to favor your son even though I am locked in an impasse with him. He is stubbornly refusing to do the right thing by Final Gift – a stupid name for an elegant filly, by the way – or even to act in his own best interest."

"I have told him the same, Edmond. He doesn't listen to me either."

"That's the crucial difference. He *will* listen to me. I will do whatever is necessary to insure that outcome. At this point I realize that you will try to block my efforts and protect him."

"Only if you use unfair or illegal methods."

"I can't have you sitting in judgment on my methods."

"What are you trying to tell me, Edmond?"

"Richard, you are a Baltimore aristocrat of the old school. Those are the three things I hate about you. As an aristocrat, you have always looked down on me. I was just a dumb ex-jock who happened to inherit some money and a company from his father. I blundered about, taking stupid risks only your brilliant legal mind and good connections could save me from. You see me as a blue collar dolt; someone to look at down your long, thin nose."

There was shocked silence on the other end of the line. Huddleston chuckled. "I know you think I'm a hot-headed fool. When I get pissed off, I see that superior smirk on your face. Let's see, where are we? Oh yes, old school. Old is the important word. You're an old man, Richard. The juices have dried up – if you ever had any. You're just playing not to lose. I play to win. And finally, you are Baltimore. You can't think outside this chummy little Charm City. In short, Richard, you are old and way too cautious. I don't need someone to watch out for me, keep me out of trouble and protect me from myself."

Richard Dawson broke in. "Edmond, I don't understand what you're getting at. We've been a great team."

Huddleston made his voice warm and friendly. "Don't think I am ungrateful. You taught me a lot, particularly when I was getting started. This is a new day. I'm not a green kid any longer. I can plot my own course. Someone who sits around worrying that I will make a mistake is just in the way. The current situation is a prime example, particularly since you have a vested interest in helping your son instead of me. Am I making myself clear? I don't need you any longer, and I don't want you around."

"I take it that you are firing me as counsel. Very well."

"I am. I will be offering the job to Richard, Jr. on the condition that he leaves your firm. Dickey understands that I make all the decisions. I'm the ship captain, and I'll give him assignments to carry out below decks. He understands that I'm smarter than he is. I'm smarter than you as well – a fact you never recognized. You're just a technician, and you're too old to even be a good technician. You can send my final statement. Of course, feel free to count this conversation as a billable hour."

With that, Huddleston hung up the phone. He wore a broad smile. He had waited a long time to tell off that pompous old son of a bitch. It felt good. It felt really good.

Now he was free to deal with the old bastard's stubborn kid. He had a few ideas.

CHAPTER 25

When Bogey heard his father's voice on the phone, he had a moment of panic.

"Hello, son," his father said. His voice sounded flat and tired. Bogey's anxiety mounted.

"What's wrong Dad?"

There was a long sigh on the other end of the line. "I need to tell you something, something that has me rather upset." One of his long pauses followed. Bogey's breath caught in his throat. He was light-headed.

Don't let it be bad news about her.

"Edmond Huddleston has fired me."

Bogey was able to breath. "Dad, even if it's bad for business, it may be for the best. Huddleston is losing his mind." He told his father about Waller and Huddleston's probable role in the horse's death.

His father gasped. "God help us. Your brother is leaving me to become in-house council for Huddleston."

"I can't believe he's doing this to you. Do you want me to call him and warn him about Huddleston? He's going the wrong way here."

"Edmond is going power mad. He's a dangerous person, and Dickey is blind to that." The old attorney's voice was heavy with regret and apprehension. "Your brother thinks he's gaining his freedom from my control even though I tried to give him room to grow. He's my son, and I love him, but he's not a strong person."

"He always seemed strong," Bogey protested. "He'll be okay."

"No, son. He isn't honest and tough like you are. You often annoyed me, but I respected you even when your decisions terrified me. Dickey, on the other hand, is vulnerable, particularly since he doesn't know he is."

"What can we do? Shall I call him?" Bogey asked again.

"No. That would only make things worse, especially if Huddleston learned of the call. We can pray for him, I suppose. Nothing else."

CHAPTER 26

The next morning, after feeding, exercising and bathing the four horses now in his stable, Bogey emerged from the barn to find Huddleston and Otey waiting by the Mercedes.

"Glad to see you're getting some horses. You deserve that," Huddleston said. Otey leaned against the car, his customary smirk in place.

Bogey felt heat course through his body, and he took a step toward Huddleston. He glowered at the man. "Get the hell out of here before I kill you for what you did." He was filled with impotent rage. He and his father had agreed there was no way to prove that Huddleston drugged Waller, but the urge to change frustration into attack was almost irresistible.

Otey moved off the car and stepped toward him menacingly. "Watch it, Shrimp," he shouted.

"I don't know what you think I did," Huddleston said. "I just came here to express my sympathy for your nasty run of luck. It was bad enough when you had to turn the filly out. I was hoping for a rematch in the big race at Belmont. Both my boys came back in fine shape, so we're headed up there. Sorry you can't make it."

Bogey said nothing. His jaw was clamped so hard it was aching.

"And now losing your old gelding." Huddleston shook his head. "I tried to warn you. Racing is an uncertain and dangerous game. I would hate for something even worse to happen to your little filly."

Huddleston spread his arms in a gesture of magnanimity. "I'll give you one last chance. Even though she's damaged goods, I'll still take the filly and see if I can nurse her back to health, and I'll still take Sentinel's Cry, but only if we make the deal now while it's early enough to get him advertised for next breeding season. The stallion registers will close in the next few weeks."

His face wrinkled with regret. "Unfortunately, I have to drop the job offer. I had forgotten how bad your attitude problems were. Can't have a negative person fouling up my harmonious team even if he does have talent."

Bogey said nothing.

Huddleston shrugged. "Final offer. If you're interested, we can talk price. It will be lower than last time, of course, but generous under the circumstances."

Bogey stared at him. "You through?" he asked flatly. "I have only one thing to say to you. If you come around here again, you'll regret it. That goes for fat boy too."

"That sounds like a threat," Huddleston said in an injured tone.

"That *is* a threat."

"Boss, I told you it was a waste of time talking to the shrimp," Otey snarled. Huddleston gave a resigned sigh. "I fear you were right. We did waste our good intentions, didn't we? Take me home." He paused at the open car door Otey was holding. "People usually come to regret refusing my final offers," he said and then climbed in.

Bogey watched them drive away and waited in vain for his heart rate to return to normal. He wished fervently he would never see them again, but he knew that wish was doomed. He needed Becky here. He needed to talk with her about this crazy mess.

* * *

He had been having an internal debate about Millie's suggestion to call Judy Patton. He was reluctant since he barely knew her, but he was tempted because she knew Becky better than anyone and might have a useful idea. The debate ended when she called him the next day.

"Mr. Dawson, I hate to bother you, but I didn't know where else to turn. How is Becky?"

"You haven't talked with her?" Bogey asked in surprise.

"No. Her mother says she's too ill to come to the phone."

"I haven't talked with her either. She told me she didn't want to see me, but I talk to her father. From what he says, she's not too sick to talk on the phone."

"That's what I thought. It's the witch. She doesn't want Becky to talk with the person who introduced her to horses and led her astray in the first place. On top of that, I'm not Jewish. That woman hates me."

"Really?"

"Yes. Really. She moved her whole family to Pikesville. She told Becky it was because the blacks were taking over our school, but I think she wanted to get Becky away from me. I'm pretty sure someone told her about my pony."

"Bouncer," Bogey said.

"Becky told you about Bouncer. That's great," Judy said, sounding happy.

"Yeah. We've had some pretty good talks lately – until this happened."

"Look, I shouldn't be telling you this, but I think Becky needs to see you. I think she's falling for you, and that scares her. She's never had a high opinion of guys, just doesn't trust them. I think you need to show her you won't go away even if she tells you to."

"I shouldn't be telling you *this,* but I'm in love with her. I've always had a crush on her, but this is different. I really think we should be together."

"I know her pretty well, and I think you're right."

"What can I do? She told me not to come back because it hurt to see me. By the way, she also says she's afraid of horses now."

"The witch has put her under a spell," Judy said. "She doesn't know what she wants. Of course she'll be afraid until she starts riding again. I clipped heels two years ago during the Saratoga meet, went head over keister, got trampled by a trailing horse and damn near died. Was I scared when I tried to start back? Better believe it. But I think I'm riding better than ever now."

"She sure seemed happy here before the accident."

"I'll tell you more about her. Becky had a pretty bad depression after she moved to Pikesville. Had to have therapy. She called me, said she and her doctor agreed she had to get back to horses. I was riding the Maryland circuit and got her a job hot walking. Lucky she had a good shrink who stood up to the family and helped her break away. But I think she's always been guilty about going against her mother. Maybe she sees the accident as proper punishment."

"That's complicated," Bogey said, "but I see what you're saying."

"I guess I'm saying you need to be the shrink who stands up for her this time."

Bogey was silent for a few moments, and Judy waited.

"I'll see what I can do," he said finally.

CHAPTER 27

Two days later, Bogey had to brave an autumn rain and his own fears on the drive to Baltimore. The cloth top of his old convertible had sprung a small leak, and a thin stream of water traced a jagged path down the inside of the back window.

What could he say to Becky? What if Sarah Friedman wouldn't let him in the house? What if Becky ordered him away? What if he lost his nerve and couldn't face her?

He pulled into the Friedman driveway. The two-story brick house with white shutters was large, well tended and worlds away from his second hand trailer. Bogey was seized by an awareness that he didn't belong there, wasn't worthy of this castle or of the princess within it.

He pushed the doubts away and dashed through the rain to the door. When he rang the bell, Becky's mother opened the door a crack. She frowned at him. Bogey noticed she was taller than him. Through tight jaws, she said, "I thought I made it clear that you were not welcome."

"I need to talk with Becky," he said.

"Rebecca is too ill to receive visitors," she said with finality and made to close the door.

Bogey stopped it with his hand. "Please. Just let me see her for a few minutes," he pleaded.

"Young man, get your hand off my door. Do you want me to call the police?" Mrs. Friedman said, her voice rising.

Bogey continued to hold the door open. "Go away," she shouted.

He heard a male voice behind her. "What's wrong, Sarah?" Hiram Friedman asked.

"We have an intruder. He's trying to push in," she said.

Hiram appeared behind her, peering over her. "It's okay, Sarah. It's Becky's good friend from Charles Town."

"It is not okay," she said angrily. "He is not welcome here."

"Shouldn't we let Becky decide who she wants to see?" he asked timidly.

She half turned to give her husband the full force of her displeasure. "Did you not hear me, Hiram? He is not to visit here."

Before Hiram had time to answer, Bogey made his move. "I have to insist, Mrs. Friedman. Call the police if you must."

He crowded into the doorway and slipped past her. "Where is Becky?" he asked calmly.

Hiram pointed to the stairs.

At the top of the stairs, he saw an open room. Becky was sitting in a blue wing chair looking out the window.

"I saw you drive up. I didn't expect you to get by mother."

"Wasn't easy."

"I thought I asked you not to visit."

"You did."

"Then why are you here?"

He stood in the center of the room and gave her a long, searching look.

"You look awful," he said.

"That's a great icebreaker."

"It's the truth. We don't have long. Your mother is probably calling the police on me. I came because I had to. I love you. I miss you terribly. I want you to come back with me. I'll take care of you."

He couldn't be sure, but he thought he saw something in her face, a flicker of promise.

"Oh, Bogey. You are the sweetest man, but you don't understand. I'm not the Becky you knew. I'm...I'm broken."

She began to cry, and Bogey crossed to the chair. He knelt beside her and put his arms around her. "I'll fix you. I promise."

She shook her head. "Can't fix Humpty," she said, weeping quietly.

He laughed and stood beside her again.

"What's funny?"

"That's what the kids called me in grade school, making fun of my name. Humpty Dumpty. They'd trip me and laugh."

"And now you're fixed," she said.

"When you're around."

"I can't fix anyone. I can't put myself back together again." She looked out the window again. "The cops are here already. Mother can be very convincing. The station is only two blocks away."

"Come back with me," he said. "You know you want to. Your parents love you, but not like I do. You need me, too."

She leaned back in the chair and studied him carefully.

Bogey could hear a mumble of conversation downstairs. He could make out Sarah Friedman's indignant soprano ringing louder than the other voices. Soon there were footsteps on the stairs, and two uniformed policemen entered the room. One of them was young and wiry, the other thick and graying. Both of them looked at Bogey warily.

"Mr. Dawson, we have to ask you to go with us," the older guy growled in a deep, commanding voice.

"May I ask why?" Becky said.

The policeman looked at her quizzically. "Your mother says this man assaulted her and forced his way into your home."

"Why would he have to force his way in? He is my invited guest, a dear friend. My mother must have made a terrible mistake," Becky said earnestly. "I'm sorry you gentlemen had to waste your time on this." She gestured toward Sarah. "As you can see, my mother isn't injured. Sometimes she is over protective of me since I got hurt. It's my entire fault really. I forgot to tell mother that Bogey was expected."

The policeman, now thoroughly unsure of what he had walked into, turned to Hiram standing in the doorway with his wife. "Mr. Friedman, what is going on here?"

Hiram took a deep breath. "It's pretty much as my daughter says. My wife tried to send Mr. Dawson away, but he insisted on coming in. I guess that made her angry. I'm sorry she troubled you. I tried to talk her out of calling."

"And this young man is your daughter's friend?"

"Oh yes. They have been working together for years, and they are very close friends. He came to see her in the hospital. Drove all the way from West Virginia."

The poisonous look that Sarah had been giving her husband turned murderous but also triumphant.

"He did not visit her in the hospital. I saw to that," she told the senior cop with absolute assurance.

"Yes he did, mother. You were at your doctor's office. Again, I guess I forgot to mention it," Becky said sweetly.

Sarah glared at everyone in the room, then abruptly left.

The policeman watched her exit, and then addressed Bogey. "I guess we'll be leaving. It doesn't appear that any charges are in order considering what most of the family says." He turned back to Hiram. "All respect, sir, you should get your wife under control."

"Yes, sir. I will make every effort to do that," Hiram said. "Thank you for your prompt response. I will send a letter of appreciation to your captain. He's a friend of mine."

The young policeman smiled. The older cop glared at him and shoved him out of the door. Hiram followed them.

Bogey smiled at Becky. "Thank you."

"Hey, what are friends for if they can't lie for each other?"

His smile widened. The wasted, sad, pale girl in the chair was sounding more like Becky Friedman. "Who's going to lie for me in Charles Town?"

"Okay," she said. "Take me with you."

"You mean it?"

"I always mean what I say, except when I lie. I'm not lying. Get out of here. I want to change clothes and pack a few things. You understand that I will have to go to the farm. We dropped my rental since I didn't plan to go back."

"That's perfect."

"What kind of rent do you charge?"

He grinned at her. "Let's negotiate later."

Downstairs, he found Sarah berating her husband. Her voice was hushed, which made her even more ominous. She looked up as Bogey came down the stairs and entered the living room.

"You must be proud of yourself, turning my family against me," she said icily.

"No, maam, I'm not proud of that. I just had to see Becky. I love her. Can you understand?"

"I understand that you're demented. You are entirely unsuitable for Rebecca. I forbid you to come here again. I'll obtain a restraining order if necessary."

Bogey couldn't help smiling at her.

"What is funny, young man? Do you doubt me?"

"Not at all. I didn't mean to anger you. I was smiling because you and Becky are so much alike in lots of ways. You are both beautiful and very stubborn. Frankly, I'm proud of myself for standing up to two strong women like you. It's a new feeling for me."

Sarah seemed to be taken off guard by this new direction in the conversation. Bogey could see her considering her reply, but Becky spoke from the top of the stairs.

"Please stop talking about me until I can get down there and defend myself. I'm almost ready. Just sit down, all of you, and don't say another word till I'm there."

"Please, dear. Don't trouble yourself. You should be resting after all the hubbub this young fool stirred. Remember what the doctor said just yesterday." Sarah made an effort to make her voice sweet and nurturing, but the words came out as a command.

Becky's voice became stronger, more assertive.

"Not another word, mother."

To Bogey's surprise, Sarah Friedman retreated to the flowered sofa and sat down. Hiram still stood, looking dazed. "Can I get you something to drink? Do you need the bathroom after your drive?" he asked Bogey.

"You heard your daughter. Not another word." Sarah patted the couch beside her and Hiram sat.

This time Bogey managed not to smile. The three people waited in silence. Sarah radiated restrained rage. Hiram looked shell-shocked. Bogey was fighting to contain his happiness. He was ecstatic over the prospect of being with Becky. Together every day, every night, all the time! He had to keep reminding himself that she had really said she was coming with him. She said it. She meant it.

After what seemed like a long time, but was probably only minutes, Becky came down the stairs.

Her mother stood. "Perhaps you'd like to explain yourself," she said angrily.

Becky looked at her, a strange half-smile on her face. "I'm not sure I can," she said.

"Don't be flip with me, young lady. You know what I mean." She pointed toward Bogey, but her gaze still bored into Becky. "You know that you weren't expecting him to come."

Becky paused a long moment, locking gazes with Sarah. "Actually, I was. I was afraid he wouldn't come, but I expected that he would." She turned and smiled warmly at Bogey. "Thank you," she said.

Hiram spoke. "What now, darling?" he asked Becky.

She crossed to him and hugged him tightly. "I'm going back with Bogey," she said.

"You'll do nothing of the sort!" Sarah shouted. "You are a very sick girl. You are going right back to bed."

Becky walked to her and held out her arms. "Give me a hug," she said.

Her mother backed away. Becky continued to move toward her. "I love you mother," she said.

Bogey didn't expect what happened next. The iron woman broke into tears. "No you don't, or you would let me take care of you."

"Two different things, Mom. Two different things."

She embraced her weeping mother, and Hiram hugged the both of them.

"It will be all right, Sarah," he said softly.

Bogey approached them cautiously. "I promise to take care of her," he said.

Sarah's look turned dark again, but Hiram spoke kindly. "I know that, son," he said. Then to Sarah, "He will, darling. He is a good man."

Becky backed out of the family embrace and spoke to Bogey.

"My bag is at the head of the stairs."

He fetched it and returned. She gave him her quizzical look, the one with the head cocked to the side. "Do you think you can carry the bag and me, too?"

"That would be an honor," he said. He scooped her up, and with her arms around his neck, he headed for the door.

Hiram leaped ahead to open it, and as they went through he called after them. "Stay in touch."

* * *

Bogey was pleased that the rain had stopped. There were a few patches of blue now, to the west, toward Charles Town.

Becky leaned toward him from her seat and put her hand on his thigh.

"Thank you," she said. "I wasn't strong enough."

He covered her hand with his. "I almost wasn't strong enough myself. Your mother is formidable," he said with a hollow laugh.

She patted his leg again and fell silent. Bogey glanced over. Her eyes were closed, her head resting on the back of her seat. He drove along, comfortable with the silence, assuming that she had fallen asleep.

"Now it's your turn," she said abruptly.

"What?"

"You have not only heard about my crazy family, you have experienced them live and up close. I have a mental picture of your father and brother, but what about your mother? Were you hatched? Single father adoption? Come on, give. There was a mother."

"Sure. Of course. There was a mother."

"Tell me about her."

He hesitated. "There's not much to tell. She died."

"I'm sorry. She didn't die in childbirth. How old were you when she died?"

"How do you know she didn't die in childbirth?"

"Because you are too nice to have been raised by your father alone."

"I was ten."

"So you remember her well."

He frowned. "I guess."

"You are starting to piss me off," Becky said, removing her hand from his leg and sitting stiffly upright. "Am I going to have to drag every word out of you? Tell me about your damn mother!"

"I don't really like to talk about her."

"And I didn't like you seeing all my dirty laundry. It happens in relationships. We have a relationship, don't we? Or were you just kidnapping me to cook for you?"

"We have a relationship. I hope we do."

"Then stop holding out on me. I have a right to know about your mother. Too bad if it makes you sad to talk about her."

"Doesn't make me sad," Bogey mumbled. "I get angry, and then I feel guilty about that."

"Join the club. How many times do you think I've been exactly there with my mother?"

"I wasn't mad at her when I was little. My mother was really good to me. She cheered me up when I was discouraged or down. She took up for me with my brother."

"I guessed as much. At least I figured someone gave you something besides legal opinions."

"Yeah. I loved her. I thought we were close. I thought she loved me."

"What do you mean? It sounds like she did love you."

He was getting the lump in his throat that always came with this subject. He coughed and swallowed hard.

"She didn't love me as much as her vodka. She died when I was a kid because she drank herself to death. She didn't care enough about me to stay alive."

Becky was nodding. "That hurt you terribly," she said.

They drove in silence for several miles. When Becky spoke again, her voice was gentle, tentative. "I have to say that I've never doubted that my mother loves me. I also have to say that the love she feels for me hasn't changed her basic nature."

Bogey thought about what she said.

"I'm an alcoholic. I got clean. She could have gotten treatment," he said, sounding petulant and childish even to himself.

"Yes. She could have. Did your father try to get her to treatment? Did the family ever have one of those – what do you call them – interventions? Sometimes alcoholics need help to even realize they're in trouble."

Bogey wasn't about to forgive his mother. She had deserted him when he needed her. His mind accepted Becky's line of thought, but his heart was twisted with black resentment.

He could feel Becky's eyes on him, but he refused to look her way. He stared straight down the road.

Maybe he shouldn't have gone for her. Maybe she was even more like her mother than he thought. She was trying to push him around.

She said nothing as they drove along, already passing through Frederick, rolling down 340 on the last leg to Charles Town.

Finally she spoke. "I'm sorry," she said.

The words cut through his shield.

"For what?" he asked.

"For comparing my mother situation to yours. It's not the same. I still have my mother."

He swallowed hard, fighting a surge of sadness, trying to not break into tears. "You were trying to help," he croaked.

She leaned over and kissed his cheek. Her hand caressed and massaged his neck. Inside himself, something unwound and opened. There was still pain, but he felt a loosening, a softening.

He gulped hard again. When he had control of his voice, he said, "She called me Bogey. When the kids made fun of Humphrey and called me Humpty Dumpty, she said I was really Bogey. She said I was brave and good like Humphrey Bogart."

He looked at Becky. She nodded understanding. In the late afternoon light, he could see tears glistening in her eyes.

"And she taught me the lullaby. Mighty like a rose."

Becky placed her hand back on his thigh.

CHAPTER 28

Becky was wan and drained the first week at the farm. Bogey wondered if her mother had been right. The girl was so thin, weak, and pale that he feared she needed active medical care. On the other hand, her spirits were good, and she assured him she had enough of doctors and wanted to be right where she was. He was encouraged by the return of her robust appetite. She craved his hash browns and ate them often, sometimes three times a day.

By the end of the second week, she looked stronger and had more energy. Before the third week was over, she was cooking dinner for them most evenings. By the end of the month, she took over feeding Rosie and Sentinel's Cry and was bugging him again for the hash brown recipe.

"Don't overdo," Bogey cautioned.

"Do you want to be mistaken for my mother?" she asked. "You are busier and busier at the track. You need my help." He shut up, especially since it was clear that her color and her verve had returned.

Bogey was a happy man. He had never fully known the feeling before. Becky was with him. Things were going well at the track. He won two races with the new horses his returning customers brought him. Substantial Balance, now as big and hearty as his name, won by daylight in his first start. Marshall and the other owners knew they were with the right trainer.

Each day, after he finished up at the track, he went home to exercise Sentinel's Cry and Rosie in his largest pasture. Becky leaned on the fence to watch him jog around. Then they would go in and have lunch.

One day she put down her fork and said, "I'm ready to ride Rosie. We can ride together again."

He waited.

"I'm not afraid any more," she said. "I want to start riding. I miss it."

"Sure you're strong enough?"

"Yes, mother, I'm sure."

"Wouldn't you rather ride the sentinel? He's let down. Rosie is almost racing fit. Haven't you noticed she's crazy?" he asked, fluttering his hands in mock terror.

"Don't make fun of things I said in the past. And no. Not Sentinel's Cry; I want to ride Rosie. You know I can ride a tornado."

"Sure?"

"Sure."

The next day, Bogey watched her on Rosie. Having Becky back in the saddle scared him, but he could swear the filly understood she needed to take it a little easy.

"She behaves better for you than she does for me," he said as they trotted back.

"Of course. They all recognize the master."

He shook his head. "The best."

"The best," she agreed.

A couple of nights later, she said, "If you don't mind, I'd like to take Rosie on a long trail ride tomorrow. There's a dirt road through those woods back there."

"Why do you want to do that?"

Becky shrugged. "She's ready for more, and it would be fun."

"Are you? Ready for more?"

"Yes. Except that I'm a little stiff from the riding. I need a massage tonight. Full body massage." She fluttered her eyelashes and gave him a coy smile.

"You are a lucky girl. My hash brown potatoes are exceeded only by my skillful full body massages."

She raised her eyebrows and rolled her eyes. "I know. Excellent deep massage skills. Just what I need to be totally well again."

He went to her and lifted her effortlessly into his arms. "Just call me ole Doc Bogey," he told her as he carried her to the bedroom. "Satisfaction guaranteed."

"To think I once considered you shy and humble," she said languidly.

* * *

In mid-November, just before nominations for the New York stakes closed, a reporter named Toole from the *Baltimore Sun* called Bogey.

"I just interviewed Mr. Edmond Huddleston," the man said after identifying himself. "I asked him how he felt about losing to your filly in that Laurel race. You may want to respond to a comment he made."

"I doubt that. But I am curious. Why are you calling me now? Why didn't you call me when Huddleston accused me of breaking down Sentinel's Cry?"

"That's easy. You were a loser then. Now you have Final Gift. Cruel, but that's the newspaper game. No one cared what you thought then."

"At least you're honest."

"What about it. Want to hear what Mr. Huddleston said about you?"

"Why not?"

"Here is what he said. I'm quoting. 'I'm not sure what Dawson did to artificially fire up that filly, but she was obviously higher than a kite. My guys run on oats, hay and water, so they came back fine. We're headed for the big two-year-old finale at Belmont, but she won't make it. It's a shame he ruined the horse. She's no match for either of my colts on a level playing field, but it's still too bad he broke her down. You may remember this is not the first time he's done this to a nice horse. At least it's not my horse this time.' That's his quote. Anything you want to say before I print this?"

Bogey's anger was chilly. "Yes. I actually do have something to say. Please quote me. Are you ready to take this down?"

"Of course. My shorthand is excellent. Fire away."

"I am not sure where Mr. Huddleston gets his inaccurate information and fanciful ideas. The only thing Final Gift needed to best his mediocre stock was her superior talent. She is fine, by the way, enjoying a brief freshening at my farm. We respect the challenge of running against New York's finest, particularly I Win Again, but I am surprised that Mr. Huddleston is wasting his time by coming to the race. He should not embarrass his colts in another futile effort. He needs to find someone who knows what they are doing to manage his stable. A real horseman would choose competitive races for his string. If those colts run at Belmont, we will break their spirits. He should not even be there. It's that simple."

"Publish it just like that?"

"All of it or none of it. Just like that."

Bogey could hear the excitement in the reporter's voice. "I'd be glad to. Nothing like a war to sell papers."

* * *

Marshall Herbert called, laughing, the next morning. "Throwing it down, aren't you? I guess you've seen the Sun."

"No. I don't get it." A daily reminder of Baltimore wasn't something he needed.

"Pick up a copy. It's rich."

"What does it say?"

"It's a long article. You need to read it for yourself. I will tell you the headline says *Underdog Trainer Vows Victory in Grudge Match*. The guy writes it as though this is a showdown between Maryland and West Virginia in the Final Four. Big as the Super Bowl."

"Should bring out a few bettors."

"It is going to gall your old boss. You took it to him according to this piece. Did you really say those things?"

"I told the reporter to quote me word for word."

Marshall's voice became conspiratorial. "Would there be a race on the undercard for Substantial Balance? I'd love to be part of this one."

Bogey grinned to himself. "Let me check on that."

The next day, Bogey got a call from the *New York Post*. A day later he heard from the venerable *New York Times*.

A few days later, Becky looked up from the pile of newspapers on their dining table. "I think I created a monster. I just congratulated you for standing up to Huddleston. I didn't know you were going to war with Maryland and New York."

"This is the most fun I've had in racing. Sorry, but I love it," he said.

"The race is only three weeks away. Were you planning on taking time out from your demanding media schedule to take Rosie back to the track and train her?"

"What do you mean? I am training her. I have my best exercise rider giving her long, leisurely gallops every day. Perfect preparation for stretching out to a mile and a furlong. Just putting some happy stamina in her. The speed is there already."

"You're going to run her in a Grade I race straight off the farm?"

He shrugged. "Why not? Have you ever seen her look better?"

"But trail rides as race prep? Come on."

"Dickey Small prepped Broad Brush for the Tesio by galloping him up hill through the snow. He won. We're going to win, too."

She shook her head. "I *have* created a monster. No doubt about it."

CHAPTER 29

Edmond Huddleston ripped the Sun into shreds and threw it on the floor. "I should call the damn publisher," he ranted. "See how the bastard would feel about losing all my ad revenue. Son of a bitch."

"I told you my brother was a nut case," Dickey Dawson ventured.

Huddleston stomped around his gleaming mahogany desk, slamming his fist into it at every step. Dickey took an involuntary step back as though the staccato blasts were rifle volleys aimed at him. "He's a damn idiot if he thinks he can get away with embarrassing me like this." Bang. "You don't get to where I am by accepting defeat." Bang. "They never whipped me on the damn football field or in business." Double bang, both hands. "I'm sure as hell not going to lose to your wimpy little brother."

"He got lucky at Laurel. Your colts will take that filly of his this time," Dickey said.

"Shut the fuck up! That goddamn filly of his is a fucking freak. Like the little shit says, she could well kick all our asses if she runs. If she wins that race after all this hoopla, Edmond Huddleston will look like a fool. That is not going to happen."

Dickey shrunk back further from the bulging green eyes and the spittle laced ranting of his boss.

"The sneaky little bastard tricked me. Led me to believe the horse broke down after her last race. All the time he's secretly training her up for Belmont. He made his mistake when he shot his mouth off to that fucking reporter. Now I know what he's up to, and he's not going to get away with it. Time to take this game to the pro level. Time to get active in the pileups. Know what I mean?"

"No, sir. I don't."

"In a football game, if the other team starts getting cute, you have to rough them up a little. Remember from your playing days?"

Dickey didn't, but he thought it was smarter to nod anyway.

Huddleston went back to his custom desk chair. He leaned forward, rubbing the pigskin-colored leather arms vigorously as though he was preparing to launch himself into space. His eyes were fixed at the ceiling, studying something only visible to him.

Dickey watched him as a twitch of a smile, incongruous on his rigid face, appeared briefly. It disappeared, but his eyes narrowed and his skin color returned to its normal carefully tended tan. He studied the ceiling for a few more moments and then looked at Dickey.

"I'm sure you are wondering what you can do to help extricate me from the mess your family has created." His voice was soft yet venomous. Dickey tried to choose his words carefully.

"Yes, sir. You know there is no love lost between me and my stupid brother. How can I help?"

"Actually, there are several things you can do. You can begin by preparing a bill of sale for Final Gift and Sentinel's Cry from Humphrey Dawson to me."

"Yes, sir. Shall I leave the money amount blank?"

"Oh, no. Put in 'thirty thousand and other considerations', which will do nicely."

Dickey suppressed his immediate urge to question the low amount. He simply nodded, and then Huddleston told him about the other things he could do to help. They involved complicated travel arrangements.

CHAPTER 30

Bogey Dawson was blissful.

Each day brought new joys in his life with Becky. Rosie was dappled and shining with good health, eager for her daily long gallops through the woods. Even Sentinel's Cry seemed happier since Bogey was riding him more. These things would have been more than enough, but there were other delights.

Rosie was becoming famous. The Sun reporter came out to the farm accompanied by a photographer. Bogey's unique training approach and Rosie's beautiful rider made for a terrific human interest bit. The Sunday Sun featured a big spread with many photos devoted to them. Headline: *Super Filly Frolics in Laidback Preparation for Showdown Race.* First sentences: "Bogey Dawson's absolute confidence in Final Gift – Rosie, to her friends – has dictated a playful training schedule as he readies her for a big test against Maryland's and New York's best colts. In a sport where trainers choose their words carefully, Dawson says casually, 'She'd be ready to beat anything out there even if they make me use Otey Musgrove as a rider – and that boy is fat.' You might say the man is sure the horse some call 'The Country Queen' will conquer all."

Becky shook her head over his audacity and tried to damp down his provocations, but he just winked at her. "Hey. No use hiding the light under a bushel. Says that in the good book or somewhere."

"But you're deliberately goading Huddleston and Otey."

"Hey, all in good fun. It's just a horse race."

"Are you sure your Mr. Huddleston sees it that way?"

She had to admit the flurry of publicity had its advantages. Two more of Bogey's old owners called, sending horses, booking mares to Sentinel's Cry and cheering his ongoing efforts to aggravate Huddleston.

Their fame spread as far as the west coast, triggering a call from Fats.

"Damn, Dawson! You're beginning to sound like a man. Keep on kicking the SOB's ass."

"I'm having the time of my life. Becky thinks I'm going overboard."

"That's what women say to their men. It's their job to try and keep us out of trouble. Not that they want to succeed."

"Could be. Sometimes I think she's enjoying the whole thing. Her father called. He's loving it."

"It really sets up this race. Belmont owes you. The crowd and the handle will be out of sight."

"Yeah. All the horses will have their cheering sections."

"Count two more in your camp. We're about to put a wrap on our sale. Millie and I will be in West Virginia within a week, and we'll head up to New York when you go. By the way, where should we stay in Charles Town?"

"Man, I don't know the answer to that one. The town is fading along with the track. I wish we had room to put you up here, but the trailer is pretty small."

"No. I don't want to listen to you guys making love, and you sure don't want to listen to us. Millie is a screamer."

"I'll ask around, but listen. The main thing is that you're coming. That makes everything perfect. I can't wait to thank Millie for her good advice."

"And me. What about me? Are you glad to see me, too?"

"No. But I guess Millie needs an escort."

"Hey, don't carry this big man thing too far. I can still kick your ass."

"And the horse you rode in on, panty waist."

"No fair. You have the best horse."

"That's what I'm telling the whole world. By the way, I should be able to pay back your loan soon."

"Don't rush. Spend your extra dough on Becky. You guys have been living Spartan too long. Believe me, with the payday we're about to get, money is really no object. I don't know what the hell to do with that kind of cash, but between Uncle Sam and Millie, I'll get plenty of help in figuring it out."

"My heart bleeds for you in your time of worry."

"As always, my sincere thanks for nothing."

* * *

After a little research, and with Becky's strong support, Bogey made a reservation for Fats and Millie at the Turf Motel. Becky then traded on her status as an employee to get them one of the most desirable rooms.

They met the plane at Dulles. As Fats and Millie walked toward them, Becky exclaimed, "What a handsome couple! Millie is gorgeous."

She was a big woman, almost as tall as Fats and strong looking. She had an open, freckled face set off by wildly exuberant red hair. She moved with an easy athletic gait that had Fats hustling to match strides. She enveloped Becky in a bear hug. "I'm so glad to finally meet you. I've heard great things."

"Same here," Becky said. "Welcome to the country roads."

Millie looked at the two guys who were hugging warmly. "You have yourself a cute little guy there," she said.

"I admire your hunk. He's a handsome brute."

"Are we going to have some fun when we can get together alone and pick at their faults?"

Becky grinned at her. "I can hardly wait," she said.

The four of them chatted together happily on the drive to Charles Town. Becky had insisted Fats should sit in the front seat with Bogey, apologizing that the back seat was too cramped. "I think my cheap little guy planned to be single forever. He loves this ragtop."

"I'll take up for him. This Mustang is a classic. I want Jim to use a little of his windfall to buy me one. I think they will be collectible. Excuse me, but I love cars," Millie said.

Millie made Becky's irrepressible prattle seem demure. As they drove on, Bogey heard Becky gradually step it up, her polite welcoming reserve giving way to a nicely competitive wish to have an equal say. He smiled. This was going to be an interesting friendship between these two gals.

In the front seat, Fats was regaling him with amusing stories of the adventures involved in selling the company.

"All the bidders wanted to tie me to long-term contracts. If I had wanted that, I would have just taken the company public. An IPO might have made even more money, but I'd definitely have to stick around a few years. I want to do something else. You know me, Hump. I get bored easily."

"So how did it turn out?"

"We sold to a big IT company with loads of guys smarter than I am. I just have to give them a month to help with any transition issues. They don't really need that. I have all the bugs out. The system is totally clean."

"And what then? What's the new thing you want to do?"

"Don't you ever listen to me when I talk to you?"

"You're going into ballet?"

"No, stupid. I told you my long-term plan years ago. I said to you, 'When I get rich…' "Fats let the phrase hang, looking expectantly at Bogey.

"Sorry. I guess I forgot."

"We were going away from Charles Town, not toward it at the time." Once again he waited.

Millie spoke up crossly from the back seat. "Jim, that was decades ago. How do you expect him to remember?"

"Well, it was important. It was an important night in his life. He should remember."

Insight struck Bogey. "Oh, sure. Prom night. The night I discovered thoroughbreds. And on the way back you said that when you got rich we would go into the horse business together."

"I said we'd *take over* the horse business. We can, too. I've got money, and I've got some great ideas of how we can use computers and your horse genius to put us on top."

Bogey gave him a searching look. "You're serious, aren't you?"

"Serious and excited. I know I'm new in the game. I can handicap, but you'll have to teach me the rest. I want to immerse myself in a whole new world if you'll let me."

"Wow. Just give me a minute to get my head around this." Bogey knew he sounded reluctant, but he hated pressure for quick decisions on anything he hadn't thought out.

"I know that. I wasn't going to drop it on you so quick, but you asked, and I guess I was eager to blurt it out."

Millie's irritation was clear. "Jim, I asked you not to spoil this. We were all happy till you started popping off."

"It's okay," Becky said. "Bogey thinks well, he just thinks slow. Actually, I believe it's a great idea. Bogey is the best horseman I've ever seen. Jim could be the partner that launches him on the national stage."

"My plan exactly," Fats said enthusiastically.

"Well, my plan is to wait until we hear what Bogey wants," Millie interjected in a firm voice. "From what Jim tells me, the man is doing just fine as is. Maybe he doesn't want his old buddy flying in to turn everything topsy turvy."

Bogey began to feel like a kid whose family is discussing him while he is in the room. "Calm down everyone. Fats and I will talk this through. Like Becky says, my slow motion brain needs some time."

When they pulled into the parking lot of the Turf Motel, Bogey assumed his guests would want to rest up from the long flight, but Fats had other plans.

"If you have the time, as soon as we register, I'd like to see your operation, here at the track and then at the farm. We're both dying of curiosity."

"It's not much to see," Bogey warned.

"Buddy, you have to stop poor mouthing yourself. I'm excited and happy. Can we do it?"

"Sure. Let's do it."

Becky turned to Millie. "Would you mind if Bogey took me to the farm and then came back for you? I would like a chance to straighten up, maybe put together some supper for us to have later."

Bogey was caught off guard by the request, but Millie said, "Actually, I'd like a chance to freshen up, if anyone should think to ask." She raised an eyebrow and glared at Fats.

"Sorry," he said. "Forgot my manners. Forgive me, I'm psyched up."

She grabbed him roughly. "Forgiven, for the umpteenth time," she laughed.

"Let me help you with the bags," Bogey said.

"No need. But one thing, Becky. Don't even think about supper. I have dinner reservations for the four of us. We need to celebrate selling one company and, if slow poke is ready, to talk about starting another," Fats said, with a sideways glance at Bogey, and then followed Millie into the hotel.

As Bogey turned onto Washington Street, he was shaking his head. "Can you believe that guy? After all these years, still thinking about our boyhood daydream." He looked over to catch Becky's reaction. She was looking away from him, and he saw a tear slide down her cheek.

"I'm sorry," she muttered. "I didn't think it would hit me like this."

Bogey couldn't imagine what she was talking about. "What's wrong?" he asked, bewildered.

"The track. I can't do it. I can't go there."

"Because of the accident."

She nodded silently and began to cry harder, her shoulders shaking. "I thought riding Rosie would make it okay. I tried. Honest to God, I've tried."

Bogey pulled the car off the street and stopped. He leaned over to pull her to him, but she resisted. "It's so damn dumb. See, the worse thing is that I have no idea what happened."

"You don't remember the runaway hitting you and your horse?"

"I remember coming to work, and I remember waking up in a hospital bed, nothing in between. The doctors have fancy words. Antegrade and retrograde amnesia. Wipes out the before and the after. Leaves a hole in your life."

"That's spooky."

She nodded. "I have weird nightmares filled with dread."

She looked at him imploringly. "Do you understand? I always felt safe and secure on a horse. In fact, that was the only place I felt really sure of myself. On horseback I knew who I was and what I was doing. Horses made me sane. Now the idea of riding at the track terrifies me. It's different at the farm. I'm not afraid there."

She hung her head and wept harder. After a time, she said, "I'm a silly little girl, scared of the dark."

"I'm scared too. I'm always scared," Bogey said.

Her head snapped up, and she looked at him quizzically. "I never saw you scared. You'd pet the devil if someone put a saddle on him."

"Horses don't scare me. Other things do."

She sniffled. "Like what?"

"First on the list, losing you. Sooner or later you'll realize you're too good for me."

"That one's not so bad. Keep it in mind and treat me right," she said and even managed a wan smile. "What else?"

"I hate to tell you."

"Since you're trying to make me feel better, you have to tell all."

"I'm scared that I'm just lucky. Picking a good horse is so subjective, maybe I just got lucky once or twice."

"Uh huh, what else?"

"Right now, I'm scared by Fats. This dream of his is scary. I'm not afraid we'd fail. I'm afraid we'd succeed. I don't think I can handle a large stable. Even in Maryland the most horses I ever had was twenty. I only had five guys working for me, and I couldn't keep up with payroll, scheduling, and paper work – all the things involved in running a business. I just want to play with the horses. I'm not really grown up."

She turned in the seat and knuckled the tears off her cheeks. She leaned into him and kissed him. "What the hell. I guess us kids can play house together and decide later whether we want to grow up," she whispered in his ear.

She sat quietly for a moment, and then she spoke again. Her tone was uncertain as though she was afraid of spoiling the moment. "Maybe I shouldn't say this, but I think there is one more thing you're afraid of. I think you're afraid of your temper."

He stiffened. "Why do you say that?"

"Because you lean over backward to stay out of arguments – always Mister Nice Guy – except when it comes to Huddleston. I saw something very different behind your eyes when you were talking to him. Frankly, it scared me a little. I dig at you, but you never get pissed. What will happen when you get mad at me?"

"I'll never get mad at you," he protested.

"Please! Do not underestimate my inner bitch."

* * *

Back at the Turf, Becky slipped into the restaurant bathroom to repair her face while Bogey rang the room to explain the change in plans. His friends were just as happy to see the farm now and do the track the following day.

At the farm, Fats, now appropriately attired in jeans, flannel shirt and sneakers, couldn't finish looking at one thing for bouncing to the next. Walking the barn aisle, he spotted Sentinel's Cry,

"Jesus, Dawson. This is a great barn you built, but can we take this guy outside so I can really have a look at him?"

Once outside, viewing the full impact of the magnificent stallion, he couldn't stand still, pacing back and forth in open-mouthed wonder. "Oh my God!" he kept repeating.

Rosie, attracted by the excitement, galloped up to the paddock fence. Fats spotted her and darted away for a closer look.

"Oh my God. She's a vision! We'll come back to him. Let's go see her," he called back.

"Do you mind if I take a moment to put him up?" Bogey asked.

Fats missed the sarcasm. "Sure, but hurry."

Each new treasure triggered new enthusiastic plans. Rosie and the stallion: "You know what you have here? You've got your foundation mare and the next number one stallion. Look out Broad Brush, here we come."

Walking the pasture, with Rosie trailing them and sometimes resting her head on Bogey's shoulder, Fats said, "Look at this grass! Good soil here.

Not so many of those infernal rocks sticking up. Is any of the adjoining land for sale? We suck up all we can get. How much per acre around here?"

Bogey was unsure of what to say, but Fats wasn't waiting for answers in any case. He flitted ahead, as giddy as a college boy inside the Playboy mansion. After the first hurried flight, he circled back and took a more leisurely tour of everything. His appraisal became more measured, but his excitement did not. After the second tour, he faced Bogey. His eyes were wide but his manner was all business.

"A diamond in the rough. I can't believe what you've done here." He put his hands on Bogey's shoulders and fixed him with a pleading gaze. "You got to let me in, Bogey. You got to."

"Look. This is small time —"

"Listen to me, old friend. I've had a good time playing in cyberspace, but I'm beginning to fall into the monitor. Do you realize how all this looks to me?" Fats waved his hand around the farm. "It looks like freedom. Another life."

"Fats, you know I love you. I just don't know how much I'm up to."

"Come on, Captain Catastrophe. Roll with me here. We could be a hell of a team."

* * *

They dinned at the historic Bavarian Inn in Shepherdstown, enjoying the ambiance, the food, and the company. "I think I must be Bavarian somewhere back in the family. I love this food!" Fats exclaimed.

The middle aged waitress wore her dirndl with pride and hovered over the party after Fats started his meal with a Schwarzwaelder Kaese Spaetzle and followed up with a hearty Bavarian Sauerbraten, not leaving a morsel on either plate. The waitress beamed at him. "Did you enjoy the meal? I can tell you appreciate real German food."

"Perfect," Fats said, giving her the thumb and index finger circle that signals total approval.

"Where does he put all that food?" Becky asked Millie. "He doesn't have an ounce of fat on him."

Millie laughed. "He always eats like that. I'd weigh a ton, but he burns it off."

"It's her fault," Jim said. "She's way too sexy."

"He does burn a few calories that way," Millie agreed amiably.

"Wow! I don't know about these friends of yours," Becky joked.

"I hope they don't offend my delicate flower," Bogey said.

They joked their way through the food and groaned when Jim asked to see the desert menu. He ordered for everyone and then sat back.

"Do you guys mind if I am serious for a minute? I don't want to spoil a great evening, but I have an idea rolling around in my head."

Bogey spread his hands in surrender. "Spit it out."

"Okay. Here it is. Obviously, my life got off to a slow little fat boy start. Except for my buddy here," he gestured at Bogey, "I didn't have any friends, and I took a lot of crap from other guys. My only good point was that I was reasonably smart."

"Yeah, reasonably," Bogey said. "You brilliant son of a gun."

"Like I was saying, reasonably smart and very imaginative. I couldn't perform physically, so I turned to science fiction, mathematics and finally electronics, and I've enjoyed it all. But I went too far that way. I've lived in my head and electronic extensions of it. Luckily, I met Millie who, thank God, saw something in me. She brings me back to reality to some extent, but at this point, I want more of the real world."

"Not that again," Bogey said.

"Oh yeah. I've talked this over with Millie, and she's with me. I want to get into the thoroughbred business."

Bogey shook his head in slow resignation. "You really are serious, aren't you?"

"Think a minute, Bogey. You know how fascinated I've always been with the game. I love thoroughbreds. Maybe it has something to do with my lack of athleticism, I don't know. Maybe I loved the swift and powerful way these animals can move."

"Spare us the psychoanalysis," Millie said drily. "You know you don't see yourself as a poor little fat boy any more."

"No, but I recognize limits. I want to be involved in something physical, active, outdoors. I can't think of anything better than racing."

"What would you want to do in the business?" Becky asked.

"I have no idea. That's why I'm bringing it up. Maybe I'm only qualified to be an owner. I sure as hell have the money to hit the market. Keeneland would love me. With my cash and Bogey's skills, we could be a hell of a team."

"I don't know, Fats. That might be a great idea. You'd learn very fast, and we could work together great. It's just that right now there are so many loose ends in my life."

"He means me," Becky said without rancor. "We need to sort out our relationship since my injury. This kind of closeness is pretty new to both of us, and we're pretty old dogs to be mastering this trick."

"No trick," Millie said flatly. "You just shut your eyes and roll on. If the chemistry is there, it will sort out."

"Well, we've exploded a couple of test tubes," Becky said.

"Great chemistry," Bogey agreed. "I wasn't really talking about our relationship. I was thinking of Rosie, our responsibilities to her. Settling things somehow with Huddleston, what to do if the track shuts down – lots of stuff."

"Sure. I understand," Jim said. "I just wanted to get this out on the table. I'm in no hurry."

"I'm wondering what that asshole Huddleston will come up with next. He is one mean bastard," Millie said.

"Especially since Bogey the Terrible insults him in print every chance he gets," Becky said.

"I love it," Fats said. "It even made the *Chronicle* back in California. This is great for racing. Seabiscuit takes on Majestic Prince again."

"Why prod the bull?" Becky asked, glaring at Bogey.

"For one thing, I want people to know about Rosie," Bogey said.

"And for another —?"

"To make Huddleston angry. He does dumb things when he's mad. I want to flush him into the open and shoot the rascal down once and for all, gosh darn him."

"Watch your language, Mary Poppins. Ladies present," Fats said.

Becky laughed aloud. "He is! He is Mary Poppins."

"Except he expects his umbrella to collapse in any breeze," Fats joked.

"I don't know about that," Bogey said, still serious. "I do know that Huddleston isn't going to give up until he gets what he wants. The prodding I've done lately is nothing compared to my great sin."

"What was that?" Millie asked.

"I told him no."

Fats raised his beer glass to Bogey and spoke to the rest of the table. "The asshole should take that 'no' seriously. Our boy may be Mary Poppins, but you don't want to make him angry. Let me tell you a story that he would never tell."

"Shut up, Fats," Bogey said. "Don't tell something stupid."

Fats waved the objection aside. "I think I mentioned that I took a lot of teasing back in high school. We both did. You ladies will find it hard to believe, but we were not the BMOC studs at our fancy boys' school."

"Come on Fats. They aren't interested in ancient history," Bogey protested.

"I am," said Becky. "Let him tell the story."

"Well, as I was saying, we were the butt of lots of crap, and mostly we just took it. Bogey tried to ignore it, but I talked back. One day three of the football jocks decided I needed a lesson. They started pounding on me. I tried to defend myself, but I couldn't do a single pull up back then. I was a blob. I guess it made them mad that I even tried to fight. They were really hurting me. It was way past the bloody nose stage. They knocked me down, and then two of them picked me up so this big bruiser could really tee off on me."

"That's really wrong," Becky said. "That's not bullying. That's assault."

"Yeah, I guess that's what my pal here decided. He walked up between me and the big guy and yelled 'Stop it'. That really amused them. They all started laughing. The guy pushed Bogey aside and started to wind up to really smack me."

Fats paused. "That's when the tornado struck. I swear Bogey flew at them so fast I only saw a blur. The big guy hit the ground. Then one of the two holding me had his feet swept away, and he landed on his butt. The last guy let go of me and took a swing at Bogey. He didn't even come close. Bogey kicked him in the head. Well, the biggest guy got back up. He was really furious. He charged, and Bogey did some kind of side flip and kicked him in the belly." Fats laughed. "I never heard such a whoosh when the air went out of him. He just lay there trying to catch his breath."

"Wow," Becky said to Bogey. "I knew you were strong as an ox, but I didn't know you had skills."

"It's nothing to brag about," Bogey said. "It caused a lot of trouble for everyone. I worried about the kid I kicked in the head. He had headaches and dizziness for weeks, maybe a concussion. I got suspended for two weeks, almost expelled. My father got sued by one of the kids' families. What I did was dumb."

"Maybe so. But we never got teased after that," Fats said. "As far as I'm concerned, those guys had it coming."

"Violence is never good."

"Thus spoke Mary Poppins," Fats laughed. "Still Huddleston should be careful."

CHAPTER 31

Over the next ten days, Fats was true to his promise. He didn't talk about going into business with Bogey. However, as he saw the horses Bogey had at the track and learned about his growing success as a trainer, he clearly had to restrain himself.

"Boy, when I think about where Huddleston dumped you and how far you've clawed back, I almost feel like bragging on you. Of course, you're probably just a lucky so and so."

"That's what I think," Bogey agreed.

"Speaking of Huddleston, what have you heard coming from him?"

"Nothing. He's not popping off in the media. He hasn't contacted me."

"Makes me nervous," Fats said.

"Yeah. I just keep my eyes open. He'll try to pull something. I don't think he has any great pull with NYRA to mess me up there. My finances are okay thanks to you. He's probably looking for an angle."

"Maybe one final offer you can't refuse."

Bogey cringed. "Don't put it that way."

Fats laughed. "I just meant lots and lots of dough and a really posh job."

"I think he knows that's a waste of time."

"Like you say, we'll just be alert."

"Yeah. He won't just go away. You can bet on that."

* * *

The plan was to leave for New York three days before the race so that the horses could have a couple of gallops over the Belmont track. Substantial Balance would be going, too. Bogey had found an appropriate race for Marshall's colt on the stakes undercard. With his newfound financial well being, Bogey had arranged for a professional van company to transport the horses. On the Wednesday before race day, he would trailer Rosie in to the track so she and Substantial Balance could load up for the journey to New York.

Fats and Millie left on Monday. His friend had insisted on putting everyone up at the elegant Garden City Hotel, just minutes from the track. "That's too expensive. You don't need to do that," Bogey objected.

Millie chided him gently. "You need to let someone be nice to you." She smiled at Fats. "I would love to stay at a fancy place like that. All of us worked hard. Now we're rich and you're famous. We deserve it."

"I'll have to buy some clothes," Bogey said.

"That's for sure," Becky said. "You'll want to look sharp in the winner's circle."

Bogey had never been so happy and excited. He really wasn't worried about the race. Rosie was ready to give her best, and he felt that would be good enough. If it wasn't, there would be another day. With a special horse, special friends and a love more special than he had ever hoped for, Bogey felt blessed.

The entire Charles Town crowd – even those who once made fun of him and jeered at Becky – came around to wish him good luck and to assure him of their support. Harry Collins volunteered to take care of his other horses while he was away. One of Harry's grooms would drive out to the farm to feed Sentinel's Cry. Bogey thanked him and assured him that he would be hiring an assistant once he returned so that he wouldn't have to keep leaning on Harry.

"Nonsense," Collins said. "It's an honor to help out. I admire you, Dawson. You've not only proven yourself, you've made all of us proud. I don't know what's going to happen to this track, but even if it goes belly up, you've let us go out in style."

Bogey was taken aback by Harry's extravagant praise. "It's nice of you to say that," he managed.

Tuesday, the day before vanning to New York, was busy for Bogey. He took care of all last minute details, did up the horses and dropped by Harry Collins' barn to give him a hand written outline covering the status of all the horses he'd be leaving behind. A final check of the tack room assured him that all supplies and feeds were there and well labeled for easy use. When he got into the Mustang to drive out to the farm, it was almost two in the afternoon. He was getting hungry, but there would be plenty to snack on at home. He drove away, looking forward to seeing Becky and Rosie.

As he drove along his pasture fence, he saw that Rosie wasn't in the field. That was surprising since Becky usually finished her gallop before lunch. He pulled up to the house and went in. No one answered his call, and the small house was empty. He went out into the yard and called out for Becky again. Again, only silence. He wandered to the back of the trailer and looked at the small area where Waller's memorial sat silent under the spreading tree, knowing that his actions were pointless. The willow was motionless in the still air, its drooping golden leaves hanging limp and purposeless. Bogey began to panic.

Where was Becky? Could Rosie have thrown her? Had they both suffered some mishap on the trail ride? Had some residual of Becky's injury suddenly struck her? Guilt over the possibility that he had let her return to riding prematurely flooded him.

Suddenly he realized what else was bothering him.

Sentinel's Cry was nowhere to be seen!

Normally when Bogey's truck turned into the drive, the stallion ran to the fence of his paddock, snorting and neighing for attention. Where was he?

His growing sense of alarm expanded when he looked in the barn and found it empty as well. His trailer still sat where he had left it, the hitch arm resting on a cement block. The November day was sunny and warm, but a chill of fear raised the hairs on his neck. His mind was numb, empty of explanations or even speculations. Only questions tumbled there. What could have happened? How could both Rosie and Sentinel's Cry both be gone? What should he do?

He stumbled back to the house and went in. Who could he turn to? Who could shed some light on the strange situation? He only had one neighbor – the nursery. Maybe someone there saw something.

The kid who answered the phone knew nothing, but he called the owner to take over.

"Yeah, how can I help you?"

"My name is Dawson. I own the ranch just down the road from you."

"Oh yes, Mr. Dawson. Nice place. You ought to let me dress it up for you with some nice plantings next spring."

"Right, right," Bogey said impatiently. "Today, at this moment I need some information."

"Of course. What would you like to know? We do have some fall sales going that might interest you."

"No, it's not about that. I just got home and my – my wife is gone along with both of my horses. Did you see her leave?"

"I don't know that I saw her but, now you mention it, I did see a horse van go by and stop at your place. I was busy and didn't see what happened then, but later it did come back by headed to the highway. That's all I know."

"Thanks," Bogey said. He hung up even more puzzled. Whose horse van? Did it take Sentinel's Cry away? Would Becky have arranged for a van to take both horses somewhere? For what possible reason? Wouldn't she have called him at the barn if something important had come up?

He couldn't stand still. He paced in circles around the room, trying to think what he could do next to solve the problem.

The phone rang.

Wonderful! It was probably Becky with the answer to all his questions. He rushed to answer it.

"Hello."

"Hello, Shrimp."

CHAPTER 32

The voice was unexpected, but it took Bogey only a moment to absorb the reality of the situation. His head cleared, confusion replaced with a cold rage. He was silent. He knew what was coming next.

"Hello, hello. Are you there, Shrimp? Surprised to hear from me?"

"What do you want, Otey?" Bogey kept his voice calm and even.

"Well, I just want to have a little chat with you. Try to do a little business with an old buddy, that's all I want."

"Why should I talk with someone like you? I have no business to do with your kind."

"Oh, come on old buddy. Your girl friend and your horses are already over here. You need to come join them."

Once again Bogey opted for silence. He waited. When Otey spoke again, his voice was a little less assured.

"Do you hear me? I've got your girl and your ponies. You better get your butt over here pronto. Hear me?"

"Let me speak to Becky."

Otey laughed. "Can't. Bitch was yelling and spitting. Had to gag her. She ain't talkin' right now."

Bogey's voice did not betray the fear in his heart. "Listen to me, Otey. If you let her go now and let her verify that she is free to drive the horses back here, I won't hurt you, and I won't report this to the police. I'll just forget the whole thing."

That provoked a hearty laugh. "Damn, I'm not so scared now. You ain't gonna hurt me! *You* ain't gonna hurt *me*! Now that's a damn relief to me, I can tell you that." He choked on a fit of laughter. He finally regained control.

"Now, Shrimp, let me tell you what you're gonna do. You are gonna look in the top drawer in that desk where you're standing. You're gonna pick up that fancy cell phone I put there just for you. You're gonna get in that rattle trap of yours, go out to Old Leetown and head back toward Charles Town. After while, I call you and tell you where to come. When you get here, we'll do some business, and then you can have your she-cat back."

Bogey stayed calm. "Otey, I know that you're doing this because Huddleston told you that you had to. He's getting you into a world of trouble. Do you want to end up in jail?"

Now Otey sounded almost bored. "Don't call no one. Don't talk to no one. If you do, your girlie will pay for it. That's all. Get the phone and get in the car, right now." He hung up.

CHAPTER 33

A couple of hours earlier, Becky Friedman had been carefree.

Rosie had loved her gallop through the woods, pricking her ears and prancing happily along. Becky let her go a mile or so further than usual since the filly showed no signs of boredom and certainly no evidence of fatigue. In fact, when they left the woods and went through the gate back into the pasture, the horse snorted in protest and was reluctant to head toward the house. She kept turning her head to look back at the riding trail they had just left.

Becky had a moment of worry. Was the filly that fit or were they being too gentle with her? Would she be ready to run a mile and a furlong against top competition, or would she tire in the stretch? Her trust in Bogey's judgment and Rosie's vibrant glow of health reassured her. Things would be fine.

Becky laughed as the filly tugged at the reins. "Just be patient, Rosie girl. You'll get plenty of serious running in a couple of days."

She didn't notice the truck and trailer on the other side of the barn until she had dismounted, tied up Rosie in the aisle and removed the filly's saddle. As she carried the saddle and blanket toward the tack room, she saw the vehicles through the doorway. She put the saddle on its rack and stepped back to look, wondering why they were there.

She'd find out once she cooled and settled Rosie. She picked up a hoof pick and slid it in the side pocket of her jeans and stepped back into the barn aisle. She reached for a bucket.

There was a rustling behind her.

Rosie blasted the air with an angry squeal.

Becky was encircled by strong arms that crushed her and almost cut off her breath. The bucket crashed to the ground.

Becky couldn't move. It was as though she was enveloped by a soft, yet unyielding mass. A heavy odor, a musty mix of cheap cologne and sweat, almost nauseated her. She screamed.

"No funny jokes for me this time, Tiger?" a familiar voice asked.

Her wrists were suddenly jerked behind her and bound together. A rough hand pushed her against the wall, and she was pinned there while her head was pulled backward.

She twisted to see who was holding her, and then she spat full in Otey Musgrove's face.

"You bitch!" he shouted.

She felt him grab her pony tail, and then her face was smashed into the wall. She let out an involuntary cry of pain.

Rosie screamed in full alarm, a high pitched screech. Becky could hear her stamping nervously.

"We'll shut you up, bitch. Don't want you stirring up that crazy horse." She could feel him moving. "Won't be spitting on me again," he grunted.

He released her hair, but she felt his big hands on each side of her face, holding it forward while the mass of him still pinned her body against the wall. She felt something move against her cheek and then she was choking on a gag of some kind. She tried to kick backward to get Otey off her, but she was jerked violently backward, lifted and slammed to the ground.

"Need to get those feet," Otey muttered. And she felt his weight on her back, and then her ankles were bound together. She was completely helpless. "Time to get moving," he said.

He hoisted her on his shoulder and walked out of the barn. At the truck, he opened the door and she was tossed behind the front seat. She landed awkwardly, striking her elbow. An electric jolt of pain shot up her arm and into her shoulder and back. Her groan was muffled by the gag in her mouth, and she had to swallow bitter vomit to keep from choking. Unbidden tears wet her face.

Above her Otey chuckled. "Hope I wasn't too rough there, girly," he said. "Don't you cry now, or you'll get me all worried."

His words helped her calm down. She wasn't going to cry. She was going to try to understand what was happening. She heard Otey close the door. There was only silence for a while, and then Becky heard the trailer door open and the ramp go down. Quickly thereafter, she could hear a horse loading on to the trailer, shifting the floor of the truck slightly as the animal's weight pressed one side of the attached trailer. In another moment, the sounds were repeated. Another horse coming on board.

Becky considered what she had heard. It could only mean that Rosie and Sentinel's Cry had been loaded. She heard the ramp come up and the door close.

The driver side door opened, and Otey spoke. "We got to wrap up those big eyes of yours. Want to do it easy?"

She could see that he was grinning and holding up what looked like a silk scarf. "See, if you gonna give me shit, I have to bang you around and do it anyway. Gonna be still for me?"

She managed a nod and even lifted her head so that he could blindfold her. When he finished, he left the door open but went around and opened the other door. Becky heard someone climb in and then the door closed. Otey came back around, started the truck, drove away down the side road and then turned onto the highway, headed back toward town.

So there were two of them. She should have known that when the first horse loaded. Otey would not have tried to handle Rosie. He was mortally afraid of her. Who was the second man, and why did Otey blindfold her only when it would prevent her from seeing him?

The answer came to her in a flash, but she found it difficult to believe.

It had to be Huddleston. Who else would be so careful not to be seen? Even more telling, who else would Otey have opened the truck door for?

But it would be insane for a wealthy, important man like him to put himself at such risk. Still, who else would be remaining totally silent? Further, who else could cause the dolt to shut his mouth? The longer the silence reigned in the front seat, the more certain she became.

It was Huddleston.

Becky turned her mind to thoughts of what might happen next and, more importantly, how she might play a role in foiling these two.

CHAPTER 34

Bogey was only on the road for a few moments when the phone beside him on the seat rang.

"You're not speedin' or doing anything stupid are you Shrimp?"

"No. Just doing what you said. Where do I go?"

"Keep drivin'. I'll call."

Bogey thought he knew where he was headed. It had to be somewhere secluded that was large enough to accommodate a truck and trailer. Perhaps it could be a wooded area or a remote rural area, but he didn't think so. This plan was surely put together by Huddleston, and he would choose a spot that was not only safe from prying eyes but also provided good sight lines to detect and identify anyone approaching. It would also be near usable escape routes.

Bogey knew of only one area meeting all these criteria.

The Jefferson County Fairgrounds.

It made sense. It would have been easy to be sure nothing was scheduled there today. Behind the arena or in the barn areas, you would be invisible from the road. Once there, you could see anyone approaching and there were multiple exit routes if you needed one.

So what did that mean?

First of all, it meant that he was entirely on his own. No one would see them. No one would come to help or call the police. Fats was far away in New York.

On the other hand, what if he did do "business" with Otey? Bogey had no doubt that this was an effort to force him to sell Rosie and Sentinel's Cry. Why not sign the papers, accept the check and then reveal that he was coerced and void the whole contract?

He knew the answer to that question.

There would be a next time. He would be putting Becky at risk again. They would have to live looking over their shoulders, watching their backs. He couldn't accept that option.

What if he disobeyed Otey and called the police?

Maybe they would understand and come quietly, even in an unmarked car. Bogey could keep Otey busy, maybe distract him so that he would never see the second car. The police would catch him in the act. He could lead the authorities back to Huddleston. Even if the two of them didn't go to jail, the heightened suspicion of them would make it unlikely that they would move against Becky and him again.

But what if it didn't unfold that way? What if something went wrong and Otey had time to hurt Becky before the police could stop him?

His heart told him that it was a risk he could not take. He would have to first control Otey. Then he could call the police.

The decision gave Bogey a measure of relief. He was sure it was the proper course of action. Now he could give himself up to the anger burning within him, white hot but harnessed and malleable. Bogey knew this rage well. It was always lurking just under his calm exterior. Normally he was alarmed when it threatened to take control of him, but today it was a welcome companion.

Beside him the phone began to ring.

CHAPTER 35

Becky felt the truck leave the road. It bumped along for several yards and then moved ahead more smoothly for awhile before coming to a stop. She heard both doors open and close. She thought she detected a faint horse barn aroma. There was no sound for several minutes. Then she could hear a distant voice through the door. She strained to listen, but the words were inaudible. The timber and cadence sounded like Otey, but she couldn't make out what he was saying. There was only the one voice, and it fell quiet after awhile. She listened carefully.

She strained at the bonds on her wrists, but they were unyielding. They felt narrow and cut painfully into her flesh as she pulled against them. The struggle hurt too badly, and she stopped. She focused on her legs, trying to loosen them, but that too was more painful than promising. Next she tried flexing her jaw from side to side and opening and closing her mouth to see if the gag might loosen. That only made her choke. Once again, the fear of vomiting terrified her, and she lay still until the queasiness subsided.

She heard the distant voice again, more briefly this time. She was sure it was Otey, and it sounded as though he might be talking on a telephone.

She bent forward at the neck, and her forehead encountered the solid back wall of the space where she lay. She pressed her face against the wall and tried to rub the blindfold upward, off her eyes, but she couldn't generate enough friction. Her nose prevented her from getting the scarf tight against the fabric on the wall. She was only irritating the skin above and below the blind. She thought a moment and came up with another approach.

The blindfold had to have a knot somewhere at the back, and the back of her head did not have a nose on it. She wiggled in the other direction, still bending her neck slightly forward, until her back was snug against the other wall. She flexed her head toward the wall, trying to feel for any lump that might be the knot in the scarf.

Becky thought she felt something and pushed back and down. She tried to scoot her body in that direction without much success, but she felt the blindfold shift slightly.

She settled herself and continued to work patiently.

CHAPTER 36

When the phone rang again, Bogey answered before the voice at the other end could speak.

"Hello, Otey. Should I meet you behind the arena or down in the barn area somewhere?"

"Damn, Shrimp. You ain't as stupid as you look. Just turn in at the first entrance and head up the hill. When I see it's you and you by yourself, I'll tell you more."

Bogey turned in at Gate 3 and drove slowly up the incline toward the arena. He wanted Otey to have plenty of time to assure himself that he was alone. Halfway up the hill, the phone rang.

"Come on up. Turn in behind the horse arena."

Bogey followed directions and saw the truck and trailer with Otey standing nearby, smiling broadly. The big man signaled him to stop.

Bogey walked toward Otey, pleased to see that the giant was relaxed and unafraid. That would make his job easier.

"Nice of you to drop by, Shrimp. Soon as you sign some papers, you and your bitch can be on your way," Otey said.

"Just a minute. I have to see Becky and be sure that she's okay before anything else happens."

Otey seemed to be considering that for a moment, but then he nodded. "See her, sure. See is all." He motioned toward the truck. "She's in there. Behind the front seat. You can see her through the window. She's fine."

Bogey moved briskly toward the truck, and Otey stepped to intercept him.

"Take it slow, Shrimp. Just look. Don't open the door. Don't say nothing." He took his place next to the truck and inclined his big head toward the window. "Have your look."

Bogey gazed in. He could see Becky behind the seat. A quick glance told him that she was bound and gagged. He spun on Otey.

"Untie her," he demanded. "She can't hurt you."

"Forget it, Shrimp. She can't hurt me, but she is too much trouble. She spit right in my face, the bitch. She yells, too."

Bogey didn't expect Otey to untie her. It was simply that he had seen more than her bound state. She had partly dislodged her blindfold, and her visible eye was wide with anxiety. But there was more. She was violently trying to shake her head as though to warn him. She blinked twice. Then blinked twice again.

Bogey just needed a moment to think. What was she trying to tell him?

There were two of them! Otey was not alone.

He should have known that on his own. That clown could not have put two spirited horses on the horse trailer.

"You wouldn't change your mind on that?" Bogey asked as though begging. He glanced all around, hoping that he looked like someone completely undone and desperate. He was, in fact, trying to see where the second man might be.

There was no one in sight. Maybe Otey had just used someone with horse skills to load the trailer. Maybe that person left once his job was done.

It didn't matter. Bogey knew what he had to do.

CHAPTER 37

Becky had heard Bogey's car drive up, or at least she knew it was him when she heard his voice. She could hear Otey speaking to him, and then she heard the two of them more clearly as they came toward the truck.

Becky hated this. All along she had realized that the purpose of kidnapping her and the horses was to force Bogey's cooperation. But she had hoped that when they contacted him, he would have the judgment to contact the authorities. She had been only slightly worried about her fate, but Bogey was another matter.

Now he was here. He sounded to be alone. He was in real danger. At a minimum, he would be forced to sell the two horses he loved to the man he hated. His career would be destroyed once again. All his hopes and his dreams for the future would be crushed.

Things could go even worse if he resisted. Otey was capable of seriously injuring him.

She had one eye free and she twisted her head to look upward toward the window. Bogey's face, tight with worry, appeared.

She tried to shout through the gag but the sounds were muffled and guttural. She could only shake her head, trying to tell him to leave. She blinked her eye twice. Maybe he would understand. She did it once again.

His face disappeared from the window, and she heard him say, "Untie her. She can't hurt you."

Untie me oaf, and we'll see about that.

The thought was heartfelt and bitter.

This time I would see you coming.

CHAPTER 38

"Okay, I guess we'd better talk business," Bogey said. His tone reflected resignation and surrender. Otey grinned.

"That's better. I'll get out the papers." He started to walk around the truck, but when Bogey didn't move, he backtracked quickly and placed a big hand on Bogey's arm.

"Oh, no, Shrimp. You stay right with me. No tricks."

Bogey spread his arms. "Okay. I'm right beside you."

They went around the truck. Otey reached into the glove compartment and pulled out a sheaf of documents. He handed them to Bogey.

As expected, they were bills of sale for the two horses. Bogey looked them over and glanced up with a frown.

"These prices are ridiculous!"

"The boss felt like your bargaining position wasn't too good right now. Sign the damn papers."

"What good will it do Huddleston? I'll go to the police, report you and void all this. You can't coerce me into agreeing to a contract."

"Why, we didn't do nothing. You signed these yesterday in front of a notary. Your brother was one of the witnesses. Me and the boss, we're in New York. Lots of witnesses seen us get on the boss's plane last night. The pilot landed us in the big city after midnight last night. We've been at the boss's condo there all night. Doorman seen us come in."

Bogey was just confirming his guess. Huddleston was too smart to leave his tracks uncovered. He wondered if his brother was actually ready to lie for Huddleston and against him. He didn't want to believe that. Right now he had to focus on this situation and his immediate plans. He looked pleadingly at Otey.

"Can you call Huddleston? I need more money than this. He probably spent more than this offer on the cover up."

"Too late, Shrimp. The boss has lost patience with you. Your smart talk to reporters didn't help you none neither. Sign the damn papers before I lose my temper and beat on you some."

Bogey shook his head sadly. "Okay, okay. I give up. You do promise you'll let Becky go if I sign?"

"Yeah, yeah," Otey said impatiently. "You can both walk out of here after I'm gone."

"Do you have a pen?"

Otey pulled out a pen and extended it to Bogey.

Bogey reached as though to take the pen but instead grasped Otey's wrist and pulled him forward to collide with his other hand, which was open, flat and rigid. The blade formed by Bogey's fingers found Otey's soft midsection and went deep. The big man's breath escaped in a great whoosh, and he doubled over, his eyes bulging. Bogey spun to the side, pivoted and aimed a kick at the back of the giant's knees. Otey screamed and dropped to the ground.

Bogey was on him, pinning the big man's right arm to his body. He drove the heel of his hand toward Otey's chin, but the giant moved quickly and the blow glanced off the side of his forehead.

To Bogey's surprise, Otey began to laugh. "That's what I always needed. Never could get going in a game till I got hit a couple of times."

With amazing agility, the big man jumped to his feet, shedding Bogey like a spare wrap.

Bogey had to dance aside to avoid a rush from Otey. As he went by, Bogey caught him in the neck with a kick and squared away to face another charge.

This time Otey was more cautious. He approached slowly, faking one way and then the other, watching Bogey carefully.

Bogey went on the attack. He danced forward and aimed a kick at Otey's groin. As his leg extended, a meaty hand the size of a baseball glove encircled his ankle and Bogey felt himself fly through the air. He slammed into the ground face down, banging his head with a hollow thud. Vision was fuzzy, and his legs wouldn't push him up. He could hear Otey's heavy footsteps thudding toward him. He tried to roll out of the way, blinking and tossing his head to clear it.

He was too slow, and the crushing weight of the man landed on him and choked the air out of his lungs. A flash of panic intruded on the cold rage that had fueled him. He couldn't let this powerful, massive man gain complete control. Bogey knew he needed to gain some distance from Otey before the giant used his mass and strength to crush the life from him.

Otey stood, holding Bogey in a stifling bear hug. He shook him almost playfully. Bogey's feet weren't touching the ground. He dangled helplessly in the hulking giant's vice grip.

Otey began to tighten the hug, doing it gradually, enjoying it. Bogey could hardly breath.

"You wanted to fight, Shrimp? How you doin' now?" Otey laughed.

But the laugh was hoarse.

Bogey could feel the giant's labored breathing. He could hear him panting, his shoulders heaving. The giant was drenched in sweat, though it was a cool day.

Maybe there was hope.

Bogey made a fist with his right hand, protruding the knuckle of the middle finger. His upper arms were pinned, but his right elbow was free. Using this small leverage, he struck viciously at the back of Otey's hand.

The iron grip holding him loosened, and Bogey reached quickly for Otey's little finger and twisted it with all his power.

He was free. When he dropped to the ground, he immediately struck backward and caught the other man full in his crotch. He heard a cry and an intake of breath that told him his blow struck home.

His head was clear now, and his legs were obeying him once again. The involuntary impulse to cradle and protect the testicles after they are struck gave Bogey the opening he needed. Otey's hand went to his crotch. The big man was hunched slightly forward.

This time Bogey's kick, backed by every ounce of his strength and his rage, flew to its target. It struck Otey's round head just above the ear with a hollow thump. The giant fell slack and heavy, banging the other side of his head on the trailer.

Bogey moved forward cautiously, ready to strike again. There was no need. Otey was out.

Bogey didn't waste a moment. He raced to the door of the truck, already tugging his work knife from his pocket.

He threw the front seat forward and leaned in and cut Becky's arms free. He slashed the gag from her mouth, and she spit it out, coughing and spitting. He was leaning in further, planning to free her legs when a cold voice spoke.

CHAPTER 39

Since Otey and Bogey had stayed close to the truck door, Becky could hear their conversation clearly. When Bogey agreed to sign the papers, she breathed a sigh of relief. Thank goodness he was doing the sensible thing.

Then she heard the sound of a violent struggle and her heart sank. She felt a swirl of conflicting emotions. Her anger called for Bogey to pulverize the fat devil. On the other hand, her love stirred fear, a terrifying certainty that worse things would befall her beloved if he did win the fight. Huddleston was somewhere around. He was more dangerous than Otey. It would be better if Bogey lost and was forced to sign the sales papers. Better to lose the horses than to lose his life.

The grunts and sounds of fighting continued until finally she felt the truck move as a large body fell against it. A moment later, the door flew open and Bogey was cutting her arms free and then removing the gag.

She struggled to clear her throat so she could warn him. It seemed to take an eternity to recover enough to shout a warning.

It was too late.

Huddleston spoke calmly. "Close the door, Humphrey. Drop the knife on the ground."

CHAPTER 40

Bogey wasn't shocked to see Huddleston walking toward him, but he was taken aback by the revolver the man had leveled at his chest.

He closed the truck door as ordered and faced Huddleston.

"Do you really need that? Are you going to shoot me?" Bogey was proud of himself. His voice revealed none of the fear he was feeling.

"We'll see. You've been pushing things, and I've had enough of you. Your brother warned me that you were a little bit crazy. I think he underestimated you. I think you're a whole lot crazy."

"*I'm* crazy? Who is threatening someone with a gun over a race horse?"

"It's not about the horses any more. They're just the scoreboard, you might say. They'll show I never back down, and I always win. I warned you from the start Humphrey. I always win."

"Please don't call me Humphrey. I told you I'm Bogey."

Huddleston laughed dryly. "See, that proves you're the crazy one. I'm pointing a gun at you, and you want to argue over your name."

"Well, see, it's not about the name anymore. Bogey doesn't back down either."

"You'd rather die than lose?" Huddleston asked, conversationally. "Pick up those papers."

Bogey picked up the bills of sale that Otey had dropped when he first hit the man. He gazed calmly at Huddleston. "I'm hoping that you will have sense enough not to do something that would get you a death sentence. Don't you realize that my father would suspect you right away if something happened to me?"

"Probably," Huddleston agreed, "but as my inarticulate associate explained so haltingly, I'm not anywhere near this god forsaken place."

Huddleston paused to look toward Otey for a moment. The big man had not stirred. "You, on the other hand, are definitely here. If my poorly conditioned friend there is dead, you would be the one at legal peril."

Bogey looked carefully at Otey. "He's breathing."

"Doesn't really matter. Let's get down to business. Are you ready to sign the papers?"

Bogey decided he had to play for time. The fastest martial arts move was no match for the speed of a bullet and, in any case, Huddleston was keeping a respectful distance. Any effort to rush him would be futile.

Bogey knew that stalling would probably be pointless as well. How could things change for the better? No one was coming to help.

He had to try anyway.

"Look, Huddleston, you have loads of money. At least pay me what the horses are worth."

Huddleston's laugh was dry and humorless. "So now you want to negotiate. Forget it. That's where I started with you. This is where it ends. Sign the papers." Huddleston's eyes glinted, their green depths dark with evil glee. "Since we're talking negotiations, perhaps I should explain my terms more fully. If you don't sign right now, we walk into the trailer and I shoot the stallion. Still no deal, the filly goes next. Let's see. That still leaves your little sweetie. I might take a little time with her. By then you'll be eager to join them, Boy Scout that you are."

"You can't get away with killing all of us. What about the truck and trailer? You didn't produce them out of thin air. There will be a trail, and sooner or later it will lead to you."

"I appreciate your concern for me, but you should know by now that I have a plan for everything."

"Wow! You are amazing. Just for my curiosity, how have you worked out that one?"

Huddleston's voice became cold and flat. "Sign the damn papers, or you all die. That's the plan."

Otey groaned and stirred.

Both men looked at him.

Bogey watched as the giant shook his huge head and blinked his tiny deep-set eyes. When he came awake, he fixed his gaze on Bogey.

Dawson was astounded to see the big man grin.

"Damn," he said. "You're somethin' else, Shrimp. Damn if you didn't take round one. Let's go at it again."

He was hauling himself up when he saw the gun in Huddleston's hand. He jerked backward as though he had been slapped in the face.

"What the hell you doin' boss?"

"I'm doing what you couldn't. I'm forcing this fool to see reality. He *will* sign these papers."

"But, boss, you didn't say anything about a gun. You just said we had to scare him some." He walked toward Huddleston, spreading his hands imploringly.

"Does he look scared to you? I'm afraid Humphrey here is too stubborn to give in to intimidation. He needs to see that this is my best and final offer. Dead or alive."

Bogey could see Otey's alarm level rising rapidly. "Boss. I ain't goin' to death row, not even for you. Put that gun down."

"Otey Musgrove. Never question my actions."

For the briefest moment, Huddleston's gun swung slightly toward Otey to emphasize his command. Bogey was on the balls of his feet, considering a move, but the gun quickly swung back to cover him.

"Please do. Charge me. I'd love a clear reason to shoot you. I hate to shoot anyone in cold blood. I only do that when it's absolutely unavoidable," Huddleston said. He looked and sounded like someone who was enjoying himself tremendously. There was excitement in his eyes.

Bogey realized with a chill that Huddleston was intoxicated with the power the gun gave him. Maybe the man had killed before. He didn't doubt that he was prepared to kill today.

Huddleston spoke, an edge to his tone. "Enough discussion. Sign the papers. Shall I count to three for effect?"

Suddenly, on the other side of the trailer, a metal door banged, and then the trailer lurched on its axles. There was a flash of motion, some huge body moving fast, and then the ring of metal striking asphalt.

The three men turned and looked over the hood of the truck toward the sound. They saw a horse and rider flashing away toward the barns below them.

Huddleston raised his gun and aimed quickly. He snapped off a shot, but the horse and rider kept going. He leveled the gun more carefully, using both hands now to steady it, preparing for a more accurate shot.

Bogey overcame his surprise and sprinted toward Huddleston. Hearing him, Huddleston began to turn the pistol toward Dawson.

Huddleston never saw Otey, who was moving toward him from a closer starting point. The big man crashed into him, knocking him almost to the ground. The gun fired, but the bullet struck the pavement and ricocheted harmlessly away.

Otey continued to advance on his employer. He held out his hand. "Give me that gun, boss. I mean it."

Huddleston righted himself.

Bogey could see the madness in his eyes.

"Look out, Otey," he shouted.

It was too late. Huddleston raised the gun deliberately and shot Otey in the chest at point blank range. The big man dropped to one knee. His face was a mask of mingled pain and shock.

"Boss," he croaked. The single word spoke of trust betrayed, of hurt, of lack of comprehension. He collapsed.

Bogey had been paralyzed by the events unfolding before him. Even though he had shouted a warning to Otey, he never dreamed that Huddleston would kill the man who had always done his dirty work.

It was too late to act now.

Huddleston pointed the gun at him. "Does that convince you?" Huddleston asked as though posing a question to a skeptical student.

"Sign...the...papers. Otey rushed the season, but, of course, I always planned to kill him. He rented the truck and trailer."

Bogey knew there would be no turning back for Huddleston now. Huddleston's next bullet would be for him, probably not for one of the horses. He fought the urge to throw up. He felt drained and powerless. There was only a sick feeling of hopelessness. This was it.

At least Becky was safe. That was worth dying for.

CHAPTER 41

The moment Huddleston had Bogey close the truck door, Becky went to work. She sat up and looked at the ties on her ankles. The binding seemed to be nylon, apparently cut from a thin rope. She strained forward at the waist, ignoring painful reminders of Otey's manhandling earlier. The knot was behind her right ankle, awkward to reach. She bent further and managed to grasp it with her right hand. She pulled it toward the front of the leg. The slick rope cut into her already irritated skin, and she gasped. But the knot was moving. It was moving slowly, but it was moving.

She ignored the stinging pain and kept tugging.

Finally she could reach the knot with both her hands.

She studied it, wanting to take the best approach to untying it.

The knot was tight. She pulled at it with all her strength, but her fingers slipped off the slick cord.

If only she could get her teeth on that baby!

She bent herself like a pretzel. It was impossible. She pushed herself on her side, feeling under the front seats for something to cut the ropes or untie the knot.

She was so engrossed with that search that she hardly noticed the sharp pain in her left thigh. The pain grew more intense.

Suddenly she remembered.

The hoof pick!

She rolled onto her back and reached for the pointed instrument used to loosen packed soil and debris from the interior of horse's hoofs. She pulled it from her pocket, winching as the tip dug at her thigh. Gripping it carefully, she worked the point into the heart of the knot and pulled.

The knot gave gradually. She continued to shove the pick in and pry. Finally the tie released and she pulled the rope free.

She was mobile now, but to what purpose? Her mind raced frantically, examining the options.

As she had struggled with the rope around her legs, she had been able to hear the voices outside the cab. Bogey's words were clear. He was obviously close by. It was more difficult to understand everything Huddleston said, but the threat in his voice came through all too well.

There was no time to waste.

She could leap out the door and distract Huddleston, but that carried an unacceptable risk of getting Bogey shot if he used the diversion to rush the man.

Maybe she could slip out the passenger door and circle behind Huddleston. Maybe she could find something to use as a weapon and hit him with it.

She knew that was foolish.

What then?

She heard a new voice outside. She recognized it as Otey's. He was speaking loudly, protesting Huddleston's use of a gun.

A plan occurred to her, and she moved quickly, hoping to take advantage of conflict between the foes.

The door handle on the passenger side slid down easily as she pressed on it. She pushed and the door opened silently. She slid toward it on her butt and held it open with her foot. Moving silently, she eased herself out the door and stood gingerly.

Her feet tingled, not really asleep but not fully awake. She tested a short step and found that she was in control of her movement. Bending forward so she wouldn't be seen above the truck bed, she moved quietly to the gap between the truck and the trailer. A cautious peek did not reveal anyone looking her way. One step allowed her to be totally hidden behind the bulk of the trailer.

She was still a moment, listening. There was no sound to indicate that she had been discovered.

The trailer's side door was beside her. She stretched up to test the handle.

It was unlocked. The door opened with only a soft clicking sound that sounded like a rifle shot to Becky. She froze, listening. Again the voices on the other side of the vehicles continued to argue.

The door opening was probably a foot and a half from the asphalt, perhaps more. Becky crouched, measured the distance and half leapt, half stepped toward the entrance. She grabbed the doorway. Her hand slipped and she almost fell back. She gripped desperately and managed to hold on long enough to grab the other side of the doorway.

She was in.

No time to listen now. Just move. She untied Rosie, who neighed softly in greeting.

Becky pulled the filly out into the front aisle. She overturned a bucket and hopped onto Rosie's back, ignoring the blowing and snorting protests coming from Sentinel's Cry.

She leaned forward to focus Rosie on the open side door of the trailer, ducked her face into Rosie's mane and kicked the filly in the flank.

Rosie shot forward out the door. They were a little to the left of center. Becky felt a stab of pain as her left knee scraped the doorframe.

Then they were flying free.

Rosie skidded when she hit the pavement but Becky nudged her again and the filly raced away.

Becky heard a shout behind them. She pressed hard into Rosie's back, expecting a bullet at any moment.

A shot rang out followed by the whine of a ricochet. There was a second shot.

But she and Rosie went on, now out of sight behind the first in a row of buildings.

Becky breathed a sigh of relief.

She rode on at a furious pace. There was no time to waste.

CHAPTER 42

Huddleston pointed at the bleeding Otey and waved his hand airily in the direction Becky and Rosie had ridden. His eyes were lit by a diabolic gleam; a weird smile played around his mouth. "My idiot and that crazy woman of yours have sealed the deal. I have no choice now."

He pointed a finger at Bogey and shook it slowly as though he was laboriously explaining a complicated situation to a dear but somewhat slow friend.

"See, she will bring back unwanted company. It can't just be you and me making a deal any longer. I'm sure you understand. I can't be here when other people come."

"Right. You better get moving. You can vanish before anyone sees you if you hurry," Bogey said. His voice was no longer calm. It was strained and hoarse.

Huddleston's laughter was high pitched, weird, excited.

"I can't leave you here with Otey. You'd tell tales on me. Some hick sheriff might listen." He inclined his head toward Bogey and spoke in a soft voice – sharing a confidence.

"See, what happened is that you and Otey struggled over this gun and both ended up shot. Who can say different? Your lady friend never saw me. The people who saw me today saw me in New York. I'm not involved."

The man bowed as though accepting applause. "Don't you see, Humphrey, I always win because I make good plans, and I adapt quickly to change."

Bogey tried to think. His body and his brain were numb with terror. He forced himself to grapple with his situation.

He was closer to Huddleston because of the few steps he had advanced when Huddleston was distracted by Becky and Rosie, but victory was still out of reach. He'd have to cross a yard or more of open space before he could grab the gun or kick Huddleston's arm.

It was hopeless. The gun muzzle was steady steel, pointed directly at his heart. All of Huddleston's attention was focused on Bogey. The man was probably still hoping for Bogey to spring at him. That way killing him would be more fun, more sporting.

Bogey tried to keep him talking. Help was on the way. Maybe something would happen.

"This way you won't get the horses. I can't sign any contract."

"Oh, I don't know. There are expert forgers for hire, or I might just see about buying them from your estate. Doesn't matter."

Huddleston gave a good natured chuckle. "If I didn't know how much you worry about my welfare, I'd think you were just trying to live a few more minutes. I'd like to accommodate you. This little feud we've had has been fun. I get pretty mad at you sometimes, but I have to admit you've given me a better tussle than most people. Sorry though, I'm running out of time."

Huddleston brought his other hand to brace the gun.

Bogey flung himself to the ground and rolled toward him, knowing that he still made an easy target but hoping that the shot wouldn't be fatal.

He never had the opportunity.

As he rolled across the pavement, he heard Otey's voice.

"You bastard," the big man shouted.

Bogey looked upward.

Otey had found the strength to lurch at Huddleston, knocking him backward and to the ground. Otey was crawling forward, trying to get on top of Huddleston.

Huddleston had dropped the gun and was scrabbling about with his right hand, trying to locate it.

Otey lunged ahead and dropped onto Huddleston's chest. His big paw-like hands surrounded the other man's head. He seemed to be staring into

Huddleston's eyes. "After all I done for you," he said. He lifted Huddleston's head and slammed it onto the asphalt. He raised it, clearly planning to repeat the move.

Bogey dove toward the gun, but Huddleston's hand found it first. He swung it up, aiming at Otey's head.

Bogey kicked with all his strength, and his foot connected with Huddleston's wrist. The gun fired, but Huddleston's aim had been spoiled, and the bullet flew harmlessly into the air.

Huddleston tried to raise the gun again, but Bogey grabbed his wrist.

Huddleston had amazing strength. As Bogey struggled to wrest the gun from him, he felt himself being lifted. He held on for dear life. but his grip was loosening. If Huddleston could free his hand, he would finish off Otey, and Bogey would be next.

Suddenly there was a loud, hollow thud and all resistance stopped. The gun slipped from Huddleston's limp hand as his arm dropped to the ground. He was still.

Bogey stood. A stream of red blood and grey matter oozed from the back of Huddleston's head. A thin trickle of red came from his ear. His eyes were open, full of surprise but sightless.

Otey was slumped across his chest. His hands lay lax on either side of Huddleston's head, slowly being painted red by the flowing blood.

Bogey felt for a pulse in his neck.

There was none. He didn't even need to check Huddleston.

He looked at the two bodies beside him. The whole scene seemed unreal. All the rage within him drained away, replaced by some weird sense of regret, even of guilt mixed with his relief.

It was Huddleston or me, he reminded himself silently, *one of us was going to die.*

He repeated it aloud, but it didn't really help. He ignored a growing stench of death and body waste coming from the dead men and sat down heavily on the asphalt, too drained to move.

CHAPTER 43

Bogey didn't hear the pickup approach, but he looked up when it screeched to a halt. Becky jumped from the passenger door and ran to him. A man in overalls came out of the other door and reached back to a gun rack to grab a rifle.

"Are you okay?" Becky asked. She knelt beside him and studied his face carefully.

"I'm fine. Just need to catch my breath." He had an anxious thought. "How are you and Rosie?"

Becky laughed. "Rosie is fine. She's tied up at the caretaker's house. I have a couple of cuts, bruises and scrapes. I may need a lot of loving care."

The man walked anxiously toward them. "Are there any more kidnappers?" he asked. He looked around the area, his rifle at the alert. "I called the sheriff, but I came on in case you needed help."

"No," Bogey said. There aren't any more. Just these two." He indicated the dead men.

The fair grounds caretaker looked at the bloody pile curiously. "What happened to them? Did you kill 'em both?"

"No. Their evil did," Bogey said. "I'll explain it to you and the sheriff at the same time. I'm pretty tired."

A siren sounded out on the highway.

Becky turned to the caretaker.

"You've been great. Can I ask one more favor?"

"Sure."

"Would you drive back and water our horse; be sure she's okay?"

"I'll do that and be right back." Bogey recognized that the fellow was a little reluctant to go.

"Don't worry. I'll be sure you hear the whole story."

The caretaker grinned. "Thanks. I don't usually get excitement like this."

Becky hoisted Bogey to his feet. "Don't get lazy on me. Help me up in the trailer. I have to see to Sentinel's Cry." He did so.

When she came back, he said, "Soon as the sheriff lets me, I'll check out Rosie. This kills any New York plans. I just hope she's not injured too badly."

He boosted Becky up to the trailer door. She turned and looked back at him. "We girls are tougher than you think, Captain Catastrophe. Rosie may be just fine."

* * *

The sheriff, Jeff Crawford, his badge said, was broad shouldered and tall. His rugged face was deeply tanned, and under the jauntily tipped brim of his lawman's hat, his eyes were patient and observant. He took in the scene, leaning down to look carefully at the corpses but touching nothing. Straightening, he studied Bogey and Becky and then turned to his deputy.

"Run back into town and fetch some sandwiches and coffee for Mr. Dawson and his lady."

Seeing that Bogey was startled that he called him by name, the set face of the lawman split in a wide grin.

"Hell, Bogey everybody in Charles Town – probably everybody in West Virginia – knows you. You're pretty much our hero. You and that filly. I'd send you on your way right now to take care of your horse, but I need to get the full story for my report. I don't want a lot of second guessing from the Ranson cops or the state guys."

He pointed at the bodies on the ground. "I bet I know who they are. I've been reading Huddleston's attacks on you in the papers. I've heard rumors about that character from some of my buddies in Maryland. They've never been able to pin anything on him, but there are plenty of suspicions. That's him and his sidekick, right?"

It took two hours for both of them to go over the events of the day. The sheriff listened carefully and was finally satisfied. While they talked, seated on the bleachers inside the horse arena, an ambulance came for the bodies.

* * *

When they had vanned the horses back to the farm and cared for them, it was after ten p.m. Becky was yawning, and Bogey was dead on his feet. He called his father and Fats to assure them they were unhurt. Becky called her father and Judy Patton. On their calls, both of them pleaded fatigue and promised more details later. Finally, they sat back on the couch and looked at one another.

Bogey sighed. "Rosie seems amazingly okay, doesn't she?" he said.

"Of course she does. Rosie is going to be fine. Now it's time to take care of your house filly." Becky held out her wrists, showing the angry welts on the outsides of both. She winced when she tried to bend her left knee to remove her riding boot.

"Help me out here," she commanded.

He took off her boots, revealing less severe purple lines across her legs.

"Get the pants off," she said.

He gingerly began to pull on her jeans. She couldn't contain a gasp, and he stood, alarmed.

"Get them off," she said through clenched teeth.

He pulled them off and saw the angry oval abrasion on the outside of her left knee. Pulling off the pants had torn some of the scab, and blood and tissue fluid was oozing down her leg.

"That looks really painful. Do you need some aspirin?"

"No, it's not bad when nothing is rubbing it. Just put a bandage on it."

He started away to get supplies, but she called him back. "I need you to check my thigh too."

At first he didn't see any problem, but when he looked more closely, he spied the round puncture wound with a small comet's tail of red above it.

"I'll clean it out with peroxide and rub some antibiotic ointment on it. What did that?"

She grimaced. "My hoof pick. It got me loose from the knot holding my legs. I forgot I had it until I rolled right onto the point."

"Tomorrow you have to have a tetanus shot. God knows what germs are on one of those."

"Always good to have a boyfriend who does his own vet work," she joked feebly. "The first thing I need is a hot shower, then you can vet away."

She stood carefully and took off her shirt and bra.

Bogey had seen the slight bruising on her cheek, the result of Otey slamming her into the barn wall, but he was shocked by the livid purple discolorations on her chest and back. He gasped.

"Told you I had a few bumps and bruises. Be nice to me." She tossed him a kiss and limped toward the shower.

* * *

Bogey awakened at four a.m. remarkably refreshed. He crawled out of bed quietly, taking care not to wake Becky. He felt sure she hadn't gotten much sleep with all her aches and pains.

He made coffee and toast without a sound, then fed Rosie and the stallion before jumping into the Mustang to head for the track.

He had a hard time getting to the barn. When he climbed out of the car, he found two reporters rushing toward him, each trying to shoulder the other out of the way. As if that weren't enough, he heard a shout from the track above him.

"He's here," someone yelled, and a small crowd of well wishers flowed down the ramp, ignoring a horse and rider who were coming up.

Bogey raised his hands into the air.

"I'm fine. The horses are both fine. But I can't talk with anyone. I have to take care of my horses and get back to the farm. I need to take Becky Friedman to the doctor."

The larger reporter pushed in. His jaw jutted toward Bogey. "Is Ms. Friedman critically injured?"

"No. No. Please leave me alone right now. I'll give you all the interviews you want later."

"Shall I report that you refused to reply when asked if Ms. Friedman was critically injured?" the reporter countered.

Bogey saw Harry Collins push through the crowd. The trainer grabbed the reporter's arm. "If you say anything at all about Ms. Friedman, I'll find you and break this."

The startled reporter tried to pull away, but Harry held him in an iron grip.

"Yeah, get the hell out of here, and don't bother Bogey," someone in the crowd yelled. There was a muttered chorus of agreement.

"Fine. Take it easy," the reporter said uneasily. He pulled a card from his pocket and tried to reach it to Bogey. "Call me when you want to talk," he said.

Harry snatched the card from his hand. He released the man, who walked off scowling and rubbing his arm. Harry called after him in an affable tone. "Don't think of writing any foolishness. This is West Virginia. We're tough on fools."

"Thanks, Harry. You saved my neck," Bogey said.

Harry waved his hand dismissively. The trainer was glaring at the other reporter.

"Did you hear Bogey? He said he'd talk to you later. You should leave."

"You shouldn't interfere with freedom of the press," the reporter blustered. Bogey could see he was only a kid.

"Do you have a card?" Bogey asked him.

The young reporter blushed and shook his head. "I'm from the *Spirit of Jefferson*. I don't have a card yet."

"That's okay," Bogey told him. "Just write your name and number on something. I'll call you first."

The youngster grinned. "Thanks Bogey, thanks." He pulled a scrap of paper from his pocket and began to scribble rapidly.

Harry punched Bogey on the shoulder. "Forget about the horses here, I already saw to them. Everything is fine. You're not supposed to be here, remember? You should be on your way to New York."

"I don't know if we can make it after what she went through yesterday."

"Come on Bogey," someone in the crowd pleaded.

"Yeah. We're counting on her," another voice said.

Bogey shook his head. "We'll see. I won't run her if she's not right. It'll break my heart, but I'll keep her in the barn."

"We know that," Harry said. "Good luck. Go take care of Becky."

The crowd parted to let him pull out. As he drove away, he could still hear their shouts of encouragement.

The whole thing was flattering, but it was making him very nervous.

* * *

When he helped Becky to the car for the trip to town, she was stiff but brushed off his concerns.

"I'm okay. They're only flesh wounds. Isn't that what all us fearless heroes say? Let's get the doctor thing done."

After the doctor checked her over, redressed her wounds and administered a tetanus shot, they started home.

Bogey told her about the scene at the track. She whistled. "Wow, this could get pretty crazy. How does it feel to be famous again?"

"I didn't like it the first time," he said sourly.

Her voice became more serious. "Do you think much about them being dead? It's all so creepy."

"I can't believe it really happened. At first it freaked me out. But then you got there with the caretaker. I'm almost ashamed to say I was so happy that you were okay, I didn't think of much else." He chuckled grimly. "It sure didn't interfere with my sleep, now did it?"

"It shouldn't. All you did was to try to protect us. They deserve what they got." She reached for his hand and gave him a radiant smile. "I have only one regret."

"What's that?"

"I would have loved to watch you kick that big oaf's ass. You are something else, Dawson." She took his hand and squeezed.

"I feel a little sorry for Otey, actually. Not about beating him in the fight, about him being killed. He probably saved my life," Bogey said.

"Sounded to me like Otey was getting his revenge. He wasn't doing anything for you."

"That's true, but he did try to talk Huddleston out of using a gun."

"All of that aside. I still say the world is a better place with both of them gone. Remember how Otey treated you and Rosie before the Maryland race. He was a wicked bully, and I've got the bruises to prove it."

"You're right. I keep thinking I should feel worse about two humans dying."

"People die every day. At least this time it was the right ones. It all happened for the best. I've had the thought that you wanted this all along, baiting him and all. I hope it's true."

Bogey pulled her to him and hugged her. "You are a tough woman. Let me know if I'm ever getting on your list."

"You can count on that, kiddo," she said. She kissed him and then pulled away. "We need to check on Rosie. New York is only three days away. It's decision time."

"I'll check her. You need to get off your feet. The doctor said you needed to rest that knee."

"Doctors say that stuff. You can't really examine Rosie without me to hold her and help you," Becky said as she limped out the door.

With Rosie out in the chill sunlight, Bogey went over her carefully. He walked around her, looking for any cuts, abrasions or swelling. He probed and palpated her back and chest, then examined each leg with meticulous care. He ran his hands down each limb, feeling with special care at the knee and ankle joints. He lifted each leg and flexed every joint.

"Can you walk her up and back?"

Becky walked the filly up several yards, turned and walked her back. Bogey moved to watch her walk away from him and then toward him. When she stopped in front of him, he spoke to Becky.

"Your leg okay to do it again?"

Without answering, she turned the horse and repeated the move.

"One more time with me watching from the side. If you're okay. You're limping pretty badly."

"I'm fine," she said impatiently. "Get over there and do your job. I'll take care of mine."

He moved obediently to the side and watched Rosie traverse her path once more.

"Okay. Just let me check the left front one more time."

He bent to the task, focusing most of his attention on the left ankle. He felt it, released it and then held it once more. He flexed it twice.

Bogey stood and took the reins from Becky. "Okay. Thanks for the help. I'll put her up. You go elevate that leg like the doctor told you."

She put her hands on her hips. "If you don't talk to me, the doctor is going to have to work on you. What the hell did you find?"

"I'm worried about that left front. There's a little heat in that ankle. I'll be right in, and we can talk more. Let me put Rosie in her stall."

Becky rolled her eyes. "Have it your way, but come straight in."

When he walked though the door, she was obediently stretched out on the couch, her left leg propped on one of the couch cushions.

"Happy now?" she asked sarcastically. "Pull up a chair, and talk to your patient. Anxiety can interfere with the healing process you know, and I'm anxious to know if we're headed for New York."

"I don't think we should go. I'm not sure she's one hundred percent. Are you sure she didn't hit that ankle on the door?"

"Yes, I'm sure," Becky said irritably. "If her ankle hit that door, my knee would be gone. Since my knee was way outside her ankle, and I barely got a scrape – come on, use your head."

"Yeah. I guess it was just landing on the concrete. No matter, it's still not right."

"Look, Dawson, I think I earned a vote here, and I say we head out to New York. Fats and Millie are waiting for us. You have two days before the race, and the filly is already walking a lot better than I am. Harry Collins will take care of everything here. We'll have a nice vacation. If Rosie isn't ready to run by Saturday morning, we scratch and drive back home."

"You really want to go, don't you?"

"Damn right."

Bogey shrugged. "What the heck. Let's load up."

CHAPTER 44

The van arrived at Belmont soon after they did. The media representatives didn't pounce until the horses arrived. The TV camera crew and a busty blonde with a mike in her hands pressed forward, way too close to the trailer door. Bogey approached the woman.

"You need to back away. I need room to unload the horses."

"And you would be?" she asked, not moving.

"I'm their trainer."

That brought the reporters with their mikes.

"You're Bogey Dawson?" one asked.

Bogey looked around anxiously, not sure of how to handle this without Harry's help. He nodded.

"What happened to Huddleston? Did you kill him?" one yelled.

"Your competition is eliminated. Are you happy?" another shouted.

A chubby fellow pressed forward. "I apologize for my colleagues. I just want to give you a chance to tell your side before the press shreds you."

The blonde and her cameras turned away from the trailer and focused on Bogey. He glanced from one to another, tempted to speak to the polite reporter who was smiling at him warmly and extending his mike. Perhaps he should explain what happened. He glanced at Becky, who was shaking her head and waving him toward her.

If he walked away, they would just follow. The horses had been cooped up in the trailer for over three hours. They needed to stretch and then be fed. It was already well past their normal dinner hour.

"Excuse me, ladies and gentlemen!" The voice was commanding, and the assembly fell quiet and turned to the distinguished older gentleman striding toward them.

"I am Mr. Dawson's attorney. Please understand that I have instructed him not to comment on matters that are still under police investigation. This does not imply any guilt, of course. I'm sure you realize that my client is not suspected of any illegal activity, or he would not be here."

There were protests from the crowd. Richard Dawson held up a preemptory hand. He didn't seem to raise his voice, yet his words cut through the muttering. "You ladies and gentlemen have a job to do. I'm not here to interfere with your right to interview Mr. Dawson regarding his horses or the important race. Feel free to ask any questions related to those subjects." His voice rang with authority. "Those questions can be addressed when and if you allow Mr. Dawson to do his job. At the moment, that involves caring for his horses. If you can't understand that, I will call track security. They understand the needs of race horses."

"Just a minute. Who are you?"

"I'm Richard Dawson. I am proud to say that I am not only Bogey Dawson's attorney, I am also his father."

The TV reporter waved her cameraman to focus on the old attorney. When she was sure they were filming, she addressed him. "Mr. Dawson, if your son is innocent, why does he need a lawyer?"

Richard studied her for a long moment. His expression was benevolent. "Miss, it is my professional opinion that everyone needs an attorney."

The other reporters chuckled.

The old attorney raised both hands. "Now, ladies and gentlemen, we have to move over to the trees there so that my son can do his job. If you have more questions for me, I will answer if I can. If you want to talk with my son on the open subjects, he will join us when he is free to do so." He walked into the crowd, moving slowly, herding them away from the trailer.

"You realize we're not going to be treated this way. We'll shred you," a tall, balding reporter said.

"Could I have your name?" Richard asked. His tone was friendly, but the man turned away without replying. The crowd moved away. Richard walked with them, smiling in a kindly manner.

The angry bald guy tried once more. "How will it sound? 'When asked about the murder of Edmond Huddleston, Bogey Dawson refused comment'."

Richard hesitated, his expression thoughtful. "Sensible. That would sound sensible."

"Aw, fuck it!" the reporter said and stalked away. Gradually, most of the group, including the TV reporter, joined him. Only two people remained when Bogey and Becky had settled the horses and joined Richard.

"Bogey, Becky, let me introduce Mr. Stewart from the *Racing Form* and Mr. Toole from the *Baltimore Sun*. They would like to ask you a few questions about Rosie." Bogey was pleased to see Toole was the polite, rotund reporter.

* * *

It was after nine by the time they finished the interviews. When the last two reporters left, Bogey turned to his father.

"This is getting to be a habit," he said.

Richard raised his eyebrows questionably.

"You appearing like the cavalry, saving my neck."

His father winked. "That's what daddies are for."

* * *

They got to the hotel just before ten. Fats had insisted that he and Millie would wait for them before eating. He came over to their room and ordered room service as the two of them unpacked. It came quickly, and the four of them fell hungrily on steak dinners.

Bogey and Becky took turns telling the details of their adventure; while one talked the other had a chance to attack the food. Neither of them had eaten since a hurried brunch before they left the farm.

Fats and Millie whooped and cheered as they recounted the more harrowing moments – both with the kidnappers and with the media.

"Damn," Fats exclaimed. "You two aren't just heroes. My buddies are a pair of super heroes!" He insisted Bogey had to go over his battle with Otey in more detail. "Give me every move, every blow. You've got to teach me some of that stuff."

Fats turned to the girls. "Didn't I tell you this guy was a karate phenom? That big goon didn't know who he was up against."

"I was really furious, and I got lucky," Bogey said.

"Come on, give. I want the bloody details."

Millie held out a hand to Becky. "Shall we escape this macho bullshit? You look bushed."

Fats stood. "Sorry. I know you, Dawson, you'll drag her out of bed at four or five in the morning to go look at that filly. I'll get those bloody details later."

He gathered the empty dishes and glasses, put them on the serving tray and walked to the door. "See you guys for breakfast – after you check out the horse. Call us when you get back."

Becky and Bogey were undressed and sound asleep five minutes after the door closed behind their friends.

They were up at five. When they got to the Belmont barn, both horses were happily nibbling hay. There were no reporters in sight. Rosie stopped briefly to blow and snort a greeting and then returned to her munching.

Bogey fed them, and he and Becky watched as both horses devoured every grain.

"She's certainly eating up," Becky said.

"Yeah. Let's get a look at that ankle. Do you think you can lead her out for me?"

"The leg was pretty stiff when I got up, but it's loosening up now. Feels fine."

She walked Rosie out into the rays of sunlight slanting between the trees. When she had the filly standing square, the filtered light came through in dots and dashes on the black background of her coat, like Morse code from heaven. Bogey gave his attention to the left front ankle. He flexed and twisted the ankle but Rosie did not flinch or show any evidence of discomfort. She seemed disinterested in Bogey's manipulations, instead looking around at her new setting. Her ears were pricked, pivoting and dipping toward each sound as other people arrived and other horses were led from their stalls.

Finally, Bogey stood.

"Well?" Becky demanded.

"There may be a little heat but less than yesterday. You can sure bend it all you want to. It's probably a minor soft tissue thing from the jump onto the hard surface."

"So we can run her tomorrow?"

Bogey shook his head. "Not if there is any heat. I won't run her against this kind if she isn't fully herself. As honest as she is, it could lead to permanent damage. If she's in the race she'll go full tilt."

"Why don't we tack her up, and I'll trot her on the asphalt. If she's off even a little it would show up."

"Neither one of you are ready for that. We can stay the night and check her tomorrow. I will do that for you. But still...."

"You're being Captain Caution. She's fine, but I'll bow to you. It's your horse."

"That's the same ankle where Sentinel's Cry broke down, isn't it?"

Bogey turned to see Stewart from the *Racing Form*. He hadn't heard the man approach. He studied the reporter and decided that the man wasn't trying to trap him.

"You're right. It is. I have to be sure history doesn't repeat."

The man nodded. "I never believed you knew Sentinel's Cry was lame. How did they fool you?"

Bogey told him, and Stewart nodded. "That was always my guess. Neither of us could prove it, eh?"

"Stacked deck," Bogey agreed.

"I'm sure nothing like that will happen this time," Stewart said. "Good luck tomorrow. I hope she can run." He turned and walked away.

"Seems some reporters know what they're doing," Becky said.

Bogey flicked imaginary sweat off his brow. "Thank goodness."

* * *

They caught up with Fats and Millie in time for a belated brunch. Bogey's hunger had fled, pushed out of mind by worries about Rosie. He was eager to test her against the unbeaten New York colt, I've Got You, hailed in the racing press as King of the East Coast. But only if he could be sure the race wouldn't harm her.

He felt sorry for Fats. Everyone tried to be cheerful and enjoy the wonderful accommodations, but they were all nervous. After Bogey's explanation of Rosie's status at brunch, no one spoke of it again, but it was at the front of everyone's mind.

It was a perfect fall day, and Millie suggested they go for a walk. They explored the wonders of the huge hotel, including the beautiful outdoor patio, and the ladies were free with praise and appreciation. Becky studied Bogey, who was trying to maintain a conversation with Fats. Her face showed exasperation but also affection. "Look everyone. Bogey is trying to fight it, but he really wants to go back to the stable. Would you guys like to come along?"

"Yes. Actually, I'd like to see the layout over there," Fats said. Millie nodded agreement.

Bogey was smiling at them.

"Just one minute, hot shot," Becky said. "We go over there only on one condition."

Bogey frowned. "What?"

"You cannot stand and stare at the horse. You certainly cannot examine her again today. We will take both horses out, let them graze and be horses. Nothing else, okay?"

Bogey grinned sheepishly. "Condition accepted."

CHAPTER 45

Fats had dinner reservations at the Rein. The room was elegant, and Millie spoke for everyone when she marveled, "This is like a palace in a fairy tale."

In spite of the wonderful surroundings, everyone was subdued, smothered by a fog of worry that hung over the table. The possibility of having to scratch Rosie from her most important race was depressing.

The waiter brought the wine, selected by Fats, for him to taste and approve. He sipped, then nodded glumly. "Fine." The waiter poured for everyone except Bogey, who declined.

"Not even for special occasions?" Millie asked lightly.

Becky spoke up before Bogey could say anything. "He's weird. Just doesn't like it. Never has."

'To each his own," Millie said cheerfully, raising her glass to her lips for a healthy draught. Then she stood. "I'd like to propose a toast." She lifted her glass and waited for the others to do the same. She pointed to Bogey's glass of water. "Heft it up."

"I make a toast to Rosie. No matter what tomorrow brings, she has brightened all our lives with adventure, excitement and joy." She turned toward Bogey and Becky. "And I toast you two. You took care of her all year, and you will take care of her tomorrow." She drank from her glass, and the others followed suit.

"Now," she said firmly, "stop mooning around and let's enjoy our friendship and a wonderful meal." She sat down.

"Isn't she the greatest?" Fats asked.

* * *

Even the fine dinner and good friends didn't help Bogey sleep through the night. He dozed but kept awakening, wondering what the morning would bring. The responsibility for the decision to scratch or to run pressed heavily on him. He would feel foolish if he left a perfectly sound horse in the barn. On the other hand, he would be overwhelmed by guilt and regret if Rosie broke down on the track. He got out of bed, stealthily trying to avoid waking up Becky. It didn't work.

"Scary decision coming up, eh?"

"Sorry. I didn't mean to wake you."

"I was awake, trying to be still and quiet so I wouldn't bother you."

They agreed there would be no more sleep this night. Becky made coffee with the hotel supplies, and they sat together, holding hands and talking softly, mainly about Rosie. They didn't talk about today's race and the coming decision, only about their history with her. How difficult and touchy she had been early in her training. The ways she had matured but still had her idiosyncrasies. They laughed and cried about her friendship with Waller. Becky went into more detail about Rosie's professionalism and coping skills during the kidnapping.

"She never questioned me. She lowered her head and jumped through that little door. She was probably wondering why I forgot to use the right door but, what the heck, 'if that's what Becky wants', she says. Then I have no reins, just guiding her with my hands on her bridle. It was like she could read my mind."

"You're both something else."

Becky sat forward, smiling happily. "Isn't it wonderful how people know her wherever we go? I mean she even smoothed things with the sheriff. I feel kinda famous just being associated with her."

"Yeah, it has its good points. On the other hand, fame brings the darned media. What if they descend on the farm? There goes our peace and quiet."

"Take the bitter with the sweet like you do with me."

He leaned over and kissed her. "There's no bitter with you."

"You're coming along, Dawson. When a girl fishes for a compliment, she likes to catch something."

The time passed easily, and soon it was time to dress and head for the track. They found Rosie looking out of her stall, happy to see them and eager for her breakfast. There would be no morning feed now, and if she ran, no breakfast later; not on race day.

Becky brought her out, and Bogey followed his usual slow and thorough check list of exams. Finally, he stood and rubbed his hands together, staring silently at the filly.

"Well, give," Becky snapped.

He sighed. "She seems to be fine. That ankle is cold as ice."

"So you're going to run her? I need to tell Judy."

"I'm going to run her," Bogey said firmly.

As though she could understand him, Rosie danced about at the end of her shank, making Becky follow her for a step or two. She quieted the filly and turned to Bogey.

"Are you going to be okay if something goes wrong?"

"What do you mean? Nothing is going wrong. She's fine."

Becky ignored his tone. "Something can always go wrong in a race even if the horse is totally sound."

"Huddleston browbeat me into running Sentinel's Cry. I'll never forgive myself." He lowered his gaze for a moment and then continued. "I also feel guilty about what I did to Rosie at Laurel. I got away with that, but it was still wrong."

He smiled at Becky. "Today is different. Rosie is ready to go. No one's going to harass her. My conscience is clear." He paused. "Of course, guilt or no guilt, if anything happens to this little girl, I may die of a broken heart anyway."

* * *

The morning was taken with necessary preparations. Bogey notified Judy Patton's agent and told Fats of the decision to run. A set of Bogey's silks, brand new in honor of the importance of the race, were delivered to the jockey's room.

Becky fetched some breakfast, and they waited impatiently for time to pass. A track representative came by to wish them well. Bogey almost hoped the press would come. Fencing with them would fill part of the empty minutes.

Bogey was glad that Substantial Balance's race would speed passage of the endless day. He left Becky to watch over Rosie and walked Marshall's horse to the paddock when the race was called.

The banker was there, along with Fats and Millie. Bogey's father stood on the fringes of the saddling area assigned to them.

Bogey took a moment to enjoy the setting. Everything looked bright and new in the radiant sun light. The statue of Secretariat dominated the center of the well-tended saddling area. He waved, and everyone waved back gaily – everyone except his father, who gave a stiff and solemn nod in greeting.

Bogey waved Marshall over. "I'm sorry that Judy Patton had a prior commitment to ride another horse in your race."

Marshall shook his hand. "That's not your fault. All the jockeys here are good anyway."

"That's true. Do you think you can hold him while I saddle? He may be a little pumped up, but he's a sensible sort."

"I have it under control, but I do have a question. He's fifty to one so far, and the odds seem to be rising. I haven't pushed you to put him in too tough of a race, have I?"

"Forget the odds. New Yorkers aren't going to take a Charles Town horse seriously. Your colt matches well in here. He may not win, but he won't embarrass you."

When the horse was saddled and the jockey Judy Patton recommended was mounted, Bogey walked the horse through the Belmont tunnel and turned him over to a pony rider. He sent the banker and his friends upstairs to watch the race and turned back to find his father emerging from the tunnel.

"Son, I know you're busy now. Do you have some time between this race and the one for Final Gift?"

"That's tight. I expect this horse to run well. I'll probably have to take him to the test barn."

"I understand. Just give me a moment. I have to ask you. Are you going to take legal action against your brother?"

Bogey was shocked. "No, of course not."

"Good. Not that you don't have every right. He was part of that wicked plan."

"All the same, he's my brother."

"This will ruin him professionally. I can't take him back in the firm. No one else will touch him after the facts about Edmond Huddleston become public."

"I feel sorry for him."

"Don't waste your energy. He's probably blaming you for the whole mess. I know you need to move on. One more question. Has the media still been bothering you?"

"No. They've pretty much disappeared except for the guy from the *Racing Form*, who seems pretty nice."

"Good. I spoke to track security. They will have to allow open access after the race, but they have some control over the backstretch. The final word. I spoke with the police and the district attorney in Charles Town."

"Am I in trouble?" Bogey asked anxiously.

His father smiled. "On the contrary. I think they are considering putting a statue of you and Rosie downtown."

* * *

Substantial Balance didn't make it to the winners circle. Judy Patton did. Marshall's colt got a decent ride, but Bogey wondered if the outcome would have been different if Judy hadn't had a prior commitment to ride the winner. She fired her colt to the lead and slowed the pace so that her horse had enough left to hold off Substantial Balance's powerful late run, although only by a nose.

The second place finish was good enough for Marshall. The little banker was ecstatic. He shouted to Bogey from the rail. "My boy almost did it. I'm so proud of him! Made a bundle, by the way. Had the exacta and had my guy to win and place at 60 to 1. Good job, Bogey. We'll get them next time. Good luck with the filly."

Bogey smiled and waved an acknowledgement and headed off to the test barn.

When he got the colt back to the receiving barn, there was only an hour before Rosie's race. The filly stood at the front of her stall, looking at him expectantly, eyes bright and eager, as anxious for race time as he was.

CHAPTER 46

The call to the paddock finally came, and they walked Rosie over and put her in the number eight stall. "Not the greatest post position," Bogey said.

"Oh, goodie," Becky said, putting her palms together in a silent clapping motion. "I was afraid you had run out of things to worry about."

"Oh, shut up," Bogey said and took Rosie around the walking ring. He spotted Huddleston's trainer by the three stall, where one of his colts would be saddled. The man was studiously avoiding any glance in Bogey's direction. Even when Bogey passed close to him while walking Rosie, he never met Bogey's level stare.

Bogey was diverted from this game by the arrival of I've Got You. The horse was undefeated, having powdered the best colts they could array against him. He had won both of the Saratoga stakes in addition to his maiden and an allowance race. In the flesh, he certainly looked the part. The royally bred bay with the flashy white star on his regal face towered over the other horses in the paddock. He was even taller than Rosie. The imposing colt was on his toes, prancing and snorting and tossing his head with imperial disdain for everyone around him. He was double shanked with a handler on each side.

Rosie stopped and turned her head to study the colt as he approached.

"Big devil, eh girl?" Bogey asked her. Rosie watched the colt intently for a moment longer and then resumed her calm walk around the paddock.

The paddock judge ordered the horses into their stalls, and Judy Patton emerged from the jockey's room looking splendid in Bogey's new silks. Her long tresses were pinned up under her cap, and her smile was bright. She shook Bogey's hand, hugged Becky and patted Rosie's neck. The new silks rustled with the rich sound of fresh fabric. She rubbed the sleeve between thumb and finger. "New togs. Neat."

Rosie neighed a greeting. "Hey, big lady, good to see you again," Judy said.

Rosie sniffed the silks and nodded vigorously. "You approve the new frock, eh?" Judy laughed and rubbed the horse's muzzle.

She turned back to Bogey and Becky. "The filly looks terrific. Say, you guys have been getting lots of press. I tell everyone I knew you when." She turned serious. "Are you really okay after what you went through?"

"Yeah," Becky said. "Nothing but a few nicks."

The paddock judge yelled "Riders up".

"Any directions?" Judy asked Bogey.

"The usual. Do what Rosie tells you."

"The race has everything, speed, trackers, closers. Where do you want us?"

"I'll let you and Rosie decide. Just remember, she always wants a vote."

"I do. If it's okay with her, I'd like to stay with the favorite and make a move when he does. I think he's the real deal."

Becky gave her friend a warm hug. She spoke quickly since the jockey two stalls away was already mounted. "We've got to get together."

"Victory celebration tonight."

"Right. Safe trip."

Bogey gave Judy a leg up. "Good luck," he said as the saddle creaked under her weight.

"Luck? Who needs luck?" she asked as she followed the line of horses onto the track.

* * *

Judy Patton was very satisfied with the way Rosie warmed up. The filly seemed relaxed yet on her toes, ready to run.

At the gate, I've Got You wanted to play 'Got You' with the assistant starters. He shied away from the gate, ignoring his jockey's efforts to push him forward. Two of the starters approached from either side and locked their arms to form a sling around the horse's rump in order to push him into the gate. He rewarded them with a vicious kick that sent them scurrying out of range. Another starter appeared with a long whip, which he snapped loudly behind the horse. I've Got You responded by rearing high on his hind legs. His jockey jumped off.

There was a brief conference, then a starter opened the front doors of the six gate, and they led the colt forward without the jockey. I've Got You had apparently had enough fun with them. He walked calmly into the gate, they closed the front door, and the jockey climbed back aboard.

Judy Patton and Rosie had watched the show calmly. "Ignore him, girl. He shows off like this every time."

The filly did just that. She walked into the gate without any fanfare and stood quietly while the last two horses loaded. Her gaze was focused straight ahead, down the track.

As expected, Huddleston's speed ball colt shot out of the starting gate and went straight to the lead. Two New York colts took up the chase, setting just off the leader. I've Got You dropped over to the rail, a length back in fourth place. Rosie followed and settled off his right flank.

They continued that way around the clubhouse turn and down the backstretch. As the lead colt entered the far turn, the race caller's smooth voice took on a note of urgency. "And now I've Got You has started his move. He is destroying this field like a flash of dark lightning!"

The giant bay moved to the race leaders in a few bounds and flew by them in a blur of motion. The race call grew even more excited. "I've Got You has widened by three, now four lengths on the field as they head into the stretch. He's running off with this race. I've Got You has got these."

Judy Patton couldn't hear the race call clearly, but she saw the bay get the jump on them and still sat chilly until Rosie rounded the turn and looked down the stretch. She gave the filly a moment to assess her task and then clucked to her and put her weight forward in the saddle.

Rosie's stride lengthened. They passed the three horses the colt had passed and took aim at the fleeing I've Got You. The big colt had four lengths on them and was running easily.

Looking squarely at her opponent, Rosie dropped even lower to the track, and her stride widened once more. Judy smiled. The race caller finally noticed what was happening.

* * *

Bogey could hear the race call clearly, even over the noise of the crowd.

"Now here's Final Gift mounting a rally in the middle of the track. She is actually closing ground on the unbeaten leader. This is becoming a horse race! Now she's moving to challenge for the lead. The finish line is coming! It's I've Got You, Final Gift, neck and neck. She's passing him! Final Gift has done it! Final Gift the winner by a head. The Country Queen has checkmated the King and conquered New York."

The crowd roared its approval. As Rosie trotted back to the winner's circle, many fans stood, applauding and calling out her name.

Waiting in the winner's circle, Becky and Bogey embraced. Fats, Millie, Marshall and Bogey's father arrived laughing and pounding one another on the back. Becky waved them into the winner's picture.

Bogey shook Judy's hand, and the photographer took the picture of the happy crowd with their triumphant horse. Judy hopped off and hugged Becky before turning to remove her tack and head off to the scales.

She looked back at Becky. "So we celebrate tonight?"

"Absolutely," Fats answered. "We have a table at Rein, plenty of room. Bring family, bring friends. It's party time."

"Wow, at the Garden City! I will bring a friend."

"Good," Fats said. "And bring your dancing shoes. We'll be dancing on the ceiling. That includes you and Mr. Herbert, Mr. Dawson. We expect you to show us the classic moves."

Marshall declined with thanks, explaining that he was heading back to Charles Town. The senior Dawson shook his head as well. He spoke to Bogey. "We can talk more tomorrow. I'll let you know of any further developments."

When Bogey moved to lead Rosie to the test barn, the filly stopped and pulled him toward Becky. She nuzzled the woman and waited to be petted. Only after Becky hugged her and said, "Well done, sweetheart, Becky is very proud of you," was Rosie willing to head for the test barn.

CHAPTER 47

Dinner was a festive occasion. Judy Patton brought her "very good friend", Parker McGowan. He was short, blonde and powerfully built. His bright blue eyes and rosy cheeks spoke clearly of his Gaelic heritage, and his easy, athletic way of moving fit his history as a skilled jockey.

Parker's comfortable sociability made him easy to know, and his obvious adoration of Judy immediately endeared him to Becky.

The three women were gorgeous in their best outfits. Millie had insisted they had to have new frocks for the occasion, and with the help of the concierge, delivery was arranged in time.

Becky was breathtaking in a svelte orange creation that clung to her frame and showed an alluring cleavage. Her raven hair was down, a striking contrast to her fair skin. She had demurred that the dress was too low cut, but Millie pressed her. "Make every man in the room envy Bogey Dawson."

Millie was turning some heads herself in an emerald princess style dress that set off her flaming red hair. A delicate orchid, nestled in the crimson locks above her right ear, echoed the contrast dramatically.

Judy's tan gown, with its high collar, was more subtle but it suited her petite beauty. Her blonde tresses were coiled high on her head, emphasizing the elegant sweep of her long neck.

Each of the three men probably thought his companion was the fairest of all, but Bogey was absolutely sure of it. He glanced at Fats and Parker and saw that they were as spiffed up as he was. They wouldn't embarrass their lovely dates.

Once they were seated at the table, Judy rose and raised her glass. "A toast. I offer a toast to Rosie, the best horse I have ever had the honor to ride – and who is so smart she is probably wondering why she wasn't invited to the party."

Everyone laughed and raised their glasses to affirm the sentiment. Judy sat back down and turned to Bogey. "I mean it. About her being smart. It's hard to believe this was only her third race. When I rode her at Saratoga, she was distracted, looking around, green as a cucumber – never changed leads. She won that race, in spite of herself, on raw talent. Today she was pushbutton. I could have put her any place I wanted. Without me really trying to control her, she seemed to know the big guy was the one to beat, so when I nudged her over to track him, she eased into it like it was her idea."

"Yes, she's smart and she's spoiled," Becky said. "She wouldn't leave the winner's circle until I hugged her and bragged on her. You didn't see that one."

Judy laughed. "No, but I'm not surprised. Soon she'll demand a carrot or two."

"Well, she deserves a truckload," Fats said. "I could buy them for her with the money she won for me today."

"I'll just say one more thing and then let the famous trainer have his say. I'm talking about acceleration! That girl has gears, several of them. When I clucked to her in the stretch, she almost ran out from under me. Make no mistake. Your Rosie is a very, very special race horse."

"Do please, please make her stick to the promise to shut up," Parker said. "I'm starting to get jealous of your fine filly. That's all she will talk about. I've never seen her this high on a horse."

"She has all the elements of greatness," Judy rushed on. "Speed, courage, competitive spirit and remarkable intelligence. I will shut up about her for now. I have some words for the two of you later," she said, indicating Bogey and Becky.

"That sounds strangely ominous," Parker said.

"You know what I'm talking about, Parker. You protect me from my little bit of fame. They're going to be badgered constantly, by the media, by fans, possibly by some nuts."

As if to underline her point, a couple wandered over, recognizing them and offering congratulations.

"We'll talk about that later," Parker said.

Fats jumped into the slightly awkward silence with another toast. "I propose a toast to the world's best horse trainer, who happens to also be the world's best friend, my buddy Bogey Dawson."

Bogey nodded acknowledgement and then stood, water glass in hand. "I am full of thanks. I drink to friendship, loyalty, beauty and, especially, I drink to love." He looked lovingly at Becky and then sat down quickly.

The skilled waiters moved forward with the first course when the toasts ended, and the group focused on eating and chatting with each other. The evening began to run down during the dessert course. All of them, and especially Becky and Bogey, had been running on adrenalin and precious little rest.

Judy promised to keep her comments brief. "Do be concise," Becky said. "I don't want to have to carry this dude up to the room."

"Okay," Judy said. "I meant what I said about Final Gift. She is special, a once in a lifetime treasure. I want you to really enjoy her. The sky is the limit on the race track; I truly believe she can and will do whatever you ask of her. Just know that many otherwise rational people treat great horses like movie stars, like rock stars. They want to bathe in reflected glory. They long to see their idols, to read about their idols, to see them on TV. The media will hound you in order to satisfy the need."

She saw that Bogey was nodding. "Looks like you've already had a taste."

"Yes, of the good and the bad," he said and yawned.

Judy chuckled. "Okay, I'll wind this up. Your situation may turn really crazy. You're a sexy couple. You've escaped from danger in a heroic manner. Rosie is the Cinderella story, a princess. You will get many avid women fans, and they can be really pushy. They will all fall in love with Bogey."

"You can skip that part. He already had that in Maryland. Groupies think he's cute. They don't know how he snores," Becky said.

"And don't think for a minute you're safe down in the wilds of West Virginia. They'll find you. Your neighbors will hate you for the traffic and trespassing problems you will bring them," the jockey went on.

"Darn, maybe I should just get her beat," Bogey said. "They'd leave us alone then."

"Ain't gonna happen," Judy said. "Any time you run her, she'll win or die trying."

"Let me throw in one thing here," Parker said. "I heard tonight, the slots bill didn't pass at Charles Town. The owners have threatened to shut down. I didn't want to say anything earlier."

"Too bad," Bogey said. "We have to get back tomorrow so I can work out contingency plans with my owners. If they close the track, I assume they'll throw us all out."

"Yes, you have your work cut out," Judy said. "I'll let you get some sleep. Just one final point. I have Parker to protect me from the media and the fans as needed. You need someone to buffer you, to keep all those people from taking over your life. A publicist, someone."

"We'll talk about it," Becky promised.

"Just one final, final, *most* important word. Don't you dare ever let anyone else ride Rosie. I'll come whenever and wherever you're running. I am her jockey. Don't forget it."

"Don't think of padding your bankroll on this girl anytime soon. She's going to the farm for some well earned R&R. Right, Bogey?" Becky said with mock solemnity.

Bogey shrugged. "The boss has spoken."

CHAPTER 48

Charles Town Racetrack did indeed close its doors in December 1994, but, as it turned out, Bogey didn't have to move all the horses. The horsemen were able to get an injunction to prevent their eviction from the stalls at the track.

He continued to train at Charles Town although it meant vanning to Maryland, Pennsylvania or New York to race. That was an inconvenience, but the task was softened by purchase of a truck and a fancy new trailer – actually the same model that had been used in the kidnapping.

He asked Becky if using that van would stir unpleasant memories.

"Are you kidding? It was my moment of glory, and it somehow cured my fear problem. No bad dreams, no fear of the track." She paused, "Besides, it really is a swell trailer. You can even use the side exit in a pinch."

Fats accepted a temporary consulting job at IBM down the road in Leesburg. He and Millie rented a house in Charles Town for the time being, but Fats continued to lobby Bogey to form a partnership.

Harry Collins confirmed a suspicion that had slowly grown in Bogey's mind.

"I got to tell you this, even if you never speak to me again," Harry said one day, slumping in a chair in Dawson's tack room.

"Whatever it was, and I think I know, there is nothing that would stop me being your friend for life. You have helped me through some difficult situations."

"No," Collins said. "I put you into those situations."

"You mean because you kept Huddleston informed about things happening here?"

Harry's head snapped up. "How did you know?"

"He obviously had a knowledgeable source. There weren't that many people who knew what I was doing and had horse sense enough to know what it meant."

"I'm so ashamed. When it started, I didn't know you, maybe I even half believed some of the bad stuff floating around. He seemed a solid citizen. He offered me money, and you know how broke everybody around here has been. At first, he was just asking general questions about everything around the track. He claimed he was thinking of buying it. Only later did I figure out that he was only really interested in you."

"Look. Forget it. It's understandable, and, besides, you've made up for it many times over. You should have accepted some money for all the things you did for my horses. Since you didn't, I guessed that you were trying to make up for something. Like they say, 'No good deed goes unpunished'."

"I do want you to know that I had nothing to do with what happened to Waller."

"Please, Harry. I know that."

* * *

Judy's predictions about fans and the press becoming a nuisance proved true for a few weeks. After some discussion, Bogey and Becky decided to accept Millie's offer to handle the problem. She proved to be excellent. They changed their phone number, and Millie only gave out her cell number. She conferred with them on all requests for interviews, whether coming from newspapers, magazines or TV. Dealing with the fans that actually came to the farm, hoping for a glimpse of Rosie or of them, was trickier. Finally, they built a gate to prevent vehicular traffic from turning down the lane to the farm. Millie negotiated a deal with the nursery to provide parking space for farm visitors. The free parking area was clearly marked, and signs directed traffic there.

When the curious parked, they were met by students who were trained to conduct walking tours around the perimeter of the farm while pointing out areas of interest and identifying the horses. Once winter began in earnest, the flow of visitors slowed and became a trickle that no longer justified all the effort.

Millie was very restrictive when it came to recommending acceptance of interview requests. Early on, Becky and Bogey agreed that they did not want to grant any TV talk show requests. Some of the procurement staff of the major shows were affronted and became insistent, sometimes abusive. Millie hung up on them and ignored their calls thereafter.

As promised, Bogey gave his first press interview to the callow lad who had demanded "freedom of the press". He also agreed to interviews with the reporters who had reported his comments prior to the race – at least those who reported them accurately. Stewart from the *Racing Form* and Toole from the *Sun* had an open door.

After two months during which Rosie did not run and Becky and Bogey stayed away from dead bodies, the media found other stories to pursue.

On a sunny day in February, right after a six-inch snow fall, Bogey and Becky rode Sentinel's Cry and Final Gift into the snowy woods. On the return, he reined up at the edge of the woods and looked at their pastures.

"Our little wonderland, eh?"

Becky flashed her brilliant smile. "It is that. You know, I sorta dread Rosie going back to the track. I've never been as happy as I have been this winter."

He nodded. "I agree. But Rosie wouldn't be. You know she loves to race. She's getting a little hard to handle."

Becky scowled and turned in Rosie's saddle to glare at him. "Speak for yourself, wimp. She's just having a little fun with me," she said.

EPILOGUE

In March of 1995, the Charles Town track reopened when management and the horsemen finally reached a working agreement. Rosie was back in serious training, bigger, sleeker and more beautiful than ever. Despite Becky's doubts, Bogey nominated her to the Triple Crown races.

"If she's not begging to go, we don't have to enter," Bogey said.

"But the Derby. They always have a cavalry charge out of the gate. All those big colts."

"Don't worry," Bogey assured her. "I won't let her hurt any of them."

On this day in early April, Bogey was running late at the end of the morning's work. He had a full stable now, and even with the skilled grooms he hired, there was a lot to do. Besides, when he finished all the work, he always had to spend a little quality time with Rosie.

At the farm, he wasn't even out of the car when Becky came running. She was racing toward him, waving wildly. He felt a moment of alarm.

She was shouting. "You're not going to believe this. My mother. *My mother* called me!"

"That's great," Bogey said, relieved. "I must say it's about time. So she's burying the hatchet? Does that include me?"

"Especially you." Becky broke into hysterical laughter. "She was very apologetic about imposing and very understanding that you might not be able to help her. She wanted me to know it would be okay if you couldn't."

Bogey frowned. "What in the world are you talking about? What does she want from me, for goodness sake?"

Becky giggled convulsively, then finally gained self control. "She wants tickets to the Preakness for her and five of the most prominent members of the temple sisterhood. Knowing us has made mother very important at temple. She says the ladies wondered if it might be possible – was there *any* chance they could 'meet' Rosie personally." Becky held out a vertical palm, the universal stop signal.

"Ignore her promise that it will be okay if we can't make those arrangements; she's lying. If she can't come through for these power brokers, she'll be mortified."

Bogey knew how important this call was to Becky, but he played along with her offhanded manner. "So your mother is talking to us. And making nice." He kissed her and then murmured in her ear, "Didn't I tell you we had a wonder horse?"

"Horses," she said. "Don't forget Waller."

He held her very close. "I will never forget Waller," he said. "He saved my career, and he saved my life."

She leaned back and looked at him curiously. "Saved your life?"

"He brought you into it."

"Bogey man, you sure can sweet talk a poor gal."

They were quiet, enjoying the moment. Then Becky spoke thoughtfully. "Maybe they're all wonder horses. I've noticed lots of people at the track, especially those who aren't born in the game, are snagged on something. Maybe the horses help us shake loose." She studied his face. "Did you ever think about it that way?"

"No," he grinned. "But that doesn't mean it isn't true."

CPSIA information can be obtained at www.ICGtesting.com
Printed in the USA
BVOW07s0214250614

357305BV00001B/51/P

9 781456 312404